STOCKHOLM RANSOM

By

S. K. Vall

Copyright © S. K. Vall 2017
This book is sold subject to the condition that it shall not, by way of trade or otherwise, be lent, resold, hired out, or otherwise circulated without the publisher's prior consent in any form of binding or cover other than that in which it is published and without a similar condition including this condition being imposed on the subsequent publisher.
The moral right of S. K. Vall has been asserted.
ISBN-13: 978-1545400166
ISBN-10: 1545400164

In loving memory of Sita Devi Xavier
XXX

For those who encouraged me to fly towards my dreams,
Let's soar

This is a work of fiction. Names, characters, businesses, organizations, places, events and incidents either are the product of the author's imagination or are used fictitiously. Any resemblance to actual persons, living or dead, events, or locales is entirely coincidental.

CONTENTS

Prologue 1
Chapter 1 3
Chapter 2 22
Chapter 3 43
Chapter 4 56
Chapter 5 65
Chapter 6 77
Chapter 7 89
Chapter 8 107
Chapter 9 124
Chapter 10 145
Chapter 11 174
Chapter 12 197
Chapter 13 217
Chapter 14 229
Chapter 15 247
Chapter 16 254
Chapter 17 261
Chapter 18 278
Chapter 19 291
Chapter 20 303
Chapter 21 309
Chapter 22 328

A special thank you to my mother, father, and all my family and friends.

Prologue

I couldn't see at first, the daggers of sunlight piercing through the leaves in the canopy above were blinding. Obscured, everything was a blur. I was running but my pace was beginning to slow down. What was that smell? Which direction had I come from? I didn't know, nor could I say how long I had been running. Rotten leaves had littered the forest floor, and combined with the drugs in my system my footsteps had become uneven. The foul stench of death flavoured the icy mist that clung between the trees and the splintered twigs bit at my ankles. I was numb from the cold, but I couldn't stop. I had to get as far away from that place as I could, but where was I running? The trees seemed to go on for miles in every direction. The harsh whispers of the wind rustled the branches with delight. I remember wondering: had they tried to search for me? Of course he must have, my father was one of the most influential men in the world, and he had both the connections and funds to search the entire country. *So why could he not find me?*

"Ow." I fell and the cold floor smacked my half

naked body hard; the leaves were giving away my whereabouts. The damp, stagnant mud soaked through the rags which I used for clothes. I was in a state; whatever drug he had given me might have been enough to kill me.

"Help," I tried to shout, but my voice was a mere whisper. My entire body was covered in a plume of purple bruises. He had beaten me to a pulp; agonisingly I struggled to my feet. The drugs had kicked in fast and my heartbeat had slowed down, I struggled to breathe. All I could do was run, but the drugs were strong and I was delirious. Run. Just keep running.

Darkness crept inwards from the edges of my vision.

Chapter 1

4 weeks later

"Sukhi is home," cried a loud voice from the top of the staircase. A thirteen-year-old girl with luscious black hair and bright blue eyes beamed at Sukhi. Her cheeks were filled with blossoming colour and her eyes glistened with aluminous joy. She rushed down with eagerness, thumping her feet heavily down the creaky floorboards. The smell of rustic, antique oak loomed the hallway. Sukhi breathed in the air and she knew she was home.

"Serena," said Sukhi, swooping in for a hug from her sister but flinching as she tried; her bruises made her feel mangled and incapable of doing many things. The life had drained from Sukhi's face; pale and dry-lipped. Her eyes were drained and her hair had frayed. A small glimpse in the mirror, and she knew she was no better than a dead corpse that had rotted over the years.

"You're finally home. I'm so glad," said her sister, unable to release her tight grip around Sukhi.

"Yes, but I might end up back in hospital if you

don't let go," said Sukhi, unable to breathe.

"Sorry."

"I missed you too, Ducky." She planted a small kiss on her cheek before looking around the house and noticing how empty it had become.

"Where is the rest of the household staff?" said Sukhi, looking around the house with confusion.

The hallways were eerily quiet, the large corridors that used to have bustling maids cleaning and maintaining the house had all disappeared. It was so silent that a pin drop could be heard. The dust drifted through the air effortlessly and would cling to her father's rustic antiques.

"Father fired them, except Chess of course… Come, let's go sit in the lounge and relax," Serena said, pulling Sukhi's hand with impatience.

"David, I think Sukhi needs to rest," said Karen, who was Sukhi's stepmother but Serena's biological mother.

"Yes, you're right. Sukhi, why don't you rest instead?" David leaned in to offer his arm and help her. "I'll have Chess bring some tea and biscuits for you?"

By looking at her father's face she could tell he had not handled her disappearance well. His face had withered, enhancing aristocratic cheekbones, but dark circles loomed around his eyes.

"Relax, no need to fuss or bother Chess. I'll be fine, besides I need to have some sister-sister time with Serena."

"But—"

"Don't worry, honestly."

David's face faltered. As the light shone through the windowpane from the hallway, he could see his daughter's large bruises more evidently. David curled his hands into large fists, attempting to swallow the anger that had risen inside him.

"I'm just glad you are home and safe now," he said, his grip tightening around her.

Serena gripped onto Sukhi's hand hard with impatience. "Come on... let's go."

"Alright, alright," said Sukhi; her footsteps were uneven due to the large splintered cuts that had wounded her calves.

"Suks, do you think you will be okay now?" Serena gripped her sister's hand harder; it was clear the family were suffering, and holding onto her was giving them some form of comfort.

"Of course, you have no idea how happy I am to be at home again."

"Are you though?" asked Serena raising an eyebrow.

The hallway was dark and surrounded by historic family portraits of her father's ancestry. The only light shone from the large stained-glass window pane of her family crest. The grey wolf filled with the colours of silver, red and royal blue. The light dusty air wavered around the musky antiques that clung to the walls. Sukhi stumbled, grabbing hold of a small ledge and almost knocked down the family photo portraits that were encased with silver frames.

"Watch out, they're expensive," said Serena.

Sukhi closed her eyes for a few moments, taking in

the darkness that seemed to swallow her surroundings. Her mind had still not come back to reality and it was clear she had not fully recovered.

"Are you alright?"

"Sorry, I'm just a little flushed at the moment."

Serena placed the palm of her hand onto Sukhi's forehead and held it there for a moment or two; she then assessed her own head to see if Sukhi was normal.

"You are burning up, do you think you might be catching something?"

"I feel fine, I think I just need to sit down for a while."

Sukhi stumbled again, desperately trying to recoup herself. Her temples began to throb harder as she furrowed her forehead, but her body could not stop shaking.

"Suks, are you sure?"

Sukhi opened her eyes, she tried to make sense of her surroundings and get back to reality.

"Yes, I'm fine."

"Were you thinking about the kidnapper?" said Serena, worried by her sister's unusual behaviour.

"No, not at all. I think the hospital just gave me some strong medication."

Serena gripped her sister's hand even harder.

"I'm fine, Ducky." A faint smile waned on the side of her dried lips.

"You can't fool me, I'm your sister."

Sukhi laughed, now feeling more at home.

As they entered the lounge, Serena walked towards a small chest, carefully disguised as a ledge, by another large stained-glass window. This one was of a grey wolf hunting a stag. She opened it, pulled out two large fur blankets and spread them onto the couch with large cushions propped up to help Sukhi's back. She pressed a button on a remote which unfolded two foot rests from the couch and motioned Sukhi to sit next to her.

"We have a new family therapist by the way," said Serena.

"Really? What happened to Dr Blease?" asked Sukhi.

Dr Blease had been their family therapist since she could remember.

"He's retired and had recommended his protégée."

"I suppose Karen didn't take it well then?" said Sukhi, who knew all too well how much Karen had relied on Dr Blease in dealing with her anxiety and stress.

"She did surprisingly, she thinks Dr Meller was a good replacement. Dad didn't really like him at first, but he's warmed up to him."

Serena's face started to glow as she moulded herself, locking into her sister's arm. A huge grin started to unravel from her lips.

"I should mention, he's really good looking as well."

Sukhi, rolled her eyes, noticing her sister's smile had turned into a Cheshire cat like grin.

"Like mother, like daughter," Sukhi laughed.

"What's that supposed to mean?"

"Perhaps you should go for boys your own age."

"Well, William Seymour asked me out before we broke up for summer."

"Oh no! Not Lord Seymour's grandson?"

"I said no, before you get any ideas."

Sukhi looked towards the windowpane and saw how grey clouds had started to form; it was clear torrential rain would hammer down judging from the darkness of the clouds. Sukhi shifted her hair behind her ear and bit her lip. Her forehead furrowed as she was lost in thought.

"What's the matter?" asked Serena.

"Nothing…" Sukhi shuffled nervously and bit her lip even more. "How can Dr Blease leave at such a crucial time? Now our family expects me to trust some 'new' doctor? Have they lost their senses?"

Anger flowed through her veins. How could her family let Dr Blease leave her at such a crucial time? Now she was stuck with a new family therapist she knew nothing about.

"He's a nice guy, try not to give him a hard time."

Sukhi folded her arms, and continued to look out the window; a huge gust of wind smacked against the window, making Serena jump a little. The room turned colder. Serena clutched to the fur blanket more but for Sukhi the cold was welcoming; it prickled against her skin with delight, sending small shivers down her spine.

"I wish Dad would get rid of those windows and put in triple glazing like normal people," said Serena.

"You know we can't do that, those windows have been there for generations," said Sukhi.

"Urgh, our family is absolutely ridiculous."

"Why are you moaning? If I remember correctly Aunt Kritziana gave you fifteen Christmas presents last year," Sukhi queried.

"So?" Serena moaned.

"At least you get benefits," she laughed. "Alright, let's watch some TV."

Serena grabbed the remote and switched on their large, seventy-six-inch curved screen TV; no doubt her father had purchased the best TV that would not really fit into their antique surroundings.

"Breaking news," said the reporter.

Of course Sukhi would be in the spotlight for some time.

"The city's 'it' girl has come back from the dead, yet won't share her accounts of what really happened."

"Oh for God's sake, not this nonsense." Sukhi's face turned red with anger. "Why won't they just leave me alone?"

"Is she a victim? Or just an attention-seeker? We have our leading psychologist here with us today to shed some light on the situation..." the broadcaster continued.

"Suks, don't worry. No one pays attention to the media anyway, everyone knows they're a bunch of liars ever since Brexit and the collapse of the

European Union."

"It doesn't give them an excuse to invade into other people's lives."

Serena changed the channel hastily.

A few moments later the housekeeper, Mrs Cheshire, came bustling in with her black and white uniform. She was large and had aged significantly over the last few weeks; judging from the large purple puffy eye bags, it was clear she had also had many sleepless nights.

"'Ow are you, Miss? The moment I knew you arrived I had to check in."

"Chess, no need for formalities," beamed Sukhi as she rose from her chair to hug her housekeeper. Chess embraced her fondly.

"Oh. But Miss, I was so worried for you." The housekeeper shed a few tears and fussed around Sukhi. "My dear child. I don't know what I would 'ave done if something awful 'appened to you."

"Well, I'm home and safe now; so no need for those tears, Chess." Sukhi held her arm in hope that it would comfort her.

"'Ow you look so withered away, and those ruddy bruises. 'Ow's about a warm chocolate milk for you and the lil' miss? I'll add some of those marshmallows, just the way you like it."

"Yes please!" said Serena with hunger.

Sukhi stood still for a moment and closed her eyes again, furrowing her forehead. She placed a hand to her forehead trying to steady herself from an unnoticed stumble. She breathed deeply for a moment before opening her eyes again.

"Miss, are you alright?"

"Of course, Chess, no need to worry."

"She's right, you know, you don't seem yourself." Serena frowned, noticing her sister's consistent imbalances had become a thing.

"These meds are so strong, but I'll get better soon."

"What happened?" Serena asked inquisitively. "During your kidnapping?"

She shuffled at the awkward question, sweeping a small strand of hair behind her ear, whilst her gaze dropped to the floor.

"Nothing."

***

Three hours later and they were still stuck on the couch watching films. Serena wedged herself into Sukhi's side like glue clinging onto her arm.

"Miss?" The housekeeper came in. "Karen would like you to meet that new therapist."

Sukhi rolled her eyes and frowned. "Do I really have to?"

"She insists, Miss, and the fella is ruddy gorgeous... if you know what I mean."

"Oh no, not you too, Chess? First Serena, now you?"

Serena and Chess both eyed each other with large grins spread across their faces.

"Guess I might as well meet this doctor."

"'Urry up now, otherwise I'll have Karen wring my throat," said Chess.

"Yes, yes I'm off."

Sukhi sighed and rose from the chair slowly, disentangling herself from her sister who stirred making to follow Sukhi. "It's okay Ducky, you stay and watch the rest of the film. Chess, will you keep her company?" Serena scowled, folding her arms before dropping back onto the couch with a huff.

"Come straight back," Serena said, "and then tell me your thoughts on our new doctor."

"Oh Miss, please don't give 'im a 'ard time, 'e really is lovely," said Chess.

"Yeah, we all know what you're like with strangers," said Serena. "Scaring them off with your brutish ways."

"I haven't even met him and you're already…"

"Sukhiii…" cried an urgent voice from the hallway. Karen, the lady of the household, who was always in charge of everything, including Sukhi's welfare.

"Bloody hell, best be off then."

Sukhi could hear the two of them giggling and laughing away as she hobbled down the corridor. As soon as Karen caught glimpse of Sukhi she rushed to her side with impatience.

"That housekeeper of yours has no sense of urgency. Hurry up, we are wasting the doctor's time."

"It wasn't Chess' fault. How many times have I told you to leave her alone?" said Sukhi, gritting her teeth in pain from walking.

Sukhi turned to face Karen. "Right, sweetheart. I know this will be hard for you, as we have a new therapist and due to everything that has happened, I think I should stay with you in the sessions until you feel comfortable."

"No Karen, it's fine, honestly. I'll be okay on my own." Sukhi swayed where she stood, dizzy with the exertions of the trip across the house. The last thing she wanted to do was contemplate her feelings over the incident with a complete stranger, but it seemed she had little choice.

"Are you sure, sweetheart?" Karen looked concerned. Her disappearance seemed to have affected her almost as much as her father. They were all victims. Her father and Karen had blamed themselves whilst Chess and Serena had been sick with worry. Guilt overwhelmed her mind; her stomach began to sink further into a dark pit.

"I'll be fine," said Sukhi.

Karen nodded, and opened the large oak double doors to the library. A tall man was standing by the large marble-top fireplace that stood five feet from the floor and was encrusted with her family emblems. The oak pillars had leaf carvings vining themselves to the top. The man that stood there had a stocky build and large muscular arms. He turned to face Sukhi and greeted her with a smile. Their gazes met and Sukhi felt her spine lock instantly; she froze as his eyes bored straight into her body, they were strong wolf-like eyes. She panted slightly and lost her balance.

He was handsome; there was no question about it.

His smile was pearly white, his face wickedly angular. Judging by the stubble around his jawline he led a busy life. His hair was black, long and shaggy at the top, but neatly trimmed on either side. His hooked nose carried evidence of some distant Roman lineage. The hues of hazel and brown softened his sharp eyes.

"Sukhi, this is Dr Meller. Dr Meller this is our eldest daughter, Sukhi." Sukhi withdrew her gaze instinctively, unnerved by a feeling of intimacy in that moment despite him exuding friendliness.

"Miss Rai, what a pleasure it is to meet you. Would you both like to take a seat so we may start the session?" He spoke in a soft North American accent, slurring his words in a unique way that made his sound charismatic.

"Oh, I won't be joining you," said Karen. "Sukhi would like to be on her own."

"Ah, well it's a good sign she feels able to do so. Miss Rai, would you care to take a seat?" he said, pulling a seat out for her. As Karen stepped away and began to close the large creaky oak doors, Sukhi felt her nerves rise; she felt less at ease with herself now that she was left on her own with the doctor. Sukhi eyed the doctor with caution, noting every angle of his face to see if he was trustworthy.

"How old are you?" she asked, whilst watching his every move to catch him off guard.

"Does my age worry you? Well if you must know I am old enough to do my job, Miss Rai." He spoke with soft confidence, a distinct eloquence that suggested he came from a wealthy background.

"You didn't answer my question."

He sighed, annoyed by her impertinence. He took a seat, pulled out a notepad and pen, then started to write down something in his notepad. On occasion he would lick the corner of his lips and sweep his hand through his thick black hair. He stopped and bored into her eyes with some concern.

"I am twenty-nine and fully qualified. It just so happens I was also Dr Blease's protégée—"

"Yes, I've heard everything… What exactly were you writing down about me?"

"That's for me to know," he responded with ease.

Sukhi hobbled over to a seat opposite him, still scrutinising his every move.

His eyes traced the bruises on her face, before returning to his pad.

"Could you stop writing in that notepad of yours, please? It's making me feel uneasy."

He returned her gaze, raising his eyebrow. He shut his notepad, put his pen down alongside with the notepad and looked back at her with intent.

"You have quite a temper," he stated. "The kidnapper must not have had an easy time with you."

"Excuse me?" Sukhi was shocked by his impertinent statement.

"Sukhi, I apologize I did not mean to offend you. I want to help you. I understand that you trusted Dr. Blease and it must be difficult for you to let yourself trust me, especially at a time like this. So how would these sessions work best for you?"

"Not working with you perhaps?"

"I'm afraid your father won't let that happen. So let me ask you again, how will it work best for you?"

"Why? If I do not want you, my father will get rid of you."

"Before Dr Blease left the three of us did sit down to discuss all matters, and we agreed that I would be the best person to take over Dr Blease."

"But... that doesn't mean anything. If I do not like you... then we will get rid of you."

"Fine, would you like someone else to reveal all your secrets and hidden issues to the media? I daresay you will not find anyone as trustworthy as me... I can reassure you."

"You have some nerve... Fine, as you're the expert, you tell me how you want to work with me."

"I'm not the bad guy here, I want to help... so here is my approach. I firmly believe the best way to recover is to get to the root of the issues, and work out ways to overcome the problems that you might be encountering presently." He rummaged his hair with his hand, sweeping it to the side, but his eyes never wavered once. They were fixated on her firmly.

"Meaning you wish for me to tell you everything that happened? If this is what you want, how can I be sure that whatever I tell you won't end up in the media or to the police?" asked Sukhi.

"Your father made me sign a Non-Disclosure Agreement and I take my work seriously. It is against our moral code to inform people of our patients' state of health, no amount of money would make me sell out my career."

Sukhi tucked a small piece of hair behind her ear and bit her lip with caution. It was clear she had not made her mind up about the doctor, unlike the rest of her family who seemed besotted with his American suave and silk-like charm.

"You won't be ready yet, and I understand that it might be too soon for you, but when you are ready I'm here to help."

"I think you must have misinterpreted my silence as me considering your offer, but quite simply put I find it hard to trust people. I will try, of course, but if this doesn't work, you will have to accept us firing you."

"As I said before, your father won't let that happen."

Sukhi's eyes jolted with fire, she bit her lip again with a smile. She leaned in slowly towards the doctor, as if to allure him.

"Really?" she said in a mere whisper. "Fine, I want you to tell me honest answers when I ask you questions."

"Okay, go for it, but on one condition."

"What is that?"

"You give me a chance to be your therapist, and answer my questions."

Sukhi closed her eyes again, drowning out her surroundings. As she opened them, she saw the doctor was still staring at her. She breathed in, deeply aware of what questions the doctor might ask her. A voice in her mind screamed, "No," at her, she was not ready.

"Okay, I will answer your questions on anything except the kidnapping."

"That's fine, I'm here to build your trust, not to delve into anything you find uncomfortable to talk about."

"Okay, so tell me about your girlfriend."

"I don't have a girlfriend." He smiled whilst returning back to his notepad and jotting down notes.

"Why not? You're good looking."

"So you think I look good? To answer, I don't have time for one."

Sukhi blushed.

"Okay, what kind of women do you usually prefer?"

"Why are you so curious about my personal life?" his eyebrow arched.

"You're meant to answer my question first."

The doctor paused for a moment before answering; he motioned his neck in a circular motion to ease stress from the spine, and winced. He tilted his head to the side but sighed in despair.

"I don't know, fit women perhaps? Like cheerleaders."

"Typical response, I suppose for an American."

"Right now, my turn, let's start from the beginning of your school life."

Sukhi glared at him. "Isn't it all written in my file? There's not much to say really, I went to a boarding school, girls didn't like me, the usual teenage angst us humans go through."

"I'm aware of your bullying, but I would like to hear the accounts from your side."

Sukhi paused for a moment, eyeing the doctor warily. "I was bullied, I didn't have any friends in school; I was made to feel inferior because of my mother."

"Why your mother?"

"Whilst my father may carry the Rai family name, he married a waitress. So you can imagine the controversy at the time and how I was maimed as the daughter of a waitress."

"Did that bother you?"

"If you know nothing of our world, then let me make sense of it for you. I was considered to be tainted because of my mother's low birth, despite my father's bloodline."

The doctor was noting her unmoved facial expressions, the room was stiff and the sound of the pen scratching against the coarse paper of his notepad could be heard. Sukhi's ears began to ring softly, the grandfather clock ticking grew louder, she closed her eyes for a moment and encountered her lost memories of being bullied. The razor-swish sound of the blade that cut her hair whilst she slept, the laughs of the girls that pulled her skirt down in assembly; she remembered everything vividly. How she would run down the corridor into the cleaner's cupboard hoping they would not find her. The beatings were hard and brutal, if she ushered a word to the teachers, she would only be beaten more.

"How do you feel about the girls who bullied you?"

"It's been eight years since I left boarding school. It made me who I am today. Stronger and detached from people, it is the best way to live."

"Is it?"

"If you want to protect yourself from those around you, then yes. In my case I now have to protect myself from the media, so yes school was certainly a valuable lesson."

"Does your sister have the same issues in a boarding school?"

"No, Karen Goldreiff came from a respectable family... so my half sister is considered perfectly normal."

"Do you take joy in behaving coldly towards people?"

"All people are malicious and vindictive, as far as I'm concerned. Why should I give a damn about them?"

"Sukhi, I understand what you went through during school must have been hard, but people who hurt you should not be held accountable for others."

"When you are born into a family that holds power in this world, people don't treat you like you're a normal human being, they will do anything to have a piece of what you have. They fail to realise that I did not ask to be born into this family and that like them, I am a human being too! I have a soul! I have a life! No! People just want a piece of you, and they will slander, drag you through dirt, betray you just to have a piece of it! You have no idea what it is like to live in my world!" she yelled.

Sukhi's temper had flared, anger and hatred had been brought up to the surface and tears had begun to fill her eyes. The doctor stared at her with awe but remained calm and collected.

"So be a human being. Define yourself, don't let others or other people's actions define who you are and what you want to be."

Sukhi paused for a moment. Her eyebrows furrowed as she looked into the abundance of darkness around her. Her heart began to beat faster as her stomach fell into a dark pit.

"I'm sorry, I just got so angry. I feel so ashamed right now."

"Why is that?"

"I'm not a nice person, I treat people badly to protect myself."

"Protect yourself from what?"

"Being hurt."

Sukhi paused.

"I can tell you, Miss Rai, the affection you have towards your sister and your housekeeper are not characteristics of a person who is not nice, quite the opposite. You have a heart, you're just afraid to let anyone near it. I think the world has attacked you in such a way, it's made you think you need to be something that you're not."

"Perhaps."

"Sukhi, why do you think I'm here today?"

"To torture me, I'm sure."

"No, I'm here to help you."

Chapter 2

"Darling, give him a chance. I asked him to approach you as a friend, instead of the usual professional doctor-patient take, as I thought it might help you relax a little better."

Her father was not an affectionate or an emotional man. He was constantly busy being the heir to the Rai fortune and managing his wealth, estates and businesses. The Rai family dated back to the 1500s, a noble family stretching out all over the world. David was the second brother descendent, and the son of Nathan Rai. His eldest brother had died at twenty-eight in a freak ski accident in the Alps.

"When you went missing, I cannot tell you how worried I was. We searched frantically and never stopped. I could not sleep for many nights; so if you cannot do this for yourself, please would you do this for me. For my own reassurance and peace of mind?"

She could see by his sad, earnest eyes, he was speaking from the heart.

Perhaps my disappearance did affect him?

Sukhi sighed and gave in.

"Okay fine, I'll do it for you," she said. With her father's small nod of approval, she dismissed herself from his private home office.

Sukhi hobbled back towards the lounge, only to find Chess had fallen asleep on one of the seats, whilst Serena was watching her favourite programme on TV.

"Your walking hasn't improved."

"I'm sure it'll get better," said Sukhi, hobbling to sit by her sister.

"So how did you find him?" asked Serena, with a small smile on her face.

"Very pleasing to the eye, I have to admit," replied Sukhi. "A completely vile man though."

"Vile? So you like him?" Serena beamed with her ever-gazing glow, her interest in the doctor was obvious by how her eyes sparkled with fascination.

"I don't like him at all… shouldn't you like guys your own age, missy?"

"Really? So you must *really* like him," Serena teased.

"God no! I detest the man, I wanted father to sack him. Dad seems intent on keeping him though," said Sukhi, who allowed her little sister to cuddle up to her.

"He must have really gotten under your skin for you to *detest* him," she giggled.

Sukhi thought for a moment.

"He has commitment issues, or he is a narcissist," said Sukhi.

"How can you tell?" asked Serena.

"I have met plenty of men just like him. Oh, I forgot, he also likes cheerleaders… typical. Admiring those plastic women that jump up and down like idiots."

"I wouldn't be too sure, sis. I think he's a good man. Perhaps you shouldn't judge him too quickly, but cheerleaders you say?" Serena suddenly perked up, hearing about the doctor's interest in cheerleaders.

"Well Ducky, give it eight years and he may have overcome his commitment issues." The two sisters giggled.

"Suks, do you ever think Father will ever let us marry someone for love?"

"Why wouldn't he? He did."

"You mean he did with your mother, with my mother it was purely convenience."

Serena's face fell. "Mother has made it perfectly clear that I needed to marry someone of nobility and wealth."

"Yes, but I know Father wouldn't allow that."

"Of course not with you, you're his favourite, he actually loves you… I'm just an invisible commodity to him."

Sukhi was unnerved and felt an overwhelming sense to protect her younger sister from such malicious lies.

"I know our father, he would never do that to you and regardless of what you think he does love you… When the day comes I will argue the place down to make sure you marry for love… if that is what you want."

"It's not just Father you know, it's the entire Rai family."

"Since when have they ever bothered me?" said Sukhi.

"Exactly, they don't bother you… but they are bothered with me, Aunt Goebel wants me to be betrothed immediately to save them from any embarrassment in the future…"

"But—"

"Whether we like it or not we are just mere pawns in their lives, our family is worth over 500 trillion because we own and control the entire banking empire in the world."

"But—"

"No one will ever marry us for love… not really. They'll take one look at our name and instantly go down on one knee."

"I don't believe that is true… I believe everyone can find true love."

"Then you are more naïve than I, plus I wouldn't bother… knowing me I'll probably marry one of Father's old friends if I'm anything like my mother." Serena laughed to herself.

"Our father is different from the rest, you know this! He will never use us as commodities."

"Maybe not you, but I think for me he will."

Sukhi looked at her younger sister with sympathy, she knew to some degree there was some truth behind what she was saying. To be born to a Rai meant they were to abide by the conditions the extended Rai family had implemented.

They could not just date anyone, the man had to have come from some substantial wealth and nobility to be worthy of acceptance.

Her father had married young and was not initially the heir, but due to the sudden death of her uncle who had no wife or kids, the burden was then passed on to her father.

"To be born into such a family, is a fate worse than death," she muttered to herself.

Sukhi closed her eyes remembering those words that ushered out of her cousin's mouth.

The stoned fireplace was 6ft tall, the fire was roaring fiercely. Sukhi must have been about fifteen years old, stumbling into Uncle Jacob's study to escape the social bustles of an annual event the Rai family was hosting.

To her surprise she found her cousin Annabelle woefully crying by the fireplace. Annabelle was seven years her senior, dark luscious brunette hair with scintillating crystal-clear eyes, but all her vibrant beauty had faded as tears marked out her imperfections and the dark circles loomed around her delicate eyes. Sukhi could tell she had drank some of the Rothschilds' finest red wine, as the stench of alcohol loomed the air and an empty bottle lay across the floor.

"Are you alright?" Sukhi had asked in her timid nature.

"Oh! It's you... God, what do you want?" she moaned in a drunken state.

"Nothing... I'll leave if you wish," Sukhi said, pivoting on one foot to leave the room.

"No... come here," said Annabelle. Sukhi paused eyeing her cousin wearily. Was she to be beaten up for intruding?

Sukhi walked slowly to her cousin, who could not stop crying.

"Is there anything I can do to help?" Sukhi was afraid, she knew her cousin's temper all too well.

"Sit down here…" she ordered.

Sukhi sidled her way to her cousin and sat opposite to her on the floor.

"My father paid him… paid him a fortune and he left me."

"Who, cousin?"

"Colin Fitzgerald… He said he loved me… we were to runaway together but my father found out."

More tears flooded down her cheeks as she wailed in pain.

"My heart is breaking… and I cannot do anything," she continued.

Sukhi reached out to pat her cousin on the back, but Annabelle grabbed her hand and pulled her in for a hug. It seemed strange to Sukhi to have Annabelle hug instead of beat her for a change.

Annabelle nestled her head closer to Sukhi's ear and whispered, "To be born into such a family… is a fate worse than death."

"What do you mean?"

"Just remember that… our lives are not ours."

***

The next morning, Sukhi was woken by the wails of Chess and Serena screaming at the top of her voice.

"MUM. I WANT TO BE A CHEERLEADER," screamed Serena. Karen was trying hard to reason with her daughter, but it was impossible.

"Mrs Cheshire. Have you been putting ideas into her head?" yelled Karen.

"No ma'am, I swear I 'aven't."

Sukhi arose from her bed; as she walked towards the mirror and saw her reflection, she gasped. *What a ghastly sight,* she thought. Pale, thin and drained. Her hair was dry and flat, weeks of neglect had caused it to look so dishevelled. Her face had sunken; it was no longer filled with the blossoming red cheeks she once had. She was proclaimed once to be a natural beauty, but now she really was better off dead. The only improvement was her bruises, which had faded into a yellow and blue pigmentation, instead of the bright purple they were the day before.

Karen came running into the room.

"Have you put ide… oh dear." She could see how Sukhi was unhappy with her appearance; she had become grossly thin and weary, and her face was still pale white.

"Shall we go to the salon, and have Bernie fix your hair?" asked Karen.

Sukhi smiled wearily, but nodded in agreement.

"Make sure you drink loads of water, and we'll have a full roast dinner as well," said Karen.

"MUM. I WANT TO BE A CHEERLEADER," Serena moaned.

"By the way, Karen, that was me. I put the idea in her head."

Karen shook her head and started to laugh a little.

"Imagine what your father will say."

"I can speak to him, he'll listen to me," said Sukhi, Karen gazed at her feet for a moment before shining her ever gleaming smile.

"Yes, you're right, your father does always listen to you. How did your session with the doctor go yesterday?" Karen asked.

"Good."

Karen smiled with a slight twitch. "I'm glad, anything to ensure our Sukhi is well. I can't imagine what you must have gone through."

Small tears began to flow down the sides of her cheeks. Sukhi only sighed.

"Please Karen, don't. I do feel fine, honestly," Sukhi pleaded for Karen to stop her tears as she saw them as unnecessary.

"But Sukhi, how can you remain so calm? Shouldn't you be angry with us? With me?"

Sukhi sighed. "I can't explain why I'm so calm, but I could never be angry with you or Dad." Sukhi tried to comfort her. "The only way I can handle this is to try get back to normal. Truth is…" but no words came thereafter.

"No. The bastard who did this to you should be punished."

Sukhi placed her arm around Karen to comfort her. "It's okay, I'm here now, and that's all that should matter." Sukhi waned a perfect but painful smile. Karen sobbed; her makeup began to crawl down her angelic face, her lines of imperfections began to show. She had aged; stress and anxiety had caught up with her. Sukhi contemplated whether it was because of her own stupidity the night she had been kidnapped that had caused this entire family to fall to pieces.

"I know I'm not your mother, but I do love you like my own daughter. I feel so guilty for what happened."

"Honestly, Karen. Don't, there's no need, it was my fault."

"Over a stupid missing plate set," she whimpered.

"Karen, everything that happened that day was my fault and no one else's."

"MUM," bustled in a young teenager, who rushed into Sukhi's room. "I want to be a cheerleader. Sukhi, please can you tell Mum it isn't stupid." Karen attempted to wipe her tears away and began to show signs of laughter.

"Where did she get this idea, Sukhi?"

"Ducky has a small crush on the new doctor, and he likes to date cheerleaders."

Karen looked bewildered at discovering her youngest daughter had a crush on an older man.

"But he's so much older than you, Serena. Shouldn't you like boys your age?"

There was a small pause that caused the room to go quiet for a moment, but Karen barked in laughter. Serena didn't look too impressed.

"Oh well. Like mother like daughter I suppose," said Karen. "But Sukhi, how do you know this sort of information about the doctor?"

"He wants me to trust him, and has given me

special permission to interrogate him."

Karen's eyebrow raised quizzically. "And you went straight into his dating profile?"

"I wanted to make him feel uncomfortable, that's all," Sukhi merely stated.

"Sukhi, is it wise for you to take an interest in men so early? After everythin—"

"NO. It's not like that," she protested. "Everyone needs to stop thinking I have something for the doctor, when I honestly don't."

There was a bustling knock on the door, Sukhi knew from the drummed loud knock it was Chess. Chess opened the door and slid into the room.

"Ma'am, there is a gentleman named Jonathan Laing here to see Miss Sukhi." Karen's face dropped. Sukhi eyed the housekeeper and knew instantly Chess had given the man a hard time, she could tell by her red flushed cheeks.

"He's the young man who found 'er in the forest. 'E's a ruddy persistent little bugger I'll tell yiu that much, I told 'im 'e could sod off."

"Tell him Sukhi is indisposed, and she will not see him," said Karen.

"No. It's okay, I'll go and see him. Chess, please let him know."

"Sweetheart, are you sure you are ready to see strangers?" asked Karen. "We can have your father do a background check on him first."

"No Karen, it's okay. Besides, I have a few questions of my own."

"MUM," piped a small voice in between them. "I want to be a cheerleader." Karen sighed for a moment.

"Your father won't allow it, you know that."

Sukhi could tell that Serena was disappointed; her eyes were gleaming close to alarming tears, which Sukhi could never bear.

"Tell you what. I'll speak to Dad this evening about it and try to convince him, how does that sound?" asked Sukhi.

Serena's eyes lit up.

"Will you? You are the best sis ever!"

Sukhi attempted to make an effort with her appearance; the makeup didn't really conceal the swelling, but it had eliminated the discoloured pigmentation.

"Fuck it."

She hobbled her way down the grand staircase into the main hallway where a young man was sitting on the nearby couch. He was good-looking, had a favourable athletic build with doe-like eyes and he gazed at her with sympathy.

"Hi, you must be Sukhi, my name's Jonathan," he said, offering his hand as a welcome.

Sukhi stood back to analyse his face and features, but greeted him with her usual curt smile.

"So what can I do for you?"

He was a little taken aback. "Oh. I thought your housekeeper would have informed you, but I actually drove by to see if you were okay."

Sukhi raised an eyebrow with a smile.

"Yes, she did inform me. I would like to thank you for helping me that day."

She remained courteous, but it had occurred to her that she was looking for signs that would pinpoint her kidnapper. Fear didn't override her; her house was under intense security and protection, so no unlawful move would go unseen.

"Honestly I thought you were close to dead when I found you, so I had to make sure you were okay."

Sukhi didn't respond but continued to eye him warily.

"Don't worry, the police wouldn't let me come here until they fully interrogated me, so by all accounts I'm completely in the clear."

I don't trust you.

"If you don't mind I would like to ask you some questions about that day. Care to come into the drawing room?"

"Sure," he responded and walked freely into the room she had directed him to. As they entered, Chess set up tea and biscuits by the coffee table.

Sukhi invited the young man to take a seat. She smiled before interrogating him herself.

"I see you're doing a lot better than how I first found you," he started.

She smiled, and sat down opposite him.

"If you don't mind me asking, how did you find me that day?"

She shifted her weight side to side, as she felt anxiety build up from within. Her hands became warm and a little sweaty. She rummaged a hand through her hair, whilst flexing her feet.

"I was jogging in the forest, up near Eppingham. It was by chance I decided to take a different route and that's where I found you, lying there quite badly beaten. Admittedly I was afraid to move you; luckily there was another family nearby who helped. I tracked my bearings and got back within range, then called the ambulance and the police department to come to the spot where I found you."

"I must have looked a state," she said.

"You looked dead. But I checked your pulse and you were still breathing, thank God."

Jonathan leaned forward towards Sukhi.

"If you don't mind me asking, what happened? Do you remember anything at all?"

"Sorry, I have no recollection," she responded quickly but with composure. "Where exactly do you live?"

"By the coast, been living with my grandmother my entire life. She's a nice old woman, makes fantastic butter cakes on Sunday, you might lik—"

"So you like running then?" She cut him off deliberately; intent to show indignation.

"Yes, I've been doing long-distance running since I was eight. I guess you could say I love the outdoors and fresh air. I don't like being cooped up in the house for too long."

His eagerness and gentile mannerisms made it

impossible to picture him being the dark, sinister kidnapper she had encountered.

"What do your parents do for a living?" she asked, now paying close attention.

"I feel like I'm being interrogated." He laughed. "My folks passed away when I was young, that's why I live with my grandmother."

There it is. The kidnapper didn't have parents either.

"How did they die? If you don't mind me asking."

He sipped his tea, and his face suddenly turned solemn. "Well if you really must know, it was a car crash."

Jonathan reclined in his seat and shifted his eyes away from Sukhi; he looked straight through the grey wolf stained-glass window.

"I'm sorry, I don't really like to talk about it. Is there anything else you'd like to ask me?" he asked.

She looked at him, still scrutinising his every move, but he remained ever so sweet, no look was a lie.

"No. That's all, you may leave." She rose from her seat, and showed the door to the stranger. He nodded with acknowledgement, and with large strides showed himself to the front door.

"If you don't mind, Sukhi, may I call on you again to see how you are? Maybe with a little less formality?"

Sukhi looked up, a little baffled. She had treated the young man with contempt and no signs of interest, yet he was keen to see her again. She might have interrogated him more, but there was a small part of her that was afraid.

"Maybe."

He smiled quite serenely. "I'll take that as a yes then." His eyes lit up with innocent hope, "Nice wolf by the way. What is that, the grey wolf?"

"Yes, our family crest or something or other—"

"They are known to represent power, intelligence and supreme confidence... You don't seem like a wolf though."

"Thank you for that..." Her smile was short and curt.

"So, I'll pick you up for that date soon then?" he asked.

There was no hope, she had been tainted. She was a lost cause from being exposed to a dark world and now found herself in listless purgatory, trying to attain normalcy. Her head and mind were conflicted. She sat and closed her eyes, remembering the accounts that happened that not only distressed her but brought peace to her soul.

"I don't think that is a good idea."

"Okay, don't see it as a date, see it as friends hanging out."

As he left, Sukhi retired into the drawing room, recollecting her thoughts on the night she was kidnapped. Her finding contentment was short-lived when another knock on the door came about.

"Miss, sorry to disturb you... Detective Darryl is 'ere to see you." Sukhi sighed, knowing exactly what the detective had come for.

"Please send him in." Sukhi propped herself up in her seat. The door swung open at full force, whilst the large plump detective strode into the room.

"Ah. Miss Rai, good to see you back on your feet."

Sukhi smiled at the detective; he was a 'no nonsense' sort of man. He sniffed the air with his stout-like nose, whilst pulling his red and black braces that clung hard to his shirt. The buttons on his shirt were close to bursting and his trousers hung quite low, underneath his belly. His cheeks were large, saggy; they reminded Sukhi of a British bulldog. His grey stubble had specks of brown coffee stains, the eyes wrinkled and the straining purple veins in them suggested he had stayed up late the night before. He seemed frustrated with the fact that Sukhi was unwilling to provide useful information initially, giving him cause to think she had something to hide.

"How can I help you, Detective?" She didn't bother to beat around the bush; he was a persistent old man who was going to attempt to interrogate her again.

"Let's go over the first night you were kidnapped, shall we?"

"Well, I was at home and I had a fight with my stepmother, Karen. I stormed out of the house and went for a walk. Whilst I was walking by Lanley Bridge, a car drove up beside me. I couldn't see behind the tinted windows, then a man in a black mask came and knocked me out. At that point I can't remember anything else. I just woke up and I was caged in a room."

"Do you remember the car?"

"No, I wasn't paying any attention."

"God dammit. How could you not be paying attention? If your senses were alert you would remember the car."

"It was black maybe. I honestly don't remember." Sukhi remained calm whilst sipping her tea that had been provided by Chess, yet she could tell her answers were antagonising the detective into a state of fury.

"Whatever this man may have said to you, he cannot hurt you again. You are under immense protection, no one will let anything happen to you." She saw through the detective. He was trying to reassure her of her safety, but reassurance was not what she needed.

Sukhi laughed. "I am David Rai's daughter; I should have never been kidnapped in the first place."

I am a daughter of one of the most powerful families in the world.

The detective sighed. "I am aware that your father isn't the most favourable man amongst certain people, but unless you give me more information I can't find leads. Without leads then that kidnapper is out there on the loose and who knows, maybe someone else is in trouble."

Sukhi remained still.

I highly doubt it.

"You know my phone number. If you wish to help us find this man then you know who to call."

His face had turned red from the heat of his anger rising. Small beads of sweat dripped down his face.

He growled in anger and stormed out of the door.

A moment's peace was all she needed. She sat there for hours watching the vast landscapes her father owned from her windowpane. The high security tendered all around her mansion. There were guards and guard dogs at every entrance, police forces in every corner. She was trapped with no way of escaping.

***

In the evening, Sukhi caught her father who was pacing up and down his office; she could tell he was stressed by the number of times he had swept his hand through his salt and pepper hair. Despite his firm exterior, it was clear that he hadn't fully recovered.

"Hey Dad," she said, sidling by the door, waiting for her father to acknowledge her. His eyes still looked withered and dull. There was a large coffee by his desk, along with a stack of paperwork that racked by his side.

"Hello my dear, please come in," he said.

She walked in at her own pace, taking a seat opposite him across his table. The air had become tense.

"Dad, what's happening?"

"The board members want me to retire. They can't handle the losses our company has made in the last few months."

"So? Dad, why is this fazing you? You've never submitted to those old corpses before, why are you now?"

"Because, I've not been myself lately, I've been erratic and made some stupid decisions. They want me to hand it all over to some hotshot Cavendish kid."

"Well get your head screwed on and tell those old crows where to stick it, and if you don't then I will."

Her father smiled.

"I forget how much you remind me of your mother."

Sukhi felt a small warmth inside her glow; hearing her father talk of her mother was rare, but when he did it was admirable. Her father's face fell into the softest smile that could kindle anyone's heart.

"But you aren't here for business, I am assuming this is something to do with Serena?"

She knew her father might have imposed some fear in the other family members and staff, but not her. She was the only one who always knew how to get through to her father in a logical approach.

"Karen already spoke to you about it?" she asked. He raised an eyebrow at her.

"Yes, she did. And I've already said no."

"Dad, she's young…"

"Before you go on, I already had one of my daughters kidnapped. I was lucky enough to have her back," he said.

"Dad, I think it would be good for me to spend more time with Serena, just to build my confidence and get back out there. I'll take her to her classes and supervise her, and I'm already under heavy protection so nothing will happen to us."

Her father shook his head.

"Dad, it's taking Serena to practice cheerleading, for Christ's sake. It's not the end of the world, you have to allow me to get better, and what better way than to take Serena to some classes?"

He paused for a moment.

"If I say yes, then Clive has to bodyguard you at all times."

"I can agree to that."

"Fine then, Serena can go cheerleading." Sukhi smiled in triumph, just as she rose from her seat.

"Sukhi, there was one more thing I wanted to speak to you about."

Sukhi sat back down; she knew instantly what he was about to ask her.

"You're twenty-six years old, Sukhi, would you consider taking a position with me, seeing as you'll inherit everything? Would you take an interest in the family business? Show these old fuckers you've got more balls than your father?"

Sukhi sighed. "I'll consider it, but you know I've always wanted to go travelling."

"I know." He sighed for a moment. "But just consider it. Who knows, you might actually enjoy it."

"I'm also going to get Chess to bring you some food, Dad."

He laughed to himself. "Alright."

Sukhi picked herself up from the chair and left his office, feeling relieved she got herself out of that mess.

"Ow," screeched a voice, as a thud hit the ground.

"What are you doing there?" asked Sukhi.

"Eavesdropping, duh…"

"Well looks like you get to do cheerleading after all."

Serena jumped up from her fall and embraced Sukhi.

"I knew I could always count on you. I'm so glad you're back, please don't ever go away."

"Miss," interrupted Chess. "The doc is 'ere to see ya."

Sukhi blew a huge sigh. "Why would Dad do this to me?" she cursed to herself.

"Because you have a crush on him. I think we all do, including Chess you know?" said Serena, giggling away at her sister's profuse blushing.

Sukhi grumbled whilst walking towards the library, stomping her feet defiantly. She opened the doors and noticed how her doctor had already made himself comfortable in the master's chesterfield chair.

"Ah, Sukhi, please take a seat so we can start your session."

Sukhi rolled her eyes, and slumped herself onto the chaise-longue.

"So what would you like to talk about today?"

Chapter 3

2 weeks later

Sukhi was looking at herself in the mirror; she was no longer weary or thin. After having full-feasted meals prepared by Mrs Cheshire, she had regained her natural figure and beauty. Her bruises were no longer in sight; her black hair was full of volume, long, thick and wavy. Indeed she was back to being the natural beauty she always was. Her purple eye was no longer swollen, revealing her almond-shaped eyes; she felt restored and her feminine features exuberated appeal. Yet somehow returning to normal proved to be more difficult and strenuous than she had anticipated.

"Miss… that Jonathan fella is 'ere to see you," said Chess, swooping into her room.

"Why the heck is he here?"

"'E said, that you allowed 'im to call on you again."

That was ages ago, and I said that out of politeness.

Chess was grinning at Sukhi with red flushed cheeks.

"Well, who could blame the poor fella? You are a right ruddy knockout."

"He hasn't seen me though."

"Oh! You were on TV, Miss! All over the news."

Of course, she thought to herself, the media had hounded her the moment she departed from her house all the way to Serena's cheerleading classes. She had been so withdrawn in her little bubble at home, and yesterday was the first sighting of her return to the real world. The media were crazed over her, asking her thoughtless and vulgar questions.

"I'll go down, and speak to him." Sukhi left her room, and waltzed down the stairs with ease. It was great to have the full use of her legs, pounding down the steps with effortless speed. To feel alive again.

"Hello Jonathan, so what can I do for you today?" She eyed him, noticing how he had made some effort with his appearance. Not that he needed to, he was good looking as he was.

"I noticed you were out and about, so I just wanted to check in on you to see how you were. If I recall I did ask if I could." His lips arched upwards into a cheeky grin.

"I am well, thank you." She bit her lip, and frowned. "So what can I do for you today?"

"Well I was hoping you might want to catch some lunch; there's a small quiet restaurant, which I think you might like."

Ah. So he is asking me out on a date.

"As lovely as that sounds, I'm a little busy today, and my personal bodyguard Clive would have to come, which is a little inconvenient, so I just don't think now is a good time."

She opened her large front door to allow Jonathan out.

The gates for the drive opened and an Aston Martin drove up the driveway. Sukhi knew Doctor Meller had arrived for his session with her. The doctor had been seeing Sukhi every day since she returned. Whilst at first it was difficult to openly communicate to him, she became at ease within the second week, bypassing her childhood history.

"Hello there." Doctor Meller waved as he opened the door to leave the car.

"Dr Meller, you've come early. This is Jonathan, and Jonathan this is Dr Meller, our family therapist."

Jonathan glared at the doctor, icily exchanging eye contact. It was intense and the air had turned into ice.

"Pleasure to meet you," responded the doctor coolly. He offered his hand to shake in greeting, Jonathan took the hand and shook it with a firm grip and a stern look in his eye.

"So you're American," said Jonathan.

"Nice to know you can pick up on an accent."

"Northern by the sounds of it…"

Jonathan turned to face Sukhi, who was scrutinising the heated situation she had found herself in.

"I'll take you out for lunch tomorrow then. See you around," and with that he moved in to kiss Sukhi on the cheek hastily and had left before Sukhi could even protest or object to a lunch with him tomorrow.

"Boyfriend?" asked the doctor with a smile.

"Oh God no."

The doctor laughed heartedly, it seemed like a vain attempt to break the intense situation that had been built around them caused by Jonathan.

The two of them entered the large drawing room to begin her session.

He took a seat on the usual master chesterfield chair as usual, then broke open his notepad and pen and started writing.

"Dr Meller before we—"

"Sukhi, I honestly think we've gone past civilities, you can just call me Ash."

Sukhi made herself comfortable in the chaise-longue. Today she was prepared for the list of questions he would have for her. The truth was he had made a considerable amount of effort to build some form of trust between them over the three weeks. It only seemed right that she would attempt to start revealing the truth. He took notes on her facial expressions, realising she had made a significant recovery in appearance.

"You look very well, blossoming every time I see you, but how are you feeling?"

"Better, perhaps?" She fumbled her fingers, and bit her lip.

"What's on your mind? Are you ready to talk about the events that happened?" he asked.

He paused on his notepad, and placed the pen down. He looked up at her with his long, ever-fascinating hypnotic gaze. His eyes bore into her, but she could tell it was out of concern.

"If we are not on ceremony here, am I allowed to ask you what you have analysed so far?"

He sighed. "That is supposed to be confidential." His voice was stern and thorough, but he knew he might have to break the rules in order to have Sukhi talk.

"Well you want me to trust you, so I need to know."

He looked down at his notepad and then back at Sukhi. He placed his hands together, resting his index fingers onto his lips. He closed his eyes for a moment then nodded his approval.

"You are not showing signs of trauma; a patient who has been violated would show signs of isolation, fear, and would appear meek and quite timid, afraid to face forms of reality. On my first meeting with you, you challenged me. You had a strong mind and willpower, this can suggest many things, but it's a little hard to decipher if you won't tell me."

"I see. What else have you analysed?"

"You adapted to normal life very quickly, showing your own initiative; however, you show signs of feeling ashamed. I believe you took it upon yourself to try and be normal to override this feeling, but it hasn't worked, has it?"

Sukhi fell silent, she found herself fumbling with her fingers, unable to keep eye contact with the doctor. She bit her lip due to her nervousness that built up within. Ultimately she was afraid he would diagnose her as insane or incurable.

"Whatever you say will be confidential, but just remember I am here to help you." She took a deep breath and closed her eyes for a moment, trying to think on how she was going to start revealing the truth behind her kidnapping.

"Where shall I start?" Her voice was quaking and her lips began to quiver in fear.

"Maybe start at the point you realised you had been kidnapped."

***

"The room was cold, dark and damp; I was chained to the floor and noticed how cold steel bars had caged me in. It was like I was underground in a hidden shelter that no one knew about. The foul stench of mud surrounded me, no light shone from the outside. I didn't know how long I was out cold and couldn't get my bearings of the time or day. I screamed for help, but no one could hear me; it was like my voice had been encapsulated in a small box. The underground shelter was soundproof.

"As I rose from the floor, unable to free myself from the chains I was bound to, a large throbbing ache pinched the side of my head. It was the original blow to my head from the first impact with the kidnapper. A large bump had formed and blood had seeped down on the side of my face. I panicked at first, screaming loudly for help, but then a hidden door opened. Lights came on and an intruder walked in. He was tall, muscular judging from his physique. I couldn't see his face as it was hidden by a black mask, one that concealed every feature perfectly. He flicked a switch and more lights turned on, only to reveal to me what looked like a torture chamber. Bars chained to the wall, ropes hung from the ceiling. There was a stainless steel like operating table, but with leather fastens for the hands and feet. There were other devices, but I wasn't entirely sure what they were. Fear had mustered itself from within and I couldn't help but scream.

"The masked man turned to face me; he walked with strides towards my caged cell. My heart pounded hard against my chest, my stomach sunk into a dark pit, my throat began to swell.

"He grabbed me by the neck and strangled me hard, but stopped when my lungs could echo no sound. He didn't speak but his actions spoke clearly to me, I dared not to utter a sound.

"I sat there in silence for hours, hoping he might leave so I could formulate plans to escape, but he never did. He was busy creating his devices of torture. I hoped but knew deep down that he had the full intent to use them. After some hours he threw a blanket in my cell and chucked a plate of food at me.

"At first I didn't know whether this was some sick game he was playing, whether he was trying to feed me and butcher me afterwards, in protest I threw the food back."

***

"Do you think he was showing elements of kindness?" the doctor asked.

Her eye contact had completely diverted elsewhere. He could tell she was distracted, but trying to decipher her was a complete mystery. He needed to reassure her that she could keep talking.

"Is that what you call it?" She couldn't stop fumbling with her fingers; she bit the side of her lip harder.

***

"He opened the steel cage door that was locked, and walked into the cell. My heart leaped, urging me to instigate a plan of action to escape, but all hopes were dashed as the door closed behind him. I was trapped and had overriding fear take over as he paced himself towards me. But before I could even look up at him to see what he would do, he had pinned himself on me and grabbed my face. His hands were hidden within leather gloves; he pushed my cheeks in hard, forcing me to open my mouth. I tried to squirm myself out of his grip, I squealed in forced apprehension, but he was much stronger than me and the pain he had inflicted on my face was too much for me to bear. Tears were streaming down my face, whimpered sounds were wringed out of me, and he forced the food down my throat. At first I spat it back at him, but this only angered him; he inflicted more pain on my face by tightening his fingers around my cheeks. I cried more and couldn't take it; I had to let him have his way."

***

The doctor could see Sukhi had become restless; he wasn't too sure if this was too much for her to bear. "This was your first encounter with the kidnapper then?"

Sukhi nodded in agreement, still unable to look directly at the doctor.

"Did anything else happen on that account?"

"He finished and left me in the cell. He locked the door, leaving me on my own."

"Did he sexually assault you?"

"No, he didn't touch me in that manner on that day."

The doctor turned to his notepad, and began to write notes. Sukhi looked up, frowning in disbelief.

"Before you think I'm writing your accounts, I'm not. It's more of a progress report on your well-being which as a professional I must note down, to ensure that my work is somewhat beneficial to you."

Sukhi sighed before nodding her head in acknowledgement. She contemplated that the worst parts of her accounts with her kidnapper had not been revealed, but the difficult question she faced was whether she could tell the doctor the truth.

"You're making progress, today was a good start," he stated reassuringly. "Did you want to continue, or would you like to end the session?"

Sukhi fell to pieces, melting down all her barriers; her eyes became red and puffy as tears streamed down her face. It was clear to the doctor she was in distress, so he rose from his chair to give her a gentle pat on the back; she couldn't express herself entirely and the doctor was attempting to reassure her with comfort.

"Doctor, you have to promise me that whatever I tell you, you cannot under any circumstances inform the police."

He sighed. "I told you everything you tell me is

strictly confidential."

"Just please don't," she implored. "You said I could trust you, so I'm begging you not to do that."

"What would you like me to do?" His silky voice was an attempt to soothe her.

"Throw them off their tracks if need be, I don't care. I'll never tell you more if you dare tell them anything."

He sighed, noticing her face was red and flustered, he could see from her frown lines she was distraught.

"Okay, I won't tell them anything, I promise."

"Thank you, Ash."

"Would you like to continue your session?" Sukhi could see the doctor's eyes were burning to know more; there was a form of accomplishment that had shown in his dark rimmed eyes. Of course, he'd just had a breakthrough with Sukhi.

"Yes, I'll continue."

He rose from the seat next to her, and resumed his normal position on his chair. Instead of picking up his notepad and pen, he sat with his legs crossed and sat back comfortably on the chair. His eyes, however, had turned slightly darker than normal, as if he were enjoying the information she was telling him.

"Please continue then," he said.

***

It must have been days where we never spoke, countless hours of silence between us. I was difficult the first few times he tried to force feed me; eventually I gave up and just allowed him to. One day, during our usual routine I had the courage to break the silence, not to scream but just to speak to him. I thought I could try to appeal to his better nature, in the hope he might let me go. "Why are you doing this to me?" I asked.

He breathed slowly and deeply, remained completely still and silent. I looked up at him but couldn't see his face, it was covered behind the woollen mask, and I couldn't make out any facial lines or expressions.

"This is nothing personal." He breathed in a deep low, yet sultry voice; it was elegant yet course but roughly refined.

"Really? You bashed me on the head and threw me into a cell. If it's nothing too personal then just let me go."

"I cannot do that." His tone was harsh and cruel; calculated in a disdainful manner. Despite the contempt between us, he hadn't treated me as badly as I had imagined. I glanced at the torture devices within the room and looked back at him.

"Are they meant for me?" He paused and walked closer to me. My heart was pounding faster; I could feel the fear rise within the pit of my stomach.

He was mere inches away from my face and in a sleek slick response he uttered, "No." I could feel his breath slide down my neck, my senses had strangely heightened in a different way.

"Not unless you want me to?" he sneered.

"What do you want from me?" I asked him.

I didn't want his black masked face to get any

closer, but it seemed he had invited himself in and with a small whisper gently pressed against my ear he muttered, "Revenge."

***

"I don't think I can go on, doctor." Sukhi noticed how the doctor was watching her intently with his intense dark eyes; he had a small frown suggesting he was far more confused and baffled than Sukhi was.

"That's okay; it seems like you went through a lot. So he was out for revenge, do you know what he might have been referring to?"

"At first I wondered if it had been one of my ex-boyfriends or someone I had wronged in the past, but recently I've begun to think it might have something to do with my father."

"Being one of the most powerful and influential men in the world, I suppose he would have had many people who disliked him," he said.

"I know. I didn't think of it at the time because the kidnapper didn't make it seem like it had anything to do with my father."

"Then possibly a vendetta personally, against your father and not you."

"How on earth can anyone decipher through the countless enemies my father would have?"

"Maybe it's not the enemies in business," the doctor concluded. Sukhi realised she had been looking in the wrong places; if it were one of business then the media would be used against him. The doctor was right; if it was a personal matter then her father would have had it cleared up and out of sight.

"I think we can conclude our session for today. I'll see you the day after tomorrow."

The doctor packed his things and dismissed himself from the room. Sukhi lay down on her leather chair and was left contemplating what her next move would be. If the doctor was right, and it was a personal vendetta, would it be someone close to her? Could she get away without being monitored by the police?

"Suks," screamed Serena from down the corridor. She knew instantly it could only be Serena. "Sukhi. My classes, we need to go."

Serena ran into the drawing room.

"Oh, you had a session with Ash. Did you find out more for me?"

Sukhi smiled at her blossoming sister. "No, not in this session, but he'll be coming the day after tomorrow, so I'll find out some more then."

"He's coming back today; Dad has a session with him."

"Oh. I see." Sukhi's heart pelted as she wondered if the doctor would keep to his word.

Was it too soon? Do I really trust him?

"Can we go now?" moaned Serena.

"Of course, let's go."

Chapter 4

As if the press couldn't hound her further, asking abrupt questions of her kidnapping, Clive the poor bodyguard had to push through hundreds of photographers that wouldn't stop taking pictures. To make things worse, the police were monitoring her every move; there was nowhere she could escape to.

Sukhi was distressed; she wanted to be left alone so she could carry out her own investigation. She wanted to ensure no one knew her true intention behind her movements or she would find herself in deep water, unable to explain why things happened the way they did. She would close her eyes recalling events, thinking long and hard for any clues behind her memories. They all failed her.

The limo had arrived back at the house, Serena ran into her home with glee whilst Sukhi paced herself into the family's mansion and sighed in exhaustion, almost collapsing whilst entering the double doors.

"Miss! Are you alright?" said Chess, grabbing Sukhi's arm to ensure she did not fall.

"Yes Chess, don't worry… the usual media

wearing me out with their stupid questions."

"Those bastards, if I could show 'em a thing or two I would... Would ya like me to make some hot chocolate?"

"No. No. Don't worry about me."

"Maybe I should take the younger miss to her classes for now, give ya a break from those vultures."

Sukhi could hear male voices coming from her father's office, she knew from the husky American accent it was the doctor. Sukhi nodded to Chess in agreement to send her away, so she could eavesdrop on the conversation between her father and the doctor.

In silence she crept up to the room, so close she could smell the antique oak through her nose; the voices were clear as day.

"I don't know what I'd do; Sukhi means the world to me. Dare I say it, more than my wife or Serena," she heard her father say.

"What she has gone through is difficult, but she is making progress, I can assure you, sir."

Will he tell my father?

"I feel so guilty; this should never have happened to her. What has she said about the kidnapper? I'm going to capture that bastard and make sure he doesn't live to see the light of another day."

"She hasn't really said much about the kidnapper, I'm afraid. I think what might be best for her is a distraction to help her in these difficult times, pick up a hobby perhaps?"

He didn't tell him. He kept his word.

"What sort? I've already offered her to work with me in the office."

"Whilst that would be good for her in many ways, I think the best option would be to just let her take a hobby for now. Encourage her to do something she enjoys."

"She used to like painting, but I think she gave that up."

Would of much preferred you telling him I needed to travel Doc...

"Encourage her to take it up again, you'll be surprised how much better a patient becomes once they've taken up a hobby that opens their creativity."

"I'll try to, but to be honest I'm really not much of a good father. I've never been a family man, when Sukhi's mother passed away I couldn't bear to look at her. She was a spitting image of her mother—"

"I can understand that, it's hard to lose the ones you love the most. I can only imagine how frightful it must have been for you during those days she went missing. The main thing is you have her back now, so maybe you should make up for lost time."

Sukhi could hear her father pacing up and down the creaky floorboards; he was breaking down, lowering all his barriers to Ash. It astounded her that a man like Ash could be so good at bringing down people's hard exterior, allowing them to divulge their darkest secrets.

"You are right. But my work keeps me away from home."

"Well what's more important? Your family or the

office? Only you can decide." Sukhi leaned closer in eagerness to hear more.

"SUKHI. Why are you standing outside Dad's door?" piped a loud voice.

Damn Serena, I was eavesdropping.

"Just need to speak to Dad," she called out.

"So why are you—"

But before Serena could say another word, Sukhi smacked her hand around Serena's mouth.

Instantly Sukhi had to think quick, she knocked on the door of her dad's office, where the doctor opened it.

"Erm… hi," she grinned.

The doctor sighed.

She instinctively tried to act like she wasn't standing there the entire time, but from the sarcastic smile on Ash's face, he knew all too well.

"I think we have finished, doctor?"

"Yes sir, I'll be taking my leave." The doctor picked up his briefcase and paced himself out of the room.

Sukhi walked in and stood opposite her father's desk. As soon as the doctor had closed the door behind him, she turned to face her father. She could see again he had been working all hours judging by the large circles around his eyes. He was tired and weary and quickly attempted to pull himself together.

"Dad, I was thinking about the offer you made about working with you in the office and learning the ropes?"

"Oh yes?" He still hadn't changed his expression, the room turned stiff. "You and your sister have a knack for eavesdropping."

"What... I was not—" Her father raised an eyebrow defiantly.

Ahh, crap!

"Well besides that, I gave it some thought and would like to join you at work."

"Well that's fantastic news, can you start tomorrow?"

"I have a lunch thing tomorrow with Jonathan, perhaps the day after?"

"Jonathan, eh?" Her father curled an uneven smirk on his lips whilst raising an eyebrow, as if to mock her.

Sukhi noticed she had caught her father's attention. He had an uncharacteristic glint in his eye.

"No Dad, it's not anything like that."

"We did a background check on him. He's a good lad, not from a great family but he's a well-rounded man, with a good reputation."

"Dad. Why would you do that? I have no interest in any man right now. I'm not sure if your paranoia is feasibly warranted in these circumstances, but it's unhealthy I'll have you know."

Sukhi's father raised an eyebrow and smirked mockingly at her.

"Good one, my dear... I'm glad that you still have your wit."

Sukhi frowned and pouted at her father.

"He was our first suspect, so inevitably the police were going to run a background check on him anyway."

"I don't like him in that way." Sukhi's face was hot and flushed.

Her father laughed heartily.

"If you say so."

Her father's teasing annoyed Sukhi. The mere thought of her and Jonathan as an item made her stomach feel sick.

What if I used him to distract the police? It would be unfair to use Jonathan in such a way, but at least I would be able to have some sort of freedom to do what I want and throw them off my tracks.

"Just be careful, you know Clive will have to come with you." Her father studied her with a look of concern, as if knowing what his frivolous and wild daughter could get up to.

"Yes Dad, which is why it's not a date or anything of that nature."

"Okay, well just make sure you know what you're doing." Her father glanced at the work on his desk, indicating it was time for her to leave the office. Sukhi rolled her eyes.

"Seriously Dad…"

She walked out, slamming the door behind her. She sighed to herself, remembering this was how mundane her life had gone back to.

"Sukhi. I need to speak with you," said Serena. Her face was ghostly white, the blossoming colours had faded from her cheeks and her face looked stricken with horror.

"Serena. What's the matter?" asked Sukhi, who analysed her sister's haunted face.

"Sukhi, I think he's going to come back for you." Serena looked pale. "What are you hiding, sis?"

Serena pulled a note and a red rose from behind her, it was a mutilated, scrunched-up piece of paper, with a full-bloomed rose. It was clear Serena had pricked one of her finger with the thorn, as there were bloody fingerprints all over the note.

"Serena, go to Chess and have that cleaned up now."

"This came through the mail in a package. What is going on, Sukhi?"

"I'm surprised security didn't go through that."

"Dad has strict orders that they aren't allowed to go through our mail and post, but stop changing the subject! What the hell is going on?"

It was clear Serena had already taken the liberty to read it herself. Sukhi opened the note. In scratched marking with what seemed like a pen knife the words read out *'I'm still coming to get you, Sukhi.'* A small lock of her hair tied in a red ribbon fell to the floor. Serena's face dropped further.

Sukhi panicked, her heart lurched right to the centre of her throat. She grabbed Serena and pulled her aside, gripping onto her tight.

"Look, I can't explain... but please don't say anything."

"What will you do with the note? Are you going to show the police?"

"Serena, you have to promise me that you won't utter a word to Dad, Mum or the police, not even Chess about this note."

"Sukhi. Maybe they can help find the person who took you."

"No. They must never know, you have to promise me."

Serena sighed, unsure whether she was doing the right thing, but Sukhi looked at her with earnest. Serena could only respond with a meek nod.

"If you tell them, he will most certainly come back for me. As long as he remains a secret, he won't take me."

Serena looked at her sister, and nodded again. "Don't worry, I'll keep this a secret, but you need to tell me what is going on."

Perhaps it was slightly sick and manipulative, but I need to keep him a secret, keep him alive.

"I promise," said Sukhi, still gripping her sister with reassurance. "I will tell you everything when the time is right."

***

"I'm still coming to get you Sukhi," the voice began to echo in her mind.

As she walked into her room, she threw the beautiful bloomed rose into her bin. Her mind was racked with thoughts of the days she had been kidnapped, flashbacks of those nights where he spent his time with her. *Come and get me. I dare you,* she thought in response to his note. If she wanted answers to the questions she had, she needed to find him herself. Sukhi eyed the rose from the bin and sighed. She stared at it with bewilderment, awestruck by its beauty. In a trance she decided to strip herself in front of the mirror. There she stood completely naked, staring at her body. She closed her eyes and began to run the rose's petals against her skin, trailing it up her arm and around her collarbone. Dancing away to the soft touch that caressed her supple skin. The petals slid down the curve of her breast and she sighed with delight, venturing it down further to her abdomen. A small release of ecstasy escaped her lips but she remained unsatisfied. Annoyed.

"Why won't you come and get me?" She sighed, almost slightly in despair. "Make me feel alive again."

She moaned, trying to remember the touch of the man who held her hostage. Dazed in her wake, she slowly began to yearn for him. Feelings she had never felt before surged through her body, as images flashed through her mind. How she wished she was back with him in the small underground cellar, her escape from her imprisoned life.

Chapter 5

The next day Sukhi arose to the blinding sun that had sidled its way through a crack between her curtain and window. Just as she turned over to break away from the sunlight, a bustling housekeeper burst through her room.

"Oh, Miss, I think it's time ya woke up."

"Why, Chess?" Sukhi moaned. She turned over in her bed and wrapped herself in the warm duvet. "It's so cold."

"Because that man is here to take ya out for lunch," said Chess.

"What. Why? And what time is it?"

"Almost 1 p.m., Miss."

Sukhi sky-rocketed out of bed.

"How did I oversleep?"

"You didn't set your alarm, Miss."

Sukhi ran to the bathroom to wash, whilst Chess prepared a set of clothes for her to wear. No doubt as part of some elaborate matchmaking scheme, Chess had laid out a provocative, figure-hugging grey dress.

"Chess, I'm not wearing that," cried Sukhi from the bathroom.

"I think ya will, young lady." Chess had a mischievous grin on her face, a rare sight on her part.

"I'll wear my trackies and hoodie actually."

"No, they're in the wash, you can wear this instead."

"What? Why?"

"'Cause you've worn them three days straight."

"So… they're comfy." But Chess raised an eyebrow. "Fine, I'll wear that then…"

Sukhi grabbed the grey dress that was laid out for her and hauled it over her head; with a few tugs and pulls she finally had the dress on. She pulled up her opaque black tights quickly and pushed her feet into her leather boots.

Sukhi saw herself in the mirror. The grey dress, matched with black tights and boots, it clung tightly to her chest and waist. accentuating her slim physique.

"Dear God, he's going to think I made such an effort. Are you crazy?"

Sukhi sighed, realising there was no way to convince Chess otherwise. Sukhi rolled her eyes and stomped out of her room.

She ran down the stairs to find Jonathan waiting patiently by the door. He was dressed in jeans, and a khaki T-shirt with brown suede shoes. He looked like a hipster, nothing special.

Sukhi glared at Chess for forcing her to wear such a provocative outfit when Jonathan had made next to no effort.

"Wow," was all that he could say the moment he laid eyes on her. Sukhi could not help blushing, as she hadn't been complimented in a while. It had been a while since she had gone out with someone other than her family.

Sukhi scowled, wishing she had not been caught in such a crossfire. She wanted someone else, and the last thing she needed was her family pushing her to date someone she had no interest in.

"You look amazing." It was clear by his face that he was totally awestruck by her natural appeal; his jaw kept dropping frequently with every turn she made, and he was pleasantly surprised by her quick recovery.

"Thank you," she responded.

She put her Kate Spade shades on and left the house, half expecting Jonathan to follow.

"Where are we going?" she asked.

"Well there's a small restaurant on the top of the hill—"

"Sounds lovely," she paused and side glanced at Jonathan whilst biting her lip. "Er…Jonathan, would you mind taking me to the forest where you found me?"

Jonathan's eyes widened, he seemed a little surprised by her request.

"Okay, but I'll only take you there after lunch," he replied. "Why do you want to go there, if you don't mind me asking?"

"I just want to see things for myself, if that is ok with you?"

"Yes, that's fine, but we will go to eat at a restaurant first, then I'll take you to the forest."

Her eyes dropped and a small sigh escaped from her lips.

"You could sound a little grateful?"

"Oh I am, thank you," she said. "Sorry I'm all out of sorts today, I've had a lot on my mind."

"Well maybe you might want to tell me over lunch?"

"I rather not, it's not really important," she said.

"Hmm, well I was hoping you'd allow me to be your friend," he said.

"Why?" she asked.

"Because it looks like you need one."

***

The limo approached the restaurant that was situated on a small hill in a remote village; he was right, it was quiet. The setting was perfect as the hill overlooked the majestic city of London.

Clive opened the door; Sukhi climbed out and stood for a moment to take in a breath of fresh air, the views left her speechless. A small smile escaped her, she was left awe struck.

She turned around setting her gaze upon a small authentic Italian restaurant that was surrounded by a few shops. It was a quiet town, but quaint and picturesque. It was serene and charming it its own unique way. There weren't many people walking around, which came as a pleasant surprise for Sukhi, as she was so used to living in a society where she lived a hectic lifestyle. To find a place of peace and tranquillity was pure bliss for her.

As Jonathan came out of the limo, he took Sukhi by the arm and glided her to the restaurant. Clive followed three steps behind them as always; he seemed surprised himself by the fact there were no media or paparazzi in sight.

As they entered the restaurant, Clive took his normal seat around the front entrance whilst Sukhi and Jonathan took two seats on a table to themselves. Sukhi smiled, feeling more relaxed that she wasn't being hounded. She glanced through the menu with delight, but before she could ask for anything Jonathan had taken the liberty of ordering the two specials and a bottle of their best wine.

"So Sukhi, why do you want to go back to the spot in the forest?" asked Jonathan.

"I want to see if I can remember anything," she said with false enthusiasm.

"As a friend, I think you can trust me. What's your real intention?"

Sukhi eyed him with caution. She didn't trust him, but knew he could be of some assistance in a different matter.

"I just want to find anything that might be able to help…" She paused and lost track of her speech.

Jonathan paused and scrutinised her every look carefully.

"I see so you want to become Sherlock Holmes and find your kidnapper?" He was no fool, he could see she had a different motive.

"If there is any way I can help, I mean I was an intern in the police department and I have some impressive detective skills."

"I see."

"Can't help wonder why you won't leave it to the detectives though?"

"I guess you could say I lost faith in the system a long time ago."

"So taking you to the forest will help? How?"

"To see if anything might jog my memory, everything at the time seemed so vague," she bit the corner of her lip and dropped her gaze down to her hands.

"Won't Clive mind?"

"No… because he will be there so no harm can come to us."

He was finding it irrevocably difficult to understand the situation and pondered why she was so interested in going back to the place she was found. Was she not scared?

"You want Clive to come with you?" he asked.

"Ideally no, but I have no choice."

Jonathan smiled.

"I'll help you, but I would like you to tell me the truth."

Sukhi found herself in a precarious situation, she needed to find her kidnapper before anyone else did, and whether she liked it or not, she may have needed Jonathan more than she had initially thought. Despite herself, she knew he had a soft spot for her and decided to use this to her advantage. Under the guise of finding the kidnapper she would spend time with Jonathan and use his knowledge and skills to find him.

It wasn't her usual self to be malicious, but she was desperate to find her kidnapper; her impatience had made her vulnerable and fragile. Her stomach sunk further thinking of him.

"So what's with this *'family therapist'*?" asked Jonathan. "He's a bit young, isn't he?"

"Dr Meller? Well he's new; we've always had a family therapist since my mother died, originally it was Dr Blease, but he had to return home to New Zealand so now we have this new therapist."

"Really? I don't think it's necessary you need one, you seem to be getting on just fine."

"Thanks, but I think my father finds it is necessary."

"I don't like him, especially the way he looks at you," said Jonathan. Sukhi felt her stomach rise further, one thing she didn't appreciate was possessiveness.

"He's only doing his job; there's nothing else to it," she said.

"Could you not open up to me?"

Sukhi looked at him, weary-eyed at first; leading a man on made every feeling in her revolt. She felt awful knowing she was going to use Jonathan as a buffer and if that meant she had to keep seeing him and go on continuous dates with him, she would have to. The notion was frustrating; she felt nothing for the poor young man who was clearly quite smitten with her.

"I suppose I could," she responded, half-heartedly. "But I barely know you."

"Well get to know me then." He was self-assured in himself no doubt, probably because of the countless women that must have liked him. What was not to like?

As the two finished their meals it was only a matter of time before the paparazzi found out her whereabouts; small photographers loomed around the bushes and on the outskirts of the restaurant.

"I think it's time for us to leave." Sukhi rose from her chair and wrapped her coat around her ready to leave. Jonathan took his last mouthfuls of food, before dropping fifty pounds in cash.

He walked out from the restaurant, with Clive treading closely from behind.

Clive opened the limo door and Sukhi and Jonathan went in. Jonathan directed Clive to take them to Eppingham Forest.

"Are you sure you want to do this?" asked Jonathan, who seemed a little concerned for Sukhi's welfare. "I wouldn't want you to have a panic attack out there and for me to call the ambulance again."

Sukhi looked a little disorientated, she pondered what she wanted to find but at the same time was unsure what she was trying to look for.

"Yes," she nodded, staring outside the window,

watching the trees rush by her. It hadn't occurred to her how she might react upon arriving at the scene. *What am I looking for?* Indeed if she was looking for clues, they probably would have all been taken by the detectives for forensic analysis. *Any sign or message he might've left me perhaps?*

As they approached the forest, Jonathan kept hold of Sukhi's arm. She found it annoying he had started parading her around like she was his girlfriend; she bit her lip down and scowled at the thought of it, but continued to proceed to the very spot he had found her. Clive followed their every move within the forest; She noticed Clive showing fear in his face which was rather amusing to Sukhi. She laughed to herself.

"Here. This is where I found you," said Jonathan. His eyes never drifted away from her. "I can't help notice you aren't afraid to be here, in fact you seem a little forlorn... curious," said Jonathan.

"Can you stay quiet for a moment?"

The trees, the moss, the dank odour of the wet mud, but it was all around her everywhere. She wouldn't have been able to make out where she came from.

"Are you okay?" asked Jonathan.

"I am fine."

"Was there something you were looking for?" asked Jonathan, trying to follow her closely.

"Yes."

"What was it?"

She rolled her eyes and sighed, annoyed by the fact that Jonathan's persistent questions were not allowing her to recollect her own thoughts for a moment. She shook her head, realising there was nothing left for her and she wouldn't get the peace she needed with Jonathan around her.

"Never mind, this was a mistake."

She lowered her head and walked back to the limo with Clive and Jonathan following her closely from behind. She wanted to scream in her head, but she knew there was no point. Clive opened the door allowing Sukhi and Jonathan to enter.

"I can tell that you're upset," said Jonathan.

"Honestly, I don't care," she said without thinking, her thoughts were always on her kidnapper and she was beginning to feel disappointed in his unfulfilled promise.

Jonathan seemed confused by Sukhi's odd behaviour.

"I find it odd that you weren't afraid."

Clive was driving quite fast down the small lanes; he could tell that Sukhi wanted to be out of Jonathan's company as soon as possible.

"You're not happy with me, are you?" asked Jonathan, in his soft-spoken manner.

"No. It's not you, I don't think I was ready, that's all." She did feel sorry for Jonathan and the way she had treated him on the site, but her tempestuous nature was not something a good-natured man could handle. She needed to be controlled.

"It's fine, I should have known better and not taken you there."

Their conversation had come to an end as the two of them arrived back at the mansion; Sukhi got out, relieved she was back at home.

"I suppose you don't want to see me again?" His face had dropped.

"No, I didn't say that."

His face appeared shocked.

"But you will need to give me time and perhaps some space." Sukhi felt annoyed; usually she would put men out of their misery and tell them once and for all that this was not going to go anywhere. Whether she liked it or not, she had to use Jonathan.

She beamed a small goodbye to Jonathan, then ran back to the door and into her mansion. As she entered she screamed so loud that the entire house stopped dead in their tracks. Her father ran out of his office and darted straight to Sukhi.

"What is the matter?" he cried.

"I'm sorry, I just needed to scream," she stated.

"Did the date go that badly then?" her father mocked, but Sukhi was in no mood for fun and games.

"It wasn't a date. I'm not coming to the office tomorrow, send the doctor to see me first thing in the morning," she stated as she ran back up the stairs and straight into her bedroom, slamming the door hard behind her.

She found herself sobbing; she picked up the note that was given to her the day before, scratched with a knife, stating, *'I'm still coming to get you.'* The words echoed through her mind, hearing the voice of her kidnapper only provided small comfort.

What am I doing? This is inconceivable.

She shoved the note under her pillow and flung herself onto her bed. All she wanted was him, but she knew her anxiety and impatience were taking over her. Finally she realised she had to break her silence and reveal the truth to Dr Meller.

Chapter 6

Sukhi woke up early morning, washed and changed just in time for the doctor's arrival at the entrance of the house. As she rushed down the stairs she noticed how the doctor seemed to be wearing more of a casual attire than his normal suit and tie ensemble.

"Sorry, it was such a short notice. I hadn't prepared myself last night," admitted the doctor with his ever-gleaming perfect smile.

"That's fine, let's start now."

It was the first time he had seen Sukhi keen to start her session, although judging from her anxiousness she wasn't doing too well. It was clear she had barely slept, judging from the dark circles that surrounded her eyes.

"Are you okay?" he asked, boring his steady brown eyes into hers; her mind was too preoccupied by the constant warping thoughts of her kidnapper.

"I'm fine; we just need to start straight away."

The doctor was aware of her distress. He opened the door to the drawing room, allowing Sukhi to enter. As he closed the door behind him, he noticed she was unable to settle down.

"He never raped me," she confessed hastily.

"Ok Sukhi, calm down first," he said with his reassuring voice that began to slowly soothe her anxiousness. She took small but deep breaths and calmed herself down; she wasn't shaking as she was before. He pressed for her to take her usual seat and make herself comfortable.

He sat in the master chesterfield chair and again began to analyse her, she hated it when he looked at her in that way, but knew it was just his professional nature to be like that.

"Okay, calm down and explain."

"I don't think he ever raped me." He could tell by her tone she was frustrated.

"Right, I see, just explain what happened to me."

Sukhi sighed for a moment, remembering her first sexual encounter with the kidnapper.

***

I was locked in my dark cell; he regularly came to make sure I was fed properly. Somehow my thoughts wandered quite a lot at this point, and I began to perceive his need to ensure I was okay as an act of kindness. I began to see his actions in a different light and I'm not entirely sure why I began to feel for him. He was taking care of me...

The one time he was in my cell whilst I ate the food he had prepared, I decided to ask him different questions in false hope that he would answer them, but strangely that one time he did.

"Do you have any family?" It seemed absurd at first to ask such a strange question, but I felt like I was attempting to find some connection with him.

"Not anymore," he sighed with his slick yet sultry voice; it was deep and slow but perfect.

"What happened? If you don't mind me asking." I was half expecting him to ignore me as he usually did, but it appeared he had made himself comfortable in my cell and was more than happy to answer.

"They were murdered," he responded. It was clear he was a man of few words but I could tell he was upset by the question I had asked him. He began to bring himself up from the floor leave my cell, but in a bold move I grabbed his hand before he could walk out. I don't know what came over me, but it was the first time in days or weeks that I got a reaction out of him and I didn't want him to leave me alone.

"Don't go," I requested. I remember feeling scared and unable to take my eyes off his mask. I was unsure what I was doing, but I knew I didn't want him to leave me. He sat back down opposite me, and sighed heftily. I wasn't sure if I was getting through to him, but by all means I wanted to. He was the only person I'd had contact with over the weeks and I hated being left alone.

"I was meant to kill you." His voice was deep and husky. "But I found myself unable to do so." Momentarily I was shocked by his remark, but a strange sensation of awe came over me. He never brutally hurt me, or tortured me intentionally. Instead he just locked me in a cell and fed me. He could have done so many things against my wishes, but he didn't.

It had seemed strange at first but it had been so long that I became accustomed to a different way of life. An escape from my life.

I'm not sure what came over me, but I felt a strange urgency to kiss him. My wrists were still bound by the chains on the floor, tears slowly formed but I tried so desperately to hold them back. I moved closer to his masked face, unable to make out its structure, but as I approached his black mask, I could tell where his lips were. I approached him slowly and kissed them through his dark mask. A strange sensation rose from within, and I could feel him kiss me back through his black mask. It was rough, course and unrefined, no soft feeling, just the pure harshness of his rough mask.

But he suddenly pushed me away; I had lost my balance and found myself falling back, lying on the floor. He looked like he was panicking; he started to pace inside my cell saying things like, "No. This cannot happen. This is not what was supposed to happen. Why? What the hell am I doing?" He repeated himself with questions.

"Why can't you?" I demanded, picking myself up from the floor. I could tell I wanted him to do more, but he was just as conflicted and confused as me.

"BECAUSE, SUKHI," he yelled, but then sighed realising it was no use losing his temper. "Even if I wanted to do anything with you... I cannot."

I remember feeling annoyed, was I not attractive? Had he not found me appealing? I was hurt and confused by his comment.

"Why not? I'm allowing you to take me, I'm giving

you permission."

"It's not that, Sukhi. Even if I wanted to, which trust me I want you. Very badly. I can't allow myself to have you."

"Why not?" He could tell by the tone in my voice I was upset, and almost hurt that he wouldn't take me. He stopped pacing and came close, so close I could feel his breath through his mask pulsate down the side of my neck. I remember feeling strange sensations and pining urges for him deep within, yet he had barely touched me. He grabbed my face with his strong hands; his strength was overpowering and undeniably uncontrollable.

"Because I'll hurt you, you won't like what I want to do to you," he whispered in my ear with desperate yearning constraint in his voice.

***

The doctor's face had fallen, he was in shock and Sukhi could tell; she slowly felt warm tears flush through her eyes, but she attempted to hold them back.

"I don't understand, doctor. Why I had become like that? I'd never even saw his face."

He analysed her face, realising that this was the reason she was ashamed. She couldn't understand why she reacted the way she did and why her mind was so conflicted. But before he gave her any form of diagnosis he wanted to know more her accounts.

"Can you tell me more, Sukhi?"

Sukhi looked up at him with dusky watery eyes; he could tell she felt helpless, but she nodded with acknowledgement, fearing the worst that she would be diagnosed as clinically insane.

***

I provoked him, he was so close to me that I could easily antagonise him. I ran my hand down his chest and onto his trousers, firmly gripping below. I could feel him, large, throbbing and hungering to burst from within. He didn't really stand a chance; I wouldn't let him go despite his desperate attempts to show constraint, but he eventually gave in. I wonder now if that was a mistake. He wasn't kidding when he told me that he would hurt me, but I craved it, I wanted him.

Bear in mind I never saw his face, but he was powerful and overbearing; it was hard not to succumb to his every wish. He mounted over me, tearing away his jumper and undoing the belt to his trousers. I was in reverence when I saw his perfect muscular body, his back had been carved out by angels and his arms were cut to distinction; it was just sheer perfection. Despite his immaculate body he was true to his word, he had warned me that he would hurt me and he did. He ripped my clothes off from my body, revealing all to him. He spread my legs apart with force and knew from how wet I had become that I was submitting myself to him.

"So you want me, do you?" His voice was dark, a small sneer of enjoyment came from the sinister laugh he had bestowed.

But he didn't enter me. Instead he thrust his fingers deep, the thrust ripped inside of me, forcing me to cry out with provoking pleasure. The motion was fast and firm, with every push I was becoming more wet; my body was quaking in ecstasy, and he didn't stop until I was fully wet to his satisfaction.

"Yes you do," he growled.

He mounted in perfect position to enter me; he grabbed a piece of my ripped clothing and shoved it aggressively into my mouth, the domineering force he inflicted upon my body was pure gratification.

"You will not like this," he snarled in a darker tone.

With one hand the masked man pinned my arms above me for restraint, I was powerless and left to submit to his every command. With the other hand he hit my face with a delightful smack, inflicting pleasurable torment; this only heightened the intensity, causing my core to flutter. He hadn't even entered me and my body was craving for him to be inside. He teased me at first, letting me feel his large girth, I moaned in hope it would entice him to give me what I wanted.

In a sudden movement without warning he thrust himself inside me. I screamed, unaware of how large he was. I arched my back whilst he tilted my head, revealing my bare neck. He snarled whilst he entwined his fingers around my throat, squeezing it firmly in his grip. He was fucking me hard whilst strangling me; the shortness in breathing whilst he drove deep inside caused my senses to intensify, satisfaction that had never reached greater heights. I cried out in pain but lusted for him to do more.

"Fuck you," I told him, spitting out the piece of clothing he had pushed into my mouth. I was aggravating him on purpose; I wanted him to impose more infliction of torture onto my body, I was enjoying his full-throttled thrusts and estranged desire to cause pain.

He slapped me hard across my face. I laughed at him, enjoying his attempt to hurt me, in the hope he could take it further.

"Is that the best you got?" I was challenging him.

He stopped for a moment, and again pushed himself away, but this time he turned me over, making me bend on all fours. He shoved the piece of clothing he had ripped before back into my mouth to shut me up, he tilted me head to a side and breathed closely around my neck; the burning sensations ran through my body, forcing me to become more wet and summoning for him to enter me again.

"You little bitch. You're going to wish you never said that," he growled. I was too busy enjoying everything he was doing; he used his legs to spread my thighs apart, aggressively grabbed my waist and hoisted it up. I felt my core race and instantly my nerves had become sensitive, impulsively I knew what he was going to do, but hoped he wouldn't dare do it.

"No," I muffled with the piece of clothing that was savagely put into my mouth, but he just sniggered cruelly at my pathetic attempts of plea. He tried to push himself into my arse, but I tensed desperately, not allowing him to enter.

"Fuck, you're so small." By his tone I could tell he was frustrated, but he had made it his mission to make sure he was going to get in. I felt a sudden spit aim directly on my hole; my entire body jolted in shock. He used his giant cock to spread his saliva around the area; I knew at that point I wasn't going to escape. I shuddered, aware that I was scared and that this was not something I was going to enjoy.

He pushed his entirety into me. I let out a piercing scream of agony and torture which echoed the entire cell. He laughed with a menacing and sadistic valour; he knew tears were streaming down my face, the anguish was too exhausting.

"Your ass is so tight," he groaned, enjoying the firm tightness of my arse that I had unwittingly presented to him. The pain was unbearable; throughout the duration I whimpered and wept uncontrollably. This only imposed more satisfaction on his part as he pumped with full vigour deeper and faster. He grew bigger and I could feel him expand within me, I wanted it to end and whimpered for more in hope that he would finish. His groaning grew louder and unexpectedly a full blast of cum was released inside. He withdrew and my entire body, exhausted, abused and fatigued, collapsed onto the hard, cold stone floor.

I lay there listlessly for a while, staring into the abyss as tears continued to stream down my face. Had I asked for it? Had I really wanted it? The masked man did warn me that I wouldn't like what he wanted to do, and he was right, I didn't enjoy some parts of it. I felt ashamed.

Instinctively this wasn't something normal and I couldn't understand why despite the turn of events I had grown an immediate attachment to the masked man who was a stranger.

***

Sukhi saw the doctor's face turn into something far more serious and full of concern, he finally began to understand but knew he needed to know more to fully summarise the problems she was facing.

"I think you've done well today. I'm slowly beginning to understand the situation better, however, I don't know the full story. We'll eventually get there and work out solutions that will benefit you," he said, attempting to comfort her with reassurance.

"Am I crazy, doctor? I don't understand why I became the way I did." He could tell she was distressed.

"There's a term we use in the medical field called 'Stockholm Syndrome'. In simplest terms it's when hostages express empathy and sympathy towards their captors."

"So I'm not crazy?" said Sukhi with small relief.

"The accounts you have described resemble this, so in answer to your question, no, you're not crazy." The doctor failed to look at Sukhi; he had a look of professionalism but Sukhi could see disappointment etched on his face.

"You think I'm disturbed?"

He looked up at her with his dashing but sympathetic look. Sukhi sighed, feeling as if the one person who might be able to understand her actually thought she was troubled. He stifled a small smile, in hope that it might be encouragement.

"No I don't, Sukhi, I think you've been through a lot and I believe you're confused. No doubt this kidnapper is the reason behind your bewildered state.

But we'll take one step at a time and get to the bottom of the situation and your feelings. Hopefully this will straighten everything out for you."

They were words of comfort; she smiled. She somehow felt pressure release from her mind, like a small burden had been lifted from her shoulders. She was no longer in her fretful state, but her desire to find her kidnapper was something that burned and urged her; her impatience for him was what was making her anxious.

"How did you feel about the session?" asked the doctor, keenly waiting for feedback.

"Strangely I can't help but feel unsettled, but I do think this session was helpful."

"Well that's good, but it's natural to feel unsettled. You've released a lot of information today." He had earned her trust and respect. Her feelings had resided with a stranger and she had made it her mission to find him.

"Well, thank you for today."

***

"Ahh... Miss," said Mrs Cheshire, cleaning the furniture that resided around the hallway.

"Hey Chess." Sukhi went behind Chess, giving her a full embrace, holding her as tightly as possible.

"What's with you now?" she said, comforting Sukhi by tapping her face with her hand.

"Nothing, just feel a little better." She smiled.

"Well that's good. I 'ave something for you."

"Really? What?"

"That Jonathan fella came by whilst you were 'avin a session with the doctor, he left a huge bunch of flowers for ya."

Sukhi rolled her eyes, aware that she had got herself into a situation with Jonathan that she wished she hadn't. There was nothing wrong with him, just upon revealing to the doctor a snippet of her account, she had learnt that there were feelings for another man. A man she didn't know.

"Chess, I really don't want to see him," she moaned, hoping Chess would comfort her, but the tough old bird believed in facing reality rather than running from it.

"Well Miss, if you don't want to then don't."

Chess was right, ultimately Sukhi was in control of her own life. A startling revelation occurred for Sukhi with that thought. She needed to start working with her father in the office.

The large housekeeper bustled away with her chores, whilst Sukhi was left to contemplate her first plan of action to find her kidnapper.

Chapter 7

Sukhi had woken herself up early morning and dressed herself in her office attire; she carefully positioned her bun perfectly centred on her head. She didn't cake herself with makeup, but put on the simplest amount to look professional.

"Sukhi, it's time for us to leave." Her father was calling her from down the stairs; she quickly grabbed her small jacket and bag, then ran out of the room to meet her father. He was smiling for a change, which was a rare sight.

"This morning, I'll have a meeting with those board members, that Cavendish fellow will be there as well."

She sighed.

Sukhi sat in the limo with her father; she noticed how the first thing he did was pull out files and financial models on the properties he owned.

"Do you think you might be able to keep yourself pre-occupied?" her father stated whilst still flicking through the pages of the financial models. "Just until the board meeting is finished?"

"What? Why?"

"I just need to take care of a few things, if you are there it might make them a bit agitated."

Sukhi could feel her head becoming hot with anger and annoyance.

"Dad, what was the point of me coming in today then?"

"Yes, to learn about the business, the thing is there is a lot more to it than just financial models, banks and acquisitions."

He looked at her carefully and noticed, from her furrowed brow and red face, she was infuriated.

"So much for father and daughter time together."

"Sweetie, you know my line of work and you're old enough to understand how you and I must play our roles with those board members and investors."

Sukhi was annoyed. She had thought she would spend time with her father, but instead was to be left to her own devices.

"Fine," she huffed.

Sukhi felt disappointed with her father, she was a little excited about spending time with him to learn the business and her hopes were dashed first thing in the morning on the way to work.

Disappointment, I seem to be experiencing this a lot lately.

"I have to remind you, your Great Aunt Vera from Austria will be paying us a visit tomorrow," her father slipped into the conversation.

"How is that old bat still alive?"

"Well she wants to check in on the family, to see how we are all doing."

"Dad," she moaned. "She's such an old crow, you know she dislikes me."

"She does not, my dear. Just grin and bear it."

Sukhi rolled her eyes.

The limo pulled up to the office, and the media and photographers started to bombard them with pictures and questions. Her father opened the door, smiling at everyone as questions from all different sides were being thrown at him, primarily about his daughter. Sukhi sighed before revealing herself to the public; the media went wild. She smiled with her pearly white teeth, whilst the hounds all tried to close in on her.

Ben, her father's bodyguard, immediately started to push people away; she quickly paced herself up the stairs next to her father. The two of them walked into the office, bidding the public goodbye.

As soon as they entered the building, her father pulled his daughter to the side.

"Okay, Sukhi this meeting with Green Capital is very important; this is a make or break deal. I'm going to ask Penny to keep an eye on you, until I finish."

Penny was David's secretary, a shrewd old woman who Sukhi liked because of her sharp mind and execution style.

Penny nodded to her boss and once the acknowledgement was made, he ran off to his meeting.

"Hello my dear, how are you?" Penny asked, leaning forward with a smile on her face. Sukhi smiled back.

"Penny, I was wondering if you might be able to tell me. Which floor is administration?"

Penny eyed her up and down with caution at first.

"What is it that you are looking for, Suks?"

"It's private."

"Then I'm sure I could be of assistance," said Penny with an air raising eyebrow.

"Ok, maybe I can just go and sit in my father's office. Where can I find it?"

"Follow me, I'll show you." Penny rose from her chair and stalked towards the lift, Sukhi followed closely behind.

Penny pressed the fifth floor and the lift shot up quickly. As they doors opened Penny carried on stalking past all the offices, Sukhi glanced sideways only to notice many of her father's employees began to stare and gawk at the mere sight of her.

"Lena Renham, can you give Sukhi access to Mr Rai's office?"

The small woman creaked a tiny smile with her wrinkled lips. She was an eerie old woman with silvery grey hair and yellow sharp teeth, she reminded Sukhi of a creepy old witch from the fairy tale stories that were read to her as a child.

"Sorry, she has no right to access his office."

Sukhi pursed her lips in annoyance.

"Lena, this is Mr Rai's daughter, please give her access," said Penny.

The woman's smile dropped and, by pressing a small button to her left, Sukhi gained access to her father's private office.

"Thank you, Lena."

Despite never having been to his office, she wasn't surprised by the interior. As usual it was decorated with antiques, no doubt from Mots Road near Chelsea.

"Antiques, isn't our house already full of it?" she muttered to herself.

Sukhi charged at his Georgian-style desk, pulling out all his drawers looking for anything that remotely presenting itself as private files, but alas it was only deals, acquisitions and mergers.

After about forty-five minutes of rummaging through all the files, she pulled open the drawer took a look, but could find nothing. She slammed it shut, but as she did a small compartment from within his study desk became slightly ajar. She pulled it open and found an old golden pocket watch with a triangular symbol on it with an oval eye shape in the middle.

What's this?

She traced her finger over it and looked longingly at it, it was a symbol she recognised from her childhood, but she could not quite pinpoint when. She quickly took her phone out and snapped a picture. As she opened the pocket watch she found something engraved within – 'Pecuniate obediunt omnia'. Again, she took her phone and snapped another photo. She saw the door handle move, and quickly jumped, stuffing the pocket watch back into its compartment.

"Cough, hello there, may I ask how you have access to this part of the building?" lurked a deep voice from behind her. As she turned to face the voice, a young man with startling blue eyes and perfectly slicked back dark hair stood staring at them. He had a sharp grin and easy manner, slim build with a perfectly tailored navy suit that hugged his physique.

"Who are you?" Her eyes widened, worried she might've been caught.

"My name is Cody, Cody Cavendish." He smiled, staring at her bewildered face.

She frowned at him with dismay, remembering this was the young man trying to take over her father's businesses.

"Right… and what are you doing in my father's office?"

"Well I have a meeting with him…"

"I see, well you can see yourself out of his office until he arrives then." Her voice was austere and curt.

"You must be Sukhi." He waltzed towards, her grabbing her hand and raising it to his lips, gently kissing it. "You have such mesmerising beauty. Has anyone told you that?"

She blushed profusely, dumbfounded for words.

He was charming.

"How were you let in, without my father being here?"

"Lena had stepped away from her desk, seeing as I saw small movement behind the glass, I had assumed you were your father."

The handle turned and Sukhi's father walked into the office, slightly dishevelled from the board meeting.

"Ah, Cavendish, I see you met my daughter Sukhi."

"Completely charmed." His lips curled by the corner of his mouth into a somewhat indecent but wickedly handsome smile. She blushed again.

"Sukhi dear, I received a call from the detective. He mentioned he's managed to narrow it down to three suspects and would like you to come in and see if you can identify them."

"Oh really? So you want me to go?"

Her father looked a little bewildered by his daughter's answer. He glanced to see that she was still glaring at Cavendish. He smiled.

"Yes, don't worry, we'll discuss business over dinner."

With a small wave of his hand, Sukhi picked up her things and left his office.

***

Sukhi was somewhat annoyed her father had dismissed her very quickly upon meeting Cody Cavendish. She quickly placed her large Bvlgari shades on and walked towards the city police department to see Detective Darryl.

"Hey Sukhi!" shouted a voice from behind. As Sukhi turned she noticed how Jonathan had paced himself beside her. "Wow, fancy seeing you out in public without the media going wild."

"Hi Jonathan, sorry I'm a little busy at the moment so I'll speak to you later?"

"Oh yeah, sure, where are you off to?"

"I'm going to see Detective Darryl."

"Oh, so you're heading to Holborn? Well I'm actually walking in that direction so I might as well join you."

Sukhi was annoyed she did not come up with a better excuse, she liked being left alone, but Jonathan was insistent on joining her, and would no doubt ask her questions.

"So what do you need to see the detective for?"

"He wants to see if I can identify some suspects."

"And you aren't afraid?" said Jonathan, raising an eyebrow.

"No, why should I be?"

"Just that one of these suspects could be your kidnapper."

"Well if the police have him, then I'm out of danger."

She walked faster, keen to be rid of Jonathan's company; Jonathan coolly paced himself beside her, keeping up with her at ease.

As they turned around the corner of Tottenham Court Road, they approached the station.

"Well I think it might be best for me to take my leave," said Sukhi with a smile.

"Of course, but as I noticed Clive is not here would you like me to take you home after?"

"I don't think it is necessary, I'll find my way back," she said.

"Ok, that's fine, would you mind if I called you later just to check up on you?"

"Sure."

With a small peck on her cheek he left her. She sighed with relief.

As she walked up the stairs towards the police department she caught many glimpses from her side view of people and police staring at her. As she approached, the lady behind the reception desk took a sidewards glance and gawked. She was a young blonde with startling blue eyes, her eyebrows were painted brown and her skin was extremely orange. It was clear she had spent far too long in the sunbed.

"Oh my god... it's you!" she said loudly enough to catch everyone's attention.

"Yes, I'm here to see Detective Darryl."

"Sorry, could I ask for your...?"

"Suzy, please let Miss Rai through," said the large detective from behind her. Suzy quickly cleared her throat and pressed a button to allow the steel door to open from the side. Sukhi walked in, noticing the police were either talking about various cases or behind extensive paperwork.

"Please follow me," said the detective, briskly passing all his peers with Sukhi following very closely behind him.

He opened the door to his office which was relatively small but filled with paperwork all around his cabinets, windowsill and bookcase. The only thing that was clear was his desk, which had a side lamp, a large mug of coffee and three files perfectly situated in the middle.

"Please excuse the mess, take a seat," he offered. Sukhi took her place and sat down waiting for the detective to begin.

"How are you today, Miss Rai?" asked the detective, who sat down in the chair opposite to her.

"Very well, my father sent me in to see you to see if I can identify any suspects."

"Yes, well my detectives have narrowed it down to potentially these three men." He slid the three files over to her. With each suspect there was a mug shot of each of them holding a placard with a name and number on the front of the file.

Sukhi peeked over the files.

"Take your time, have a glance at the reports and let me know if you think any of them are the suspects." With that, the detective left the room to leave Sukhi to look through the files.

One older man who was bald, aged 52, wrinkles sidled around his eyes and his large nose was his most prominent feature. His face was untimely withered and she could tell by the large neck and saggy cheeks that this was not the man who kidnapped her.

Simon Byrd, primary suspect, aged 52.

Convicted: Sex offender, drunken disorderly behaviour, disruptive nature

Diagnosed: Schizophrenia, Dyslexia

No Occupation

Illiterate, quick temper, and suspect shows no signs of remorse in regards to Sukhi Rai. Used the term "Bitch should have been done in more." He has no moral inclination, shows a clear disliking towards David Rai.

Reason to dislike Mr Rai: Thirty years ago, the two had a dispute in a bar. Simon Byrd's family was taken away by social services, constant blame towards David. His house: walls covered with the David's picture, darts and other disfiguration towards Mr Rai's face. This suggests genuine hatred towards the man. Books found on ways to assassinate Mr Rai and large illustrations of dismembering his family.

"This isn't him," muttered Sukhi, who felt a little uneasy viewing the pictures taken from the suspect's house. He had quite vivid pictures of hacking the entire family up into pieces including Serena, which only made her feel sick. "What a disgusting old man."

Joe Cole. Aged 35

No convictions

Diagnosed: No Mental Illness

Occupation: Investment Banker

Shows signs of irrevocable hatred towards Mr Rai due to rogue trade that lost Mr Rai's company 4 million pounds in 2008 after the financial crisis., Joe was fired and arrested. FCA fined Mr Rai, Joe was never to work within an investment bank again.

"This isn't him either." Sukhi sighed again.

Sukhi looked closely at the mug shot, and felt instantly saddened by the history inflicted on the poor man. She knew it wasn't him judging by the paleness of the skin, her kidnapper was bronzed and was extensively athletically fit, whereas this man didn't have any of those primary features.

Sukhi suddenly felt disheartened that the police hadn't really narrowed it down to someone worth investigating, but then she also felt relieved that they were on the wrong tracks.

Ben Norman. Aged 48

Convicted: Drink driving

Diagnosed: Borderline Personality Disorder

No Occupation

Primary Suspect. Killed Mr Rai's first wife. Sima Rai. Accidental release in mental institution. Sima Rai was bludgeoned to death.

"What the…?"

All blossoming colour began to fade from her perfect face, her stomach sank into a foul pit of darkness, the room they were in began to close in on her. She was losing sight of everything around her. A small tinnitus ringing began to grow louder.

My mother was murdered.

Sukhi felt the walls around her caving in, her head started to spin, and slowly she began to hallucinate, unable to get to grips with her hyperventilation.

The detective walked into the office to check in on Sukhi, only to find her collapsed on the floor.

"Oh dear God! Miss Rai!" He swooped in, quickly putting her into the recovery position on the floor.

"Someone call the ambulance!" he shouted.

***

Sukhi woke up to the sound of a constant beeping and bustling around in the background, the white walls and greyish blue large curtains surrounded her. She knew instantly she was back in a hospital.

"Miss Rai, are you awake?" said the detective who was standing fairly close to her.

"Leave her, she will be fine," said a familiar voice – it was Ash. "Her father is on his way."

"What is going on?" she muttered, trying to get back to normal.

"You fainted in my office, so I got you straight to the hospital."

Sukhi slowly became more alert, remembering that her mother was murdered.

"Yes, now I remember… My mother was murdered… Is that true, detective?" she asked.

The detective's eyes widened.

"Your father never told you?" he asked.

His face faltered and was expressing a huge amount of worry. "Ah, fuck! I'm in shit!"

"Sukhi, you need to rest," said Ash, trying to calm her down again, but she pulled herself upright in the bed.

"Detective, please could I ask you one favour before my father gets here?" she asked.

"Certainly, my dear."

"Pass me your notepad and pen."

The detective passed over his leather cased notepad and Cartier pen from his pocket. She quickly opened a blank page and drew the triangle with the oval eye in the middle. She passed the notepad and pen back to the detective who eyed the drawing, baffled and confused.

"Please could you tell me what this triangle thing means? Come back to me as soon as you find out."

The detective looked at her, confused, wondering if this symbol had anything to do with her kidnapping or something else entirely.

"Of course."

There was voice shouting amongst the halls, Sukhi could hear the nurses trying desperately to keep someone calm. That voice was none other than her father's, who came stomping in to her unit.

"Detective! What is the meaning of this? How did my daughter end up back in here under your watch?" he yelled.

"My sincerest apologies, Mr Rai… I—"

"Dad! It's not the detective's fault at all, it's yours!"

Sukhi nodded towards the detective indicating that he should take his leave. Ash glanced at Sukhi and then her father and took a step back, thinking he should leave.

"No Ash, stay here," she demanded.

As the detective took his leave, Sukhi's father took her side looking completely confused.

"When were you going to tell me my mother was murdered?"

Her father's face became ghost white, all colour drained from his face instantaneously. He sighed.

"We will talk about this another time, not here."

"No, Father! I demand to know now! Why have you kept it a secret?"

"Not here! God dammit! Listen to me when I say not here!"

Before she could utter another word, her father stormed out of the ward. His face had become one warped with guilt and frustration, but Sukhi could not quite understand why. Why had he lied to her?

"Are you alright, Sukhi?" asked Ash.

As she glanced up to nod to Ash, she noticed a huge bouquet of pink wild orchids were perched on her small side cabinet.

"Who bought me those?"

"I did, wild orchids I read in your file were your favourite."

"Yes, they are." She smiled. "They're beautiful! Thank you."

Suddenly a huge nurse came bustling into her ward, quickly taking her file and checking off an entire list.

"Right young lady, you will be discharged," she prompted.

"Did you do all the thorough check-ups?" asked Ash.

"We did, and she is fine," said the nurse in a brisk and sharp manner.

"Ok, looks like I'll be taking you home," said Ash.

The nurse gave him a sweet and short curt smile before quickly taking off all apparatus that was linked to Sukhi's arm. Once she was fully discharged, Ash gave his arm to Sukhi for her to hold on to.

"That drawing you gave to the detective, may I ask what that was?"

"I have no idea, hence I gave it to the detective."

"Do you think it is linked to the kidnapper?"

"To be honest, no. It's just a symbol I found in my dad's office and I just wanted to know what it was. Why would Dad keep things away from me?"

"Maybe, like most parents, he was just protecting you," said Ash, trying to console her. "It'll be fine."

Luckily the doctor had parked around the back of the hospital away from the media and spotlight; he walked towards the passenger side of his Aston Martin and opened the door for her. She sat into his silvery dasher which was refined with red leather seats. He was a man of good taste, no doubt.

As he revved the engine to start the car, he drove speedily towards her home. The journey was simply smooth but wonderfully fast. Her imagination grew wonderfully wild as he meandered through the back streets of London to take her home, the idea of running away from the world seemed like the most perfect dream.

Within ten minutes they reached home.

"How do you feel about our sessions, if you don't mind me asking?"

"Oh. Yes. Well y... you are helping," she stuttered. "Erm, doctor..."

"You know you don't have to call me doctor all the time."

"Sorry Ash, would you mind coming in for a longer session tomorrow?"

His face perked up in astonishment, but he could tell by the expression on her face she was unhappy, and the revelation regarding her mother would be affecting her.

"I have a feeling it's not do with your kidnapping. Are you okay?"

She looked up at him with pleading eyes; he could tell that something else was bothering her.

"Is it to do with your mother?" he asked in a concerned voice. He aimed to comfort her by rubbing her shoulder, pressing his thumb near her collarbone. She naturally convened.

"No, maybe... I'm not sure."

"I guess we have more issues than your kidnapping to get to the bottom of?"

She nodded, still unable to get to grips with the revelation about her mother. The doctor patted her on her back in an attempt to make her feel better.

"I'll come first thing early morning then, and we can have a longer session."

"Thank you, Ash."

Her faint smile showed her weakness, her eyes were dark and vacant as if she were lost in the wilderness of her own dark thoughts.

"You're most welcome, Sukhi, I shall see you then."

And with that, he took his leave and climbed into his Aston Martin to drive away.

As she waved goodbye her stomach sunk further into a dark pit, her legs began to lose sensation and her heart pounded harder in anxiety.

How I wish you would come and take me away from all of this.

Chapter 8

The next morning Sukhi rose feeling lightheaded, the dark sinking feeling had not disappeared; she wanted to smile but it seemed useless. What did her mother suffer from that led her to be in a mental institution? Had her father treated her badly? There were so many questions that hounded her mind, causing her head to ache.

"Miss. The doctor is here to see ya," said Chess.

Sukhi rose from her bed, she had no intention of changing out of her pyjamas. She quickly washed her face and brushed her teeth. She didn't think she was wearing anything too inappropriate, her pyjama shorts were relatively short and her cami top was a little thin but covered most. She pulled a large ochre boyfriend jumper over her and ran down the stairs to the drawing room, where the doctor was waiting for her. His smile dropped in shock.

"Oh, I didn't realise I woke you." As he eyed her full legs which were on show, he tried to quickly resume composure and not be distracted by them. Sukhi took comfort in her normal seat.

"No. I just refused to get out of bed, and figured I couldn't be bothered to change. I apologise for my attire."

"No, that's fine." He smiled again with the same relaxed composure. "Right, where would you like to begin?"

She looked up at him with her demure glazed eyes; he could see all the light had been drained out of her, that darkness had crept in, wiping all signs of hope and happiness in her.

"Yesterday I went to my father's office, a strange turn of events happened whereby I found a small revelation about my mother."

"Okay, what did you find out?"

"My mother was admitted into a mental institution where she was murdered by an insane patient."

The doctor's eyes shot up from his notepad, his eyebrows furrowed into confusion.

"Yes, I remember you told me yesterday… but in your file, Dr Blease said you were told?"

"Told what?"

The doctor's face looked alarmed.

"I'm sorry, Sukhi."

"No, my father never told me, no one told me."

"He is very overprotective of you."

Sukhi's face fell into dismay, had her entire life been a lie? Her father had kept so many secrets from her, other people in her life knew things she didn't even know and it had now taken its toll.

"What did the file say about my mother?"

"I'm afraid it doesn't say much, but I was aware that your father wanted you monitored from a young age because of your mother's death."

"Do you know anything about her mental illness?"

"Sadly Sukhi, I don't."

Fuck my father. I hate him. How dare he…

"I need to find out about her problem, maybe that's why there was always something wrong with me."

The doctor raised an eyebrow. "Something wrong with you?" he asked.

"Because I'm in… I never… I must be mad…" She couldn't complete her sentences.

"Do you think you're in love with your kidnapper?" Ash asked.

"There's just something about him, we are linked in a strange way and that connection was so strong it made me…"

She trailed off, realising she was revealing too much. She blushed in embarrassment, as the doctor looked at her with both bewilderment and fascination. He shuffled in his chair and remained composed.

"Interesting," was all he could merely say, before making notes in his black notepad.

"Now I know I must be crazy," she followed. "Like my mother apparently."

"I see." Ash continued to examine her. "Firstly, Stockholm Syndrome happens from events, it's not hereditary."

"You don't understand… the things he did were just…"

Sukhi paused for a moment, realising she was revealing too much for her own comfort.

"Hmm… please continue?"

"Do you not think it's possible though? He had something to do with her death? My father, that is?"

"Sukhi, if you have questions regarding your mother, you need to speak to him about it. Only he can tell you the truth… Why won't you tell me more about the kidnapper?"

"I just don't want to."

"Why? Are you now protecting him?"

Sukhi paused for a moment, taking in everything the doctor was implying. He was merely stating the feelings she couldn't come to terms with. It hit her hard, but it was what she needed.

"I think I am."

***

He'd bought me new clothes as the ones we had from the previous night, when we were together, had ripped to shreds. I sat there waiting for him; I was naked, wrapped up in a small blanket he had given to me before. When he walked in, he took my hand and led me to a small bathroom that had a toilet, washbasin and an overhead shower. It had been a few days since I had washed and it felt great for the first time in ages. He watched everything I did in the shower, taking pleasure in observing my every move.

He requested me to wear the silk beige dress that he had bought. It was expensive, judging from the material and the perfect finishes, which could only imply he was making good money or he came from a rich background. I obeyed his every wish and request; I don't know why I did that but I suppose it could be because he intimidated me in many ways and I wanted to please him in any way I could.

For the first time he didn't just give me food in a cell to eat, he had set up a small dinner with a table, two chairs and a flickering flame dancing from a candle; of course he never ate with me, but he did take pleasure in watching me eat.

When I had finished the lavish meal, he got up from his seat and stood behind me, I remained still and frozen for a minute, aware that he had stood mere centimetres behind me. He pushed his hands onto my shoulders, causing my body to react, flushing a huge pulsating heat that rattled through my skin; the touch was enough to make me extremely wet and ache to have him inside of me again.

"Do not turn around." I obeyed his command with delight. He placed a silk tie over my eyes, shielding my sense of sight which only intensified all my other senses to the surface; my body was aware of his every move that surrounded me. For the first time I felt a different touch flail around the nape of my neck. It was a genuine kiss, not the harsh, course, rough ones I got through his black woollen mask. It had occurred to me in that very instant he had taken off his mask and blindfolded me to still conceal his identity.

"We are going to try something different." His voice was just as silky and sinister as before, it was also deep, relaxed and composed. He pulled me up from my seat and led me elsewhere, I in turn didn't know what to expect. He didn't like to do things normally, which only made me think he was special; his dark and elusive ways captivated my interest. I had become accustomed to his ways and had taken an enjoyment in them as well. He placed my hands in front of me, and with what felt like rope he bound them together. I then felt a cold steel cuff clink around both my ankles and felt a heavy steel bar between them. I was his prisoner as he had taken full control of my body and I liked it.

"You want me to fuck you? Don't you?" he snarled, laughing menacingly in the cold air. He pushed his body close to mine from behind, locking me in between him. I could feel warmth exuberate from him, he breathed slowly around my neck which only caused me to pine for his infliction, but all of that changed in an instant.

"There was a sudden jolt from the side of his belt, it sounded like a blade by the swish of the metal. I attempted to free myself from him, but he had gripped me firmly and I was unable to escape from his clutches. I was captured and had no control to get away.

"No." I squirmed. "Please don't," I pleaded. Tears flashed down my cheeks, every good feeling had gone in that moment. I thought he was going to kill me, I knew he had a knife on him and in some way he wanted to use it on me. My heart was racing and I was in fear of my life. A small tear began to fall down one cheek.

"Shhh," he whispered, attempting to reassure me

somehow. "I'm not going to hurt you." His dark voice was scaring me, but made me drip with pleasure. "Stop moving," he ordered.

It was like a reaction my body had become ordained to, because I stopped instantly. My breathing hadn't stopped fluctuating, but I had stopped trying to wriggle out of his grip. He used the sharp edge of the blade to caress the curvature of my breast. I couldn't stop crying, I became so afraid of him in that instant, it would only take him one powerful push into my skin and then I would be dead.

"Shhh."His husky voice echoed in my ear, but it was still not easing my discomfort. He then pushed the blade outwards to the fabric of the silk dress, I could hear the dress slowly ripping down the centre. "You should trust me more," he growled in my ear.

"Once he had lavishly ripped my beige dress with the blade he had, I heard him throw the blade to the side whilst ripping all that material off, baring all flesh to him. He coaxed me aggressively with his fingers, causing my body to crumble in earnest within his grip. The pleasure was uncontrollable and he knew that I loved his hostile ways, as soon as I was dripping wet to his satisfaction. He slammed the top part of my body onto a cold steel surface, and hoisted my waist upwards in perfect inclination for him to enter.

"No," I screamed, aware that he would hurt me like he had last time.

He chuckled to himself cruelly, knowing fully what I had protested to.

"I told you I won't hurt you," he said with reassurance. With his strong, athletic, large build he used his thighs to spread my legs wider; the anticipation of waiting was too much, but I was afraid he would not enter where I wanted him to enter. True to his word, he didn't hurt me and instead he thrust his large enormity inside, the warmth of my wetness forcing him to groan piercingly; he had driven into me harder and faster and as he kept penetrating I continuously wailed in ecstasy. The sounds seemed to have made him more ecstatic; he increased his torment by forcing deeper luscious thrusts of pleasurable pain. The full throttle of his insertions broke all walls of defence and all I could do was succumb to him.

"Fuck," was all I could whimper, as the feeling of him probing with every shove only crumbled my core.

"His hand moved swiftly up my spine and with a forceful grip he pulled a fistful of my hair. I jolted as he yanked and pulled me up into a vertical position, the thrusts at a different angle inflicted new sensations of torture like pleasure.

"You are mine, Sukhi,'" he growled, still pushing deeper. His words seemed to have greater effect on the build of my climax that was so close to bursting. "No other man will ever have you. Because you are mine."

I nodded in acknowledgement, clenching harder to embrace his enormity that was consistently inducing more wetness underneath. I could feel myself building up, I tried to stop myself from releasing, but with his final deeper large thrust I cried out in relinquishing distressing pleasure.

I'd released, the climax released fluids that dripped down my inner thighs. He stopped thrusting and pulled out his large cock; he caressed my back, soothing me to return my breathing back to normal. Once I'd calmed down he turned me around to face him, I still couldn't see and I was still standing vulnerable, tied up and ready to do his bidding. I felt his hands caress my cheeks and the line of my jaw. Judging by the fact I could feel his breath so close to my face, it almost felt like he was close to kissing me, but he didn't.

He held the back of my head and pushed me down to my knees, he roamed his hands around my hair, coaxing me to open my mouth and let him in.

"I want you to suck me, Sukhi," he demanded.

I bit my lip, contemplating whether I should have allowed him, but it hadn't taken me long to decide, and with my tied wrists I took his enormity in my hands, and opened my mouth, welcoming his erect cock.

First I teased it with my tongue, slowly licking it up and down. I couldn't see if I was pleasing him, but I could feel the pulsating through his cock. I swirled my tongue around the tip, inducing pressure and warmness around it. He groaned with satisfaction and pushed my head down onto him with some force. He was large and his infliction of deep throating nearly choked me. I pushed my head back against his hand, so I could attempt to do things my way; I think he knew otherwise he wouldn't have stroked the side of my face with gentility. I went on to suck the sides of his cock, sweetly caressing it with my tongue, swirling it around him. After the mere foreplay of teasing was done, I then went onto deep throat his large cock, sucking it hard and fast. He groaned more. I could feel his legs quake slightly as my mouth was giving him nothing but perfect gratification. I wanted him to enjoy it, show him how much I loved the fact he could equally please me, and only wanted to return the favour. I sucked him harder and faster, licking it wildly whilst smothering the rest of his largeness with the surroundings of my wet mouth. I could feel him getting larger and knew he was close to cum. I willed myself to go wilder on him, his groans grew louder. In an instant, he released. The frustration that he had built up had pulsated into my mouth with delight. The salty fluid had infiltrated my taste buds, forcing me to swallow it.

"Good girl," he stated.

***

The doctor stared at Sukhi, with a flushed red face, but he was concerned; she could tell by the severity of his frown lines on his forehead.

"Sukhi, let's be honest here, are you in love with him?"

"That's what I can't work out. How is that even feasibly possible?" She was frustrated with herself, and could see that the doctor was in shock and disbelief from everything she had just told him. "What have you analysed so far?"

"That in these actions you have demonstrated signs of Stockholm Syndrome, the man showed signs of dominance, power and authority. He became your superior and you adhered yourself to it, finding some form of attachment from his domination, but my dear can you be in love with a man having only spent four weeks with him?"

"Now you're making me sound like I'm crazy."

"You aren't crazy, Sukhi. Stockholm Syndrome can be seen as normal in some cultures and it even dates back to evolution. It's a rare problem, but nothing that can't be helped. You need to assess your feelings though, and whether you can come to terms with the fact you will never see this man again."

"No. He said he will…" Sukhi paused. "He said he would come for me."

"Did he now? Was this an agreement between the two of you?"

"No. I received a note a few days ago, and the moment I received it I became impatient and restless." She lowered her eyes, ashamed of how she really felt about him. "I wanted him."

"Sukhi, I think we can both agree you have feelings for him, why do you think that is?"

"I don't know, I've recently begun to crave him."

"Did you ever have accounts that weren't sexual between you two?" The doctor's curiosity had heightened, he was intensely intrigued by the newfound revelations from Sukhi.

"There were many times… we talked about things I suppose."

"What did you talk about with him then?"

***

I was sitting in my cell waiting for him to arrive; it got lonely down there so there were times where I did look forward to him visiting. He would bring me food and drinks, and occasionally buy a brush and small things for me. I began to appreciate the fact he would do that for me.

One day he came into my cell and took a seat on the creaky bed he had inputted for me, the planks were noisy and the edges had deteriorated a little. It wasn't a great bed but it was the thought that counted. He sat there watching; despite his face being constantly hidden behind a black mask, I could tell he was watching me.

"Sukhi, what are your aspirations?" he asked. I remember feeling quite shocked that he had taken a sudden interest in my life, and yet at the same time I felt flattered he wanted to take the time to get to know me.

"My aspirations?" I was in disbelief. "Well I suppose I always wanted to be a writer and reside somewhere in a different country."

"Why is that? Don't you love your life here?"

"No, I'm hounded by people and controlled in life, I prefer being down here."

"How so?" I remember him folding his arms; he seemed genuinely intrigued with my dissolute and idle life as the daughter of David Rai.

"I'm expected to go to public presentations, showcase a good model citizen and not have a life of my own. It's like constantly trying to be someone I'm not and live a life that's not my own."

"I see. I think you should just do what you want, even if it means escaping this country," he advised.

I laughed a little at the irony of his statement. "Bit hypocritical. You have me locked in this cell."

He didn't laugh, just remained still and allowed there to be a frozen silence between us. I desperately yearned to question him, not so I could sell him out but purely because I wanted to get to know him. He had kidnapped me for a reason, and at the time I could only think I had wronged this man previously, especially as he only told me that he wanted revenge.

"Why did you decide not to kill me?" I was afraid of what he might answer, but I desperately wanted to know.

He sighed and didn't answer for what felt like a long period of time.

"I couldn't," he stated. "And I don't think I can anymore."

"Why?"

He walked over to me, leaning down close to my face; I remember feeling nervous and unsteady, his proximity caused dizziness sensations.

"Don't mistake my kindness as a weakness."

I was frowning at him, he didn't answer my question and this only fuelled anger; admittedly I was aware that I had a terrible temper and it wouldn't take very much to set it off.

"You didn't answer my question," I demanded.

He groaned, I was treading on thin ice but I didn't care. I wanted to know why he didn't want to kill me.

"You're too beautiful. It would be a shame to see the light drawn out of that pretty face of yours," he responded.

I wasn't too sure if I was disheartened by his

answer, I guess I wanted more. But needless to say, considering the circumstances, it would be impossible for him to harbour any feelings for me. I was just 'beautiful' to him, meaning he was enjoying the fucked-up sex he could have with me and relished the fact I was enjoying it.

***

"It is very clear you developed feelings for the kidnapper," stated the doctor, who was scrutinising the situation intently. "It actually explains your behaviour from the beginning, not showing signs of trauma, or isolation."

"Is this a bad thing?" asked Sukhi, who was confused.

"Imagine this kidnapper returned to you, what would you want to happen?"

Run away.

"I don't know."

"Would you want to reveal your feelings to him?" The doctor was asking questions that that were beyond her knowledge. She had not taken the moment to understand how she felt.

"How can I do that when I don't even understand them?"

"Sometimes we cannot explain the way we feel about someone, but it is up to the individual to work it out for themselves. Now I can write a diagnosis saying you are suffering from Stockholm Syndrome, however, only you can decide whether you felt compelled to do his bidding, or whether you wanted to do his bidding."

The doctor had laid it on a plate in a very clear and concise manner. Again it delighted Sukhi to know that she had personally felt she'd made some progress. It was a case of thinking outside the box in a logical approach and the doctor aided her in doing so.

"In all of your encounters with this kidnapper, had you ever called him a name? Or did he even tell you his name?"

"He referred to himself as a master. I asked him once and he only called himself by that name."

There was a small silence, as the doctor scrutinised the situation even more.

"In your opinion, what do you think I should do?" she asked.

The doctor sighed, shaking his head in disapproval of the entire situation. "As a doctor I cannot give you my opinion, I can only help in solving any issues you may have."

"As a friend then, what do you think I should do?"

"Personally, I think you should move on, forget about the kidnapper and start a new life. What you have described to me seems unhealthy."

Sukhi scowled at his scathed comment, but she knew she had asked for it. The doctor didn't want to express his opinion but did so as a friend.

"Have you not thought to give that young handsome fellow a chance?" He had stopped scrutinising her, and wasn't prying like he normally did. Instead he sounded a lot like her father in offering advice into her personal life and strangely she wasn't angered by him.

"Jonathan. I don't know." She pouted. "I find him annoying at times and he doesn't like you very much."

The doctor began to laugh, knowing that he caused many men to become very jealous of his good looks and charming apparel.

"Oh dear, have I ruined your chances?" he laughed.

"No. Not at all, he's very persistent and just asks so many questions."

"Maybe this is an opportunity for you to have a fresh start?"

"So I should forget about my kidnapper? Just like that?"

The doctor looked like he was stumped for words; she knew by the look on his face that he thought it was a hopeless cause. The kidnapper had no intention or feelings that reciprocated the way she felt about him.

"I do think you should try to let go of him," he said. This time his voice wasn't professional, it was a friend advising another friend.

But I want him. He promised he would come...

"I think I did care for him a lot more than I thought, is that so strange?"

"It isn't strange, Sukhi, but what you have described isn't considered normal. Just attempt to move on, you might be a lot happier if you did."

She sighed helplessly. "Okay."

Suddenly the doorbell rang. Sukhi became alert and realised her Aunt Vera had arrived.

How poorly timed, she will no doubt take pleasure in my misery, relish in the fact I am secretly in dire pain.

"Oh God, not her."

"What's wrong?"

"That would be Aunt Vera."

"I see, and do you not like her?"

"Put it this way, my mother was a waitress, the rest of my extended family despise me." She sighed.

The doctor looked at her sorrowfully.

"Seriously, no need to give me that look of sympathy. I've gotten used to it."

A shrilly voice came for the corridor. "Karen. Serena."

"That is appalling, she isn't even acknowledging you, and does your father know about it?"

"Of course he does."

Chapter 9

"My dear, dear Serena. Look how you've grown so beautiful. Just like your mother."

Great Aunt Vera was an old woman with defining grey streaks of silvery hair. Like David she had a strong defining jaw and cold astute eyes.

Sukhi walked through the door with Ash, she looked down at the floor and shuffled her feet into a perfect stance.

"Oh it's you, and I'm assuming this must be one of your new beaus?"

Sukhi scowled but didn't say anything. Her aunt merely smirked.

"Well, you know what they say? Common flowers have no place in the rose bush."

"That's an odd thing to say," piped up Ash, who realised the fat old spiteful woman had gone too far. "You see roses are a common type of flower."

Sukhi looked at him with confusion.

"You are right, Sukhi is no rose, she's more like a

wild orchid, exotic and rare."

Sukhi was dumbfounded. He was standing up for her.

"Why should she fit in? When she was born to stand out." The doctor was now glaring back at the old woman who was offended by the very presence of Ash.

"Hmph... that's Americans for you," said Aunt Vera with a raised eyebrow.

Sukhi cowered again.

"I'll take my leave," said Ash, gently patting Sukhi on the back. "We will speak soon."

With a swift turn, Ash had left.

Aunt Vera turned her attention to Sukhi again, knowing full well the girl wouldn't say anything. "Could you pollute our bloodline any more, girl? With an American."

Sukhi as usual didn't respond, only bowed her head a little and ran up the stairs into her bedroom; the one place her relatives couldn't get to her.

As she got there, she reminisced how appallingly her father's family had mistreated her. There was Uncle Phillip from Germany who refused to acknowledge her existence and there was Aunt Freya who raised her concerns over Sukhi inheriting the entire family fortune as she was the eldest in the family. It was no secret that they disliked her, after all she was the daughter of a waitress. As she got to her room, she noticed her phone buzzing.

It was Jonathan.

"I'm outside, I've found out some information that will be of interest to you."

Sukhi peered out her window and saw Jonathan waving at her to come down.

"Come on."

"You're a star... you know that?" She grabbed her bag in haste, she couldn't help but feel an overwhelming relief, as an afternoon with her aunt might've killed her.

She rushed past Aunt Vera who was still praising Serena to Karen. Outside Jonathan was waiting for her by her limo. She ran up to him, not thinking twice about leaving her home.

"You seem happy."

"I couldn't stay in that house with that old bat. Take me away please."

"Ahhh, family issues again I see... Look, I talked to my grandmother who used to work a mental institute called Sepia Health Clinic, she told me your mother was admitted there."

Sukhi's face fell.

"I only found out about that yesterday."

"Yes, it is all over the news how you fainted onto the floor upon finding out your mother was murdered in a mental home, the case blew wide open into a frenzy."

"How?"

"Someone must have leaked it from the police department."

Sukhi felt annoyed about how careless her actions were in public.

"Hence I researched the location of the clinic, and found some other interesting information you might want to know."

"Brilliant, get in the limo so we can go."

The two of them rushed into the limo and she ordered for Clive to drive.

"This sort of makes me feel like Sherlock Holmes," said Jonathan.

"Well we are about to unravel the secret of why my mother was even put into a mental institute in the first place," she said. "So I guess we are a bit like Sherlock Holmes and Dr Watson."

"I daresay, we make a pretty good team," he said. "The man, Ben Norman, was a schizophrenic, but don't worry, I'll be here to protect you. He's at the facility."

The drive was twenty minutes long but Sukhi had butterflies scorching through her stomach, it was anxiousness and excitement. Was this a link to lead to her kidnapper?

They arrived at their destination, a secluded building deep within a forested mountain area. It was extremely well kept and appeared to have some wealth status behind it, judging from the inventive architect. It seemed strange, however, that it would be secluded from civilisation. She took a deep breath, slowly preparing herself. She was about to come face to face with this institution and hunt for her mother's files to find out the truth behind her illness.

Jonathan raced to the door and rang the buzzer. A whiny voice came from behind the metal rusty speaker.

"How can I help?"

"We need to speak to the manager of the facility here."

"What for?"

"Let us in and we'll tell you," replied Jonathan.

The buzz allowed them to enter the large gothic-like building, Sukhi instantly felt uneasy with the number of mental patients wandering aimlessly with cold vacant expressions of being lost in a different world. The entire scene made Sukhi feel somewhat uneasy and for the first time she felt thankful Clive would be waiting outside for her.

It was impossible to think it was Sukhi's father that would send her mother to such a place.

"Listen, you go and speak to the manager, I'm going to snoop."

"Wait…" But before Sukhi could even say the next word, Jonathan had disappeared from her side.

Teamwork, that's what this was. Sukhi was on a mission to find out as much information about her mother as possible and Jonathan was proving to be a worthy ally in her mission.

"Miss Rai? What can I do to help you?" A tall woman with large spectacles peered over the rim to analyse Sukhi's face. She was old with silvery grey streaks against her chestnut brown hair. Her lips were thin, coarse and unrefined. She frowned at Sukhi.

"I'm assuming you want to know about your mother?" she said, before Sukhi could even answer.

"Look, I just want to find out information as to why was she sent here."

"I sincerely apologise but we can't disclose confidential information." Her smile was tight-lipped and curt.

"Claire… don't you have the rounds to attend to?" said a voice from behind her.

The old woman rolled her eyes. "Yes, Doctor Smith, I'll attend to that right now." The woman sneered at Sukhi before pivoting on her foot and stomping away down the corridor, clicking away in her high heels.

"You must be Miss Rai. Would you like to join me in my office?" said the doctor. Doctor Smith was a short, stout old man with large round spectacles that amplified his black beady eyes. As they walked down the hallway, Sukhi's fear began to build as screams and laughter could be heard from the hallways. As they approached his office, she couldn't help notice all the awards and certificates that hung around his office. He was a man who loved his work, but the entire setting of his facility seemed to be a contradiction to it.

"Miss Rai, please take a seat," he said, offering his chair. "To what do I owe the pleasure?"

Sukhi thought for a moment, she had a million questions to ask about her mother, but she knew she needed more time. Time was of the essence and Jonathan would soon be finished with his snooping.

"I understand my mother was admitted here a long time ago and I just wanted to find out... why?"

The doctor sighed.

"The information regarding our patients is private and confidential."

"Please, I just want to know why she was admitted. That's all."

The doctor's lips twisted, he ran his hand across his forehead as he contemplated whether to give in. Sukhi's eyes were pleading for information, and eventually he gave in.

"Ok... She suffered from severe depression and suicidal tendencies. Our job was to ensure she could do no harm to herself or her family."

"But she was murdered?"

"Miss Rai, I can't help you further, the person you should speak to is your father. He's the one who removed all of your mother's files from here." The doctor was shifty and Sukhi knew he was lying.

"Please..."

"We have nothing more to discuss, please find your own way out," he said sternly, turning her away.

"No... I'm not leaving here until I know more about my mother."

The doctor eyed her up and down. "You have the same fire."

"I can have my father ruin your professional career."

"Oh, there's no need for that, your father knows he cannot touch me."

"What do you mean?"

The doctor laughed at her. Sukhi's blood turned cold, she felt ice run through her veins, as she knew instantly something didn't feel right.

"That's enough." The door swung open and in came Jonathan.

"I see you have brought friends," the doctor leered.

"I think it's time to leave." Sukhi could tell Jonathan wasn't happy, it seemed he was far more distressed than she was.

Could he really care?

He grabbed her arm with force and got her out of the chair. Sukhi, unable to comprehend what was happening, just followed on his instruction.

"Go to Clive now, I'll see you outside in a moment," he instructed her.

Sukhi didn't dare to cross Jonathan at that point, she could tell by his face that he was livid.

She walked out of the door and the institution, and waited for Jonathan outside. She felt a cold breeze brush past her as the wild clouds began to sweep in. She felt an uneasy presence shoot cold tingles down her spine. Something didn't feel right, and she began to worry about Jonathan.

Just before a thunderstorm was about to start, Jonathan walked out of the institution slightly dishevelled and flustered.

"What happened?" asked Sukhi.

"We have a lot of work to do." Jonathan was still

fuming with anger so Sukhi refrained from interrogating him with questions. He hurried her into the limo and requested for Clive to drive fast. He dashed files onto Sukhi's lap and continued to ignore her.

"You don't seem yourself, what happened?" Sukhi ventured to ask.

"The content of those files, are just…" He didn't finish his sentence. It was clear from the content he had found in the files, he was disturbed.

"Don't look at it, Sukhi, just trust me when I say your mother went through a lot."

This only made her more curious, but she gulped, realising there was a lot more to it than anticipated.

"My father would have covered up my mother being in a mental asylum."

"The files revealed she had a mental breakdown after she killed an entire family in a fire, so yes, your father would cover up such a matter."

"We need to find out information then, about that family."

"How would we be able to find out such information? Police wouldn't have it if your father had something to do with it."

"What if this incident wasn't something you could cover up?"

"What do you mean?" asked Jonathan.

"An entire family? They would've had friends and other family. I know my father is powerful but there are some things he wouldn't be able to hide."

"What are you trying to say?"

"He might've made it look like an accident, taking my mother out of the picture."

"So what are you suggesting?"

"Archives. All the newspaper articles from 22 years ago that related to accidents with a fire."

"Sukhi, that won't be easy."

"It'll be tedious, but I'm sure we could find something that might point to more information about her."

Sukhi could see the reluctance in Jonathan's face; he was pondering whether he had got himself into deep water and if this entire investigation would get him into serious trouble.

"Okay, let's do it," he said. "But if you turn up to a library looking at archives, the media will be all over you, especially with that news report yesterday of you fainting."

"Oh shit."

"Listen, I'm very good friends with Gabby from the library. Rather than going to the library why don't I speak to her about having the entire library to ourselves at night, or taking out the archives, that way we can both take a look through them together without the hassle of the media."

"You'd do that for me?" She was shocked about the great lengths Jonathan would go through for her. "Why are you helping me?"

He smiled at her. "Well, maybe I'm just hoping you'll like me and want to go on a date at some point, but I figured you'd need time before you could even consider that."

"Oh," she said, looking down, fumbling her fingers.

Oh dear, he really is a perfect gentleman; maybe the doctor's right and I should really give him a chance. I should just forget about the man behind the mask.

"The doctor actually told me to give you a chance; he thinks it would be good for me to move on."

"Did he *really?*" Jonathan looked completely astounded. "I still don't like him."

"You don't have to, but he's still my therapist and that won't change."

"It just seems to me he has some form of control over your way of thinking."

"I sometimes think it might be better for someone to have control over me."

"That's not right, in my opinion," said Jonathan; it was clear by the frown that had convened on his forehead that he really didn't approve of the doctor. "So are you going to take his advice then?"

"Perhaps… I'll have to think about it properly before making any rash decisions."

He was grinning with the cheeky boyish smile. "There is nothing too rash about me, I daresay."

Sukhi rolled her eyes. "Right, so I shall see you later around my house, then?"

"Of course, I probably won't get them today, but I'll try bringing them tomorrow."

"I have my session with the doctor tomorrow; you can come around the afternoon."

"See, now you wonder why I really dislike the man."

They approached the mansion and Sukhi dismissed Clive, informing him that their travels for the day had finished. Jonathan approached his car and was about to leave before Sukhi decided to stop him.

"Do you want to come in?" asked Sukhi, her face blushed a violent red, but he was wearing his mischievous grin again.

"Are you sure?"

Sukhi rolled her eyes. "Wipe that grin off your face, my family will be in."

"Doesn't look like they are," he said, still grinning with that annoying smile of his.

"Even if they aren't, my housekeeper is."

"Ah, of course, isn't she just a bundle of fun."

Sukhi could hear the sarcasm in his voice, she wasn't sure if inviting him in was the best idea, but she had every intention of trying to follow the doctor's advice. Maybe he was right; she did need to move on.

"Well, it's up to you."

"Yeah, okay." He waltzed to the front door. Sukhi rang the doorbell expecting to see Chess come bustling to the door, but no one came. This made Sukhi nervous. Jonathan was right, no one was home.

"Dammit, where's Chess?" she muttered in frustration, now fumbling through her bag to find the house key. Eventually she found it and opened the door, the alarm started to beep and Sukhi ran to the alarm, putting in the code to ensure it was switched off before the whole house blared out in wails of sirens.

"Isn't this convenient? I have you alone in your house."

"Don't get any ideas."

"I'm getting plenty."

Sukhi noticed on the small table beside the entrance a note was written, it was clear by the messy writing that it was from Chess.

Dearest Sukhi,

I've taken your youngest sister to her cheerleading practice, it will be going on for three hours today so I won't be back till 9 p.m. Your mum and father are at the town hall ball with that horrid aunt of yours, they won't be back till late. I've left some food in the fridge just pop it in the microwave for two minutes and it should be good to eat.

Lots of love,

Chess

Sukhi put the note back down on the table and sighed; she walked to the lounge and summoned Jonathan to follow.

"Is there anything that you'd like to drink?" she asked.

"Nah, I'm good thanks."

There was an awkward moment where both of them fell silent, she felt compelled to switch on the television with the remote just to break that awkward moment. Of course she would, her doctor was telling her to move on, but she felt like she couldn't. It was instant betrayal even thinking of Jonathan in a certain way. Betrayal. Her entire body and mind was repelled.

Jonathan had sidled his way closer to her on the couch; she felt an unnerving need to keep away from him. She pushed herself away and kept the corner.

"Okay. Now you don't want to be kissed?" said Jonathan, bemused by her reaction.

"Sorry."

Maybe I should try. One kiss. Would that really cause so much harm?

"You can kiss me once."

He lifted an eyebrow at her, amused yet bewildered by her comment.

"I see, and if you like it?"

"I probably won't, but no harm in trying I guess." Blunt just like her father.

He moved closer, only inches away from her. He pressed both palms of his hands around her face, pulling her in. He could see that she was frowning, yet she closed her eyes waiting to be kissed.

"With that frown, I'm surprised I'm not deterred from you."

She huffed with discontentment.

"Yet you are very beautiful, it's remarkable how pretty your face is." Sukhi opened her eyes, alarmed by that statement.

Was it him?

"But guess what? I won't be kissing you today." He pulled away and laughed at her.

"Excuse me," she protested. "Why not?"

"Because you don't want to be kissed, I can see it written all over your face." He got up from the couch and pulled his jacket around him. "I'd rather you wanted it, than force yourself to want it."

"Am I that transparent?" she asked.

"Yes." He was still smiling but it was mocking and distasteful, without another word he slammed the door behind him and walked out of the house.

She huffed, feeling rejected and embarrassed,

But to deter herself from that feeling, her mind wandered elsewhere, predominantly her thoughts of her kidnapper. It seemed to have a calming effect on her nerves when she thought about him. How her body would rile itself up thinking of him, she was merely living in a fantasy of him, whereby he would cradle her and fuck her. The thoughts of him touching her provoked sensations deep within her. All she could think of was why she couldn't get him out of her head. Why were her feelings such a way? Was the doctor right in telling her to move on?

His touch, his body, and his domineering character that controlled her fiery and tempestuous wild nature was a perfect match. Indeed someone she barely knew enamoured her, his actions were enough to make her body quake at the mere thought of him.

"Sukhi. Wake up," echoed a voice; it was him, I knew it was him. The firm grip he had about my waist was recognisable

and yet comforting.

"Yes?"

"Come with me." I felt him lift me with no effort, he was strong, his arms were beautiful and perfectly muscular; angled to perfection. He placed me onto a cold steel-like bed face down. It was the bed I had seen from my cell.

"Are you going to kill me now?"

He sighed before he spoke, that elegant huskiness in his voice was enough to make me swoon.

"You know, I can't kill you," he responded.

He was a man of few words, mysterious, elusive and unattainable. He tied my wrists down to the cold steel bed with the patient restraints.

"I'm still need to punish you."

"Oh no, please wait, don't."

He laughed; I could see the torture tools around him. Was he going to use them on me? He pulled out the gag ball and tied it around my mouth, whilst I attempted to avoid it by thrashing myself side to side. He was too strong for me; his grip around my face stopped me from squirming.

"Shh," he whispered in my ear, his voice like silky threads wrapped around my neck. My knees buckled within seconds, it was like he was trying to comfort me but the words were pointless. He knew he wanted to inflict pain on me and he had every intention. I wanted it more than anything.

I heard him unbuckle his belt, I knew in that instant he had every intention to whip me. I kept wondering if I had done something wrong to displease him.

He pulled down my bottoms revealing my bare flesh; I squirmed and flailed but all to no avail.

"You really need to stop moving, it won't help." His voice had turned dark and sinister. This worried me.

The leather belt cracked against my tender skin. The pain was unbearable, yet this was only the first whip. The next ten strokes came very hard and fast, I gripped my hands down, clawing my nails deep within the steel bed but anything I did was no comfort. There was no escape from the pain he was inflicting; I began to cry, hoping he would just stop, but he didn't. My flesh felt swollen and beaten, I knew I would bear bruises for weeks. I began to breathe deeply, taking in every whip; warm tears flushed across my face but nothing kindled his ruthless and demonic nature.

The burning sensations from the whips had turned into warmth, a small comfort. The last crack of the whip finished me. Tears were streaming down my face, but I felt all life had been drained out of me; his desire to inflict such treacherous torture had exhumed all spirit that was in me. The question of why he had to hurt me in such a way confounded my mind. I wept silently and discreetly whilst I lay there seemingly dead.

He rushed to my side, and realised the torment had taken its toll on me; he untied me with haste, the ties that had crucified my wrists.

As he lifted me he saw how lifeless I had become. I was staring into the abyss with no soul left in my eyes. He fledged his large hands around my face; shaking me in despair.

"Sukhi. Oh God, what have I done?"

All I could do was weep, he knew that he might've pushed it too far. He moved his mask upwards only to show his lips. He tried to kiss me violently in order to have some reaction, but I remained still like a lifeless doll. He gathered me up, cradled me into his arms and decided to lay me down onto my bed within the cell. Usually he would leave me, but he lay himself down beside me. I couldn't speak to him, I didn't want to.

"I'm sorry," he whispered, covering my face with gentle kisses, stroking my hair and the sides of my cheeks. He placed a small finger under my chin and lifted my head so I was face to face with his mask. My eyes stung a little from the weeping, but all he could do was bless me with sweet rough kisses as if I were the most precious thing he had ever held.

I couldn't understand why, but I needed him more than he needed me. I felt my heart wrap itself around him; we were kindred spirits, tied together by something far greater than lust. He loved me…

"Sukhi, we're home," screamed a voice from the corridors. She knew it could only be Serena. The teenager came pounding up the stairs, Sukhi knew she was going to burst into the room and fill it with light and joy.

"Hey sis, I learnt how to do the splits today," she yelped in excitement. "You think the doctor might like it?"

"Do you intend to show him?" said Sukhi, raising an eyebrow at her sister.

"I always show him all the moves that I learn." Her beaming smile was full of innocent joy, something Sukhi wished she could have back.

"Oh dear. Your father got 'imself a 'andful right there," said Chess, who seemed out of breath and exhausted from the day.

Chess bent over, grabbing her back in pain, and beckoned herself to straighten out. Sukhi knew there was something wrong with Chess.

"Chess, are you okay?" Sukhi, noticed how the colour was waning from her housekeeper's face. Had the years of service to her family taken its toll?

"Ah, Miss, I ain't getting younger."

Sukhi doubted her comment. "Chess, you can't fool me, something is wrong and you won't tell me?"

The usual glow that Chess would have blushed around her large cheeks had become withdrawn. The housekeeper eyed Serena, indicating to Sukhi that her sister should not be around.

"Ducky, why don't you wash and get changed into your pyjamas? We can watch movies till late tonight, seeing as it's a Friday."

Serena beamed at her older sister with glee and ran out of the room without a second thought.

Sukhi's attention directed back onto Chess, who was still heaving in exhaustion.

"Tell me what's going on, Chess."

The housekeeper waned a small smile across her face.

"Miss, I ain't doing too well, doctor said I 'ave cancer."

"What?"

"It's true, Miss, I've known for a while now... I was going to 'and in my notice but then you were kidnapped, and I knew I couldn't leave the family."

Immense guilt sunk in; she couldn't believe how ignorant and self-absorbed she had been to not notice a member of her family was seriously ill.

"Did you tell Dad? We can get the best doctor for you."

Tears welled up in her eyes, the large puffy glow had been totally drained. It dawned on her that her truest and beloved housekeeper was intending to leave. The darkness kept creeping in and it overwhelmed her. Sukhi knew in that moment she had to let her only family, that she had known her entire life, go.

You can't go, I am so lost right now, I need you.

"Oh, Miss, there's nothing the doctors can do… it 'as spread."

"Do you wish to leave?" said Sukhi, hoping Chess would say no.

"I'd like to go back to my 'ome."

Sukhi smiled. "I'd like to come with you. Dad knows I've been pressing on leaving too."

The old broad chuckled to herself. "Oh yes I know, you should see ma cottage in the Cotswolds in Oxford. It's small but you'd love it."

"I'd love to." Sukhi felt like crying, she knew in her heart that if she did it would show Chess that she had given up already. "You must be strong, Chess."

"I am tryin', but I do wish to go back 'ome."

Sukhi nodded in acknowledgement, she grabbed Chess and embraced her in the warmest hug. A small tear streamed down her face as she felt a part of her family was being ripped from her heart. Chess was lost for words and could only hold Sukhi with an embrace that was of a daughter.

"I'll let Dad know," whimpered Sukhi, who only held her oldest friend tighter. "He'll make all the necessary arrangements for you."

"Oh please, Miss," Chess could not contain her tears.

"You're my family, Chess, and I need to make sure you're going to be okay."

Sukhi was dealing with irreparable pain that was beyond anything she could understand. Her friend, her family, closest thing to a mother, was leaving her for good.

"Of course, Miss, ya like the lil daughter I never 'ad," said Chess, who was now in full-fledged tears that were beyond her control.

I love you, Chess.

Sukhi was in pain though, she was losing her friend to cancer and there was nothing she could do to change that. Who could console her at such a time?

Please come for me, wherever you are, I need you.

Chapter 10

The next morning Sukhi woke early, she was lost in her trail of thoughts whilst getting ready for the day. The news of her housekeeper having cancer had caused her to have a sleepless night. All she could think of was how she wanted to be wrapped in the warm embrace of her kidnapper. *How selfish*, she thought.

"Sukhi dearest. The doctor has arrived to see you again," shouted Karen from the corridor.

"Oh, that man is her doctor. So he is employed by us and has the cheek to speak to me," said a faint voice from below that belonged to that of Aunt Vera.

"Vera, let's go shopping in Westwood with Serena. That will be a nice little trip for all of us," Sukhi could hear Karen say, hustling the troupe out of the door. Once the door closed, Sukhi sighed in relief.

She glided down the stairs, her wavy hair loose and tasselled, hanging gracefully around her face. The only difference today was that she had lost all colour in her face and large puffy bags hung around her eyes.

She entered the drawing room where the doctor

had been sitting in his normal seat, waiting for his patient.

She took her seat opposite him. At first she found it hard to look at him straight in the face, but he knew judging from the dark circles she was a mess.

Sukhi's eyes dropped.

"This seems to be a rough week for you, how are you coping?"

"I'm not…"

"When will Chess be leaving?"

"Tomorrow, my father has organised everything, including her own carer for when she arrives."

"You two were close I assume?"

Sukhi's faint smile could not hide her silent tears from within. "She has been the one consistent family member I've ever had in my life."

"I see how this must be hard on you."

"Me? Forget about me. I've been so self-absorbed and selfish to not even notice that she was sick." The doctor could tell that it was guilt that had been ripping her to shreds throughout the night.

"You've been through a tough time."

"No I haven't, I'm actually perfectly fine… I'm in love with a man that I've never seen, and have been using everyone including you to hunt him down for myself."

"Come again?" The doctor raised an eyebrow. It was clear Sukhi had caught his full undivided attention; his face was full of confusion.

Oh God, he really must think I'm insane.

"The point I am trying to make here, is that I have been selfish because I've been too preoccupied in trying to hunt down the man who kidnapped me."

"You've been trying to hunt him down because you are…?"

"Yes, I'm in love with him," she huffed, folding her knees into her arms as if to protect herself.

"And you are certain of this?"

"Call me mad, but yes I am and I don't care if you think I'm insane. Diagnose me Sweden, Stockholm… Finland, whatever you call it. I'm in love with him."

"And you have been trying to track him down? How's that going?"

"I think I might be on to something."

The doctor's facial expression had changed and was now looking worried and flustered, more so than his usual calm self.

"Sukhi, you shouldn't be putting yourself into dangerous situations, the police should be in charge of the investigation."

"It's not dangerous, I'm sure he must have felt the same way."

"Did he ever tell you so?"

"No."

"Then how can you be so certain?"

Sukhi began to bite at her nails, and avoided all eye contact with Ash. She was annoyed by his lack of support, but he had become distressed by her lack of self-awareness.

"Everything you described to me isn't normal, he is a domineering sex fiend and you are a consenting submissive. You've taken his actions and made them out to be marks of affection."

"No. You think that because you don't know the whole truth of what happened."

"Now you're protecting him... Please enlighten me, Sukhi."

Sukhi shuffled her feet and bit at her nails more, she was now worried the doctor would sell her out.

"I don't want to say any more."

The doctor stared with disdain. "Well then I cannot help if you don't tell me."

"It's personal, that's all I am saying."

"How so?"

"It meant a lot to me..."

"But probably wasn't for him, unless you tell me."

"There was a point where he had whipped me."

"This sounds promising..."

Sukhi glared at him for that comment. "I was in a state of shock and I found myself unable to respond to him. He became worried and it seemed like he actually cared, he lay next to me for hours holding me close."

"Because you were upset. It doesn't mean he cared for you or loved you back, so why are you chasing something that is now just sounding like a figment of your imagination."

"Why are you so dead sure he has nothing for me?

You don't know him like I do," she shouted.

***

After what seemed like hours of him holding me. He lay there asleep next to me, topless and showing the beautiful cuts on his arms and along his stomach. I could feel the warmth of his body exuberate onto mine. There came a moment where I dared myself to move my hand and lift the mask off. I stroked the side of his neck, and gently tugged the woollen mask upwards. I lifted it slowly, revealing his soft luscious lips and then stopped. My head started to become numb as the instant fear of knowing him set about a certain amount of doubt; he might have whipped me more or worse, killed me if I knew his identity, so I stopped myself from going any further. I gently pressed a finger against his lips, they were soft and perfect, and he had a rugged amount of stubble surrounding him that enhanced his perfect jawline.

He was awake, but he wasn't startled by the fact I was touching the flesh of his face, instead he puckered his lips and tenderly kissed the finger I had pressed against him. I moved my hand to stroke his cheek and pressed my body closer to his. His hand moved about my waist as I gingerly kissed him.

"Good morning," he heaved, wrapping his muscular arms about me to bring me closer to him.

I instantly felt safe. How can I feel safe with a man whose first intention was to kill me? He was no killer to me, but someone whom I enjoyed being with despite the derelict conditions he had put me in. He kissed me, weaving his hands down to touch the warmth further down, I moaned from his touch as my body reacted instantly in immense pleasure. He turned me around so my arse was perfectly situated onto his large and hard cock. I sighed with earnest, feeling the strong warmth arouse me beneath.

"I guess you've forgiven me then?" he whispered, as he nibbled my earlobe.

I nodded, he then moved to play with the back of my neck and it instantly drove my body into extreme heightened intensity. He positioned himself above me and pulled off the small dress, revealing my vulnerable body; I had perked up to allow him to do as he wished. He wasn't rough like he normally was, if anything he was just being perfect, soft, suave and smooth. His touch seemed to have an immediate effect on every part of my body.

He positioned himself above me, still trailing his hot breath that swooped over the nape of my neck and down to my breast. He massaged them with his hands and coaxed the nipple with his warm delectable tongue, instantly driving me to arch my back.

He went further down using his tongue, I was instantaneously wet; he hit every nerve perfectly, and it instantly drove my body crazy. I was panting, desperately trying to prevent myself from letting go. He tweaked his hand around my nipple, causing a reaction; he knew I was going to climax and burst, but I was trying to hold it back.

He rose up to watch me as he pushed his fingers deep within me hard and fast, using the palm of his hand to beat again my clit. The strength was too grave for me to bear, and unknowingly I cried out with pleasure as I released.

There was a small smile on his face, as he knew he had pleasured me to new territorial heights. He was thick, large and unsatisfied, I knew he wanted his favour returned and I was more than obliging. As I grabbed him, I noticed how swollen and long he was; I stroked his large cock, thrusting it inside me.

He still took me by surprise; the girth of his cock always had its effect on the surrounding walls within me. My panting increased as he pushed deeper and harder, every thrust had thrown me into ecstasy. I clawed my nails deep into his back; he growled with an intense might that led him to kiss me with violent passion, and increase the outspoken pace he was thrusting within me.

He paused for a moment, and I groaned, frowning at the fact he had stopped.

"I haven't finished with you," he said with a rakish grin on his face. He mounted himself over me still, positioning my legs around his neck. He then continued to thrust down and harder. It was like a different sensational all over; the weight that impacted within me had heightened in immense desire. I moaned louder than ever; he placed his hand over my mouth. He knew I was enjoying everything he was doing and kept on going; I was in a different world all together and knew that I was climaxing for the second time.

The rush of heat swept over my entire body. He put my legs down and around his waist and pulled my arms up and around his neck, he then moved his hands about my waist and pulled me into him, forcing me to prop myself up opposite him. My body was quaking within his grasp. He looked up at me, noticing how my eyes were instantaneously gazing upon him. He swept a small strand of hair behind my ear and smiled with intrigue; he continued to move rhythmically, which only empowered my body to cave in to him.

The heat had built up; I noted how his muscles that had lined his back to perfection moved rhythmically, almost appeared angelic. His breathing had become wavered and distinctive, the impulse to push into him further grew and with every thrust I reciprocated by hoisting my hips and moving to his pace.

He became large and his panting and groaning grew. Instinctively I ravaged my hands through his hair, tugging it to keep in line with him. His grasp tightened about my waist, and his defined kisses about my breasts grew savage.

My breathing had become laboured, as the atmosphere grew hot and dire. He swelled larger and firmer and I knew he was close to releasing. I needed him inside me more than ever and I never wanted him to let go. The nature of this was not brutal or violent, he was not the man of a sinister nature that I thought he was, there was good in him.

"Sukhi," he breathed, almost pleading to allow him to release.

"No, not yet," I pleaded back.

He placed his thumb near my lip, caressing it softly; I voluntarily opened my mouth and greedily sucked it, sending a non-spoken message to him to keep going on. His mouth gaped open in lust as the sensations through his thumb riled him up enough to become larger. I could feel him within me, desperately waning to burst.

"Sukhi," he growled, rummaging his other hand up my back and clasping a handful of my hair. He was indeed vulnerable at this point and I couldn't let him suffer anymore, I thrust harder and faster, allowing him to build up. He gripped my straining thighs as the first spurt of semen entered me. The rest pulsated out in a soothing and massaging effect against the walls inside me.

I carefully slowed my pace down, hearing his panting calm down to a normal state. He released his grip from my thighs and lay down in exhaustion. I was still straddled between him, unsure what I should do. As I was about to move off him, he caught my wrist pulling me down to lie beside him, I obeyed his command and nestled between his arm and large chest; the room was hot and sticky from the sex. His body glistened from the sweat he had worked himself up into.

"You are going to wear me out," he exclaimed, moving to face me and playing with a small tangle of hair that fell beside my face. I didn't know how to answer; I just sighed and took comfort in his warm embrace. "I fear you're going to be the death of me," he ended.

***

"This does complicate things." The doctor's face looked far more alarmed, and Sukhi could tell. "From what you've just told me, it does seem like he grew to care for you. What happened after that?"

"That's when things changed, he would only have sex with me when I wanted it, and majority of the time I wanted him to use the equipment he had."

"So the two of you built a small understanding relationship that involved mindless sex?" The doctor's face was not its usual professional self, but more alarmed with worry.

"What have you got against him?" Sukhi asked.

"He kidnapped you! But it sounds to me like he's a psychopath and you are going into deep water by trying to hunt him down."

"He isn't a psychopath."

"I think I'm the one qualified enough to say whether he is or isn't." All professionalism had long gone; all guards were down.

"Fine, well if you really must know I did take your advice and tried to move on," said Sukhi, huffing with impatience. The doctor had started to annoy her, and huge doubts as to whether she could trust him began to cloud her judgement on matters.

"With that young fellow? And?"

"Well he's rejected me. Safe to say though, he shows genuine example that he likes me, and doesn't just want *mindless sex*."

"I see."

"Yes, I've flung myself at him."

"Why is that?"

"He seems to think I'm forcing myself to like him, as oppose to genuinely liking him."

The doctor eyed her again with fierce scrutiny. She couldn't understand why out of all days the doctor seemed extremely off. He wasn't his normal pleasant self with a favourable manner, but was portraying signs of someone who was rather annoyed by her behaviour.

"Could you tell me exactly what you did?"

"Well I threw myself on him and he rejected me." She huffed in her spoilt brat like manner. "You know, you've been a real jerk today. You told me I could trust you. Instead you've thrown back everything in my face and now you're just beginning to sound like a... jerk."

"Let me clarify a few things. I am not your friend, I am your doctor. Secondly, if I think you're a danger to yourself, i.e. taking it upon yourself to try and find a *psychopath*, then I will have a duty to inform the police, as well as have you house arrested to ensure your safety is not in jeopardy."

"Excuse me, are you blackmailing me? Who the hell do you think you are?"

"No, God dammit, Sukhi. I'm trying to make sure you don't get hurt again."

Sukhi suddenly sat back in shock, it was the first time she had ever seen the doctor lose his temper, and it had an astounding impact on her.

"I'm sorry, Sukhi, I didn't mean to shout. I'm a little angry with myself for allowing you to indulge in this kidnapper. I had no idea you had the intention of trying to find him."

"No, I'm sorry, I promise not to investigate this kidnapper anymore."

He sighed with relief. "Good. Then I don't have to

inform the police."

"However, I do want to know more about my mother," she stated.

"As long as the investigation is only about your mother, then I have no qualms. Just don't get yourself into troubled water with the kidnapper."

"Of course not."

The doctor began to calm down and bring back his professional self, yet his face was still flushed from his outburst.

Why does he care so much?

"Sukhi, I must express that I don't want you to get into trouble."

The doctor's face had turned pale white; it might have been better for him not to know that Sukhi had been running an investigation to find the kidnapper. Why had he reacted the way he did? It seemed odd that a working professional would break out of character.

"I promised, didn't I?" said Sukhi. "Did you mean it when you said you were just my doctor and not my friend?"

"No, of course not."

He sipped some water from the glass that was left on the table for him, and sighed in release of relief.

"Do you ever date your patients?" she asked.

The doctor raised an eyebrow at her; he stared at her, watching to see what she meant by her question. Sukhi was using her eyes to do her bashful gaze that normally made men quite weak.

"I don't, it's not deemed professional," he said.

"And you wouldn't want to take me out on a date?" she asked, it was bold on her part. However, she realised in such situations she needed to ensure the doctor would not rat her out to the police, even if that meant she would date him to ensure some sort of reassurance on his part. Besides, why would it be so difficult to date a man who by all accounts was 'picture perfect' to her father? He was a sincere professional, it was clear he did well for himself. Her father would look favourably on such a match.

"Sukhi, I am not prepared to answer that question."

"Answer it," she demanded, in her calm condescending voice.

He sighed and broke into a side lip grin.

"Is this to make your boyfriend Jonathan jealous?"

"He isn't my boyfriend." The look he cast upon her was quite bewitching, this young doctor was a handsome man. "I'm also following your advice, doctor."

"Oh, and what's that?"

"I'm trying to move on, as you suggested."

"It is not deemed professional, Sukhi." He sighed. "You are a very beautiful girl... but I'm not sure I would be of interest to you at all."

"How do you know?"

"So you are saying you are interested in me?" He raised his eyebrow.

"Maybe, if you weren't employed *hypothetically*

speaking and you weren't my therapist… would you want to date me?"

"Well, I think you're very beautiful so I don't see why not."

"Okay, now would you want to have sex with me?"

The doctor was taken back a little, shocked by the question he had just been asked.

"I'd prefer not to answer that."

"Well I implore you to answer that." The doctor began to frown at Sukhi, but his eyes darted around her body, taking note of her perfect wavy hair that descended around her face and draped down perfectly around the curves of her breasts. Her legs were shaped and toned, whilst her skin looked perfectly flawless and delectable.

"I suppose if we got to know each other better, and we both liked each other, then yes, sex might be on the table."

Sukhi smiled, she realised the doctor had taken a fancy to her and she would use it to her advantage; it was the reason he had broken some of his high professionalism. Yet in her mind she wanted to push the boundaries.

"That is all I needed to know. I think we can wrap up the sessions here," she said, ending further professional conversation. The doctor nodded and started to pack up his books and journals that lay around the table.

"So Sukhi, would you like to go on a date then?" asked the doctor. Sukhi turned around in slight shock and disbelief.

"But you said you don't..."

"I said it's not deemed professional and I don't tend to date my patients, but I've already broken many rules with you so I don't see the difference."

Sukhi smiled at him with glee, he was indeed wickedly handsome.

"Besides, you spending time with me might keep you out of trouble."

"Why don't you just admit that you obviously care for me a lot more than just a patient?"

"I do," he laughed, "otherwise I wouldn't be making so much of an effort, would I?"

She smiled at him.

"You know, I've never thought highly of men... but strangely your opinion matters more to me. Much more so than Dr Blease or my own father."

"Don't be too harsh on him, he's a good man." He finished packing, picked up his briefcase and stood facing Sukhi. "So how about it then?"

"Yes, I would like to go a date." She beamed at him. "Although best not to tell Serena, she might kick up a small fuss."

He laughed. "Ah, of course, my favourite patient."

He kissed Sukhi on the forehead.

"I'll speak to your father, requesting permission then."

She frowned at him, a little upset that he would have to do so. "Like I said, your father is a good man and I'm not the type to put my entire career on the line. I'm also quite traditional if you haven't noticed, so I will ask his permission first."

He kissed her forehead again and left.

Sukhi stood baffled. Was the doctor only really going to date her to keep her out of trouble or did he he genuinely really like her?

She wandered off to the kitchen where she knew she would find Chess, who was busily packing away small things. Sukhi ran up from behind and embraced her in a warm hug. She noticed Chess had been sobbing.

"Ah my dear, you ain't 'ugged me like that since you were a child."

"Chess, please don't go."

"Your father and you 'ave made this place my 'ome for twenty-eight years. Ya know... but my dear you're getting better, ain't ya?"

"Of course, but you have been the only family I've had since I was a child."

"You've got ya father."

"A ruddy lousy one."

"Loves you though, ain't good at showing it, but 'e does love you."

Sukhi began to cry again, kicking herself for feeling a small amount of happiness that the doctor had asked her out on a date and yet her very own Chess was close to going away for good.

"Can I come away with you?"

"And miss out on that date with that gorgeous young doctor?"

"Oh, how did you know that?" said Sukhi, slightly alarmed that Chess might have heard everything.

"Well you over ran, and when I went to go and see if you were close to finishing so I could cook you up something for lunch, I 'eard 'im ask ya out on a date."

Thank goodness she didn't hear the first half of my conversation with Ash.

"Don't give me that look, you think 'ighly of him. That's why you're a little bit 'appier than I've seen you, and it sounds to me like 'e cares for ya a lot more than a doctor should."

"I know, but I want to be with you."

"Now ya being silly, but I want ya to know that even if we're apart, I'm always going to love you."

Sukhi began to sob. Chess attempted to embrace and comfort her with all her might, but it was hopeless. Sukhi felt like a small part of her that was good was abandoning her.

"SUKHI!" yelled a voice from the corridor. It was Karen. "Jonathan is here to see you, dearest."

"Oh God," whispered Sukhi in annoyance. "I forgot about him."

"Dabbling with two fellas, eh?" said Chess jokingly, poking at Sukhi.

"No, this one just annoys me majority of the time."

"So why is 'e 'ere?"

Sukhi knew that the only reason he was here was to help investigate accidents that her mother may have caused many years ago.

"Urm, Chess, I've been sort of investigating incidents that might have involved my mother."

Chess's face fell and became ghostly white. "Oh. Your mother was a lovely lady though, she never did any wrong."

"Well that's not what I've found out. She suffered from depression and was sent to a mental asylum, did you know anything about this?"

Chess looked startled and alarmed. "By God. 'Ow the 'ell did ya find out?"

"So you did know? Chess, why did you never tell me?"

"You were just a child. I wanted to protect you, and your father made me promise never to mention it to you."

"But you must tell me."

"SUKHI." Karen's voice echoed from the corridors, which only made Sukhi a little annoyed.

"Coming," Sukhi replied. "Chess, don't go anywhere until you've told me everything. I'll just go see Jonathan quickly and come back."

"Okay, Miss." Sukhi noticed how Chess had looked a little worse than normal. Not only had her face turned pale and ghostly white, but she had lost weight too.

Sukhi walked outside of the room closing the large oak doors behind her. She paced herself, trying to pull herself together to face Jonathan.

As Sukhi turned to meet Jonathan, she noticed how he didn't look like his normal self. His eyes were weary and tired, it was quite clear he had been staying up late, judging from the dark circles that loomed around him.

"Hi Suks, there was quite a lot of articles but I managed to decipher through and I found a few possibilities," stated Jonathan, with his normal fixated smile.

Sukhi saw how Jonathan had made a vast amount of effort for her.

"Why did you do that? I thought we could go through it together."

"Well I didn't think you needed to go through more trouble."

Sukhi rolled her eyes and led him through to the drawing room. He waltzed in with his normal jovial manner, sitting comfortably onto the lounge chair and pulling out stacks of papers from his bags.

"There's still quite a lot to get through," he remarked.

Sukhi came about the table, hovering over the articles and noticing how Jonathan had circled quite a few headliners.

"This is great," she remarked.

"Yes but the thing is, I'm not entirely sure how you're going to know if your mother was involved."

I'll soon find out from Chess, she thought.

The two of them deciphered articles, of course

there were many highway car crashes which involved more than ten cars, or reckless lorry drivers, these were ruled out as possibilities. Sukhi suddenly became distressed, realising that the possibility of finding anything was quite slim.

Victims Vivienne Dorian and George Dorian were tragically found dead in a road accident near Capeside Moors, the two were cautiously driving, however due to severe weather conditions on the road, the car was swept off the road and the two were found dead on the scene. It is a tragic loss to society and all friends and family members.

Sukhi pulled up the article, a picture of the car completely crumpled by a large oak tree.

"That was my parents," said Jonathan, who noticed Sukhi staring at the article. "Do you think your mother might have been involved in that?"

Sukhi suddenly became alarmed, realising that if this was the case then all arrows would be pointing to Jonathan as the kidnapper. He didn't fit the bill though; his personality traits and characteristics didn't match those of the kidnapper.

But then the kidnapper was smart, he could have been a totally different person to the public eye.

"Possibly, but I wouldn't know… Let's leave that article on the side for a moment," she responded, carefully placing it to a side and looking through the other articles.

"They were great parents, you know, always wanted the best for me," said Jonathan, still pressing on the matter. A dark looming voice began to alter his normal one.

"I'm sure," she responded, acting as if nothing was bothering her.

"If your father had some doing in this cover up, I'm not sure how I would take it."

The room fell silent, Sukhi felt a jolt of nerves bundle up within her.

"Ermm... so... I need to tell you something."

"What's that?" His voice had turned dark.

"I will be going on a date with the doctor, he's erm... a really nice guy."

"Oh, is it?" His voice had returned to normal. "So he's competition."

"Actually, I asked him," replied Sukhi.

"Oh, I see." Jonathan's face had swollen into a deep red. "You know, I don't know why I bothered with you. Everyone said you were self-centred and stuck up, and I'm beginning to think they were right."

"I beg your pardon?"

"Yes, you heard me. You don't care for anyone but yourself and you seem to think you can get your way just because you're beautiful and men fall for that kind of stupidity."

He's jealous.

"Are you kidding me? You could have kissed me but you didn't."

"Yes, well I did that with good reason."

"Oh, and what was that reason?"

Both of them had raised their voices and it was quite obvious by the shaking of the drawing room door, that Serena was eavesdropping.

"Maybe because you're worth more than you give yourself credit for and I didn't want to be one of *those* guys."

"Screw you. All you had to do was kiss me."

With that Jonathan moved fast, he swooped his hands around her face and pressed onto her lips with a vast amount of hardness. It was different. She didn't have a moment to catch her breath; his lips were smaller and far harsher than she had remembered the kidnapper's to be. Sukhi kissed him back. She was hoping there was something more, but nothing.

Jonathan moved his hands from her face to her shoulders, massaging them as he pulled himself away. The situation had become unnerving, Sukhi couldn't figure out her bearings, the kiss had made her dizzy.

"Erm," was the only response that Sukhi could muster. The awkwardness had caused a stiff and cold atmosphere around them.

"I'm assuming by that look on your face you didn't like it?" said Jonathan, whose face had turned into a frown. Sukhi couldn't speak, she was dumbfounded. He took his hands off her shoulders and picked up his things.

"Wait," she replied. "I'm sorry, I wasn't ready for that."

"Sukhi, I can't help but wonder what it is you're looking for. Do you really want to investigate your mother? And do you really want to move on?" His voice seemed calmer.

She stood still, aware that the entire situation had become tense.

"I do want to move on, but I think with you I've been forcing myself. I'm sorry..." She sat herself back into her seat.

"Oh really?" his voice had turned dark, black and sinister. This time when he looked at Sukhi it wasn't one of compassion but one of extreme loathing. Sukhi became frightened. The darkness that had overpowered him began to make her feel nervous. "How would you like it if I asked the police to investigate my parents' death? Maybe your mother had some part." His voice was calm and twisted. The rush of fear overwhelmed Sukhi to the bone; he began to behave more and more like a psycho.

"No, wait. I..." She attempted to hide the fear that had become clear on her stricken face and shaky voice.

"Why should I listen to you? After all, you've just been using me for your own gains."

"No, it wasn't like that."

He laughed at her, mocking her desperate pleas. It was clear that Jonathan was not the man he had appeared to be when he initially met her. However, the fear of knowing his true colours impaled an adverse effect on her, fear and panic had overridden her.

"Sukhi, was anything I did good enough for you?"

"Jonathan, please stop. I'm going to ask you to kindly leave."

The comment antagonised him to react more. "All I wanted to do was help you, but you're just as selfish and self-centred as *your father*."

Sukhi had begun to shake in fear.

"Please just go," she muttered.

Without another word he grabbed his things and walked out of the door. She was left baffled and frightened.

You need to forget about him.

Sukhi was left to collect her thoughts, she remembered the things that the kidnapper did to her, but wondered whether it was smart to go chasing after someone she didn't know. The room was silent again, until a door slammed open awakening her from her deep thoughts.

"Why didn't you tell me?" said a small angry voice at the door. It was Serena who was no longer beaming her beautiful smile, instead she was glowering with anger towards Sukhi. Her arms were folded, with her foot tapping on the floor. It was clear she was waiting for a good explanation from her older sister.

"You knew I liked him," she barked, still tapping her foot with clear contempt towards her sister.

"Oh dear, who told you?"

"Chess told Mum, and I was eavesdropping."

"Sweetheart, this isn't really a date; it's just a dinner."

"That's what she said."

"Why do you like him so much?" asked Sukhi, who invited her little sister to sit next to her on the couch. Her arms were still folded and her face was still scrunched up in fury.

"Because he looks good." The small voice was shrill, which only amused Sukhi even more.

"Anything else?"

"He saves lives. He might as well be a superhero, which I actually think he is."

"He's not one of those doctors, Ducky."

"You don't know that, he told me he liked saving people."

Maybe not that kind of saving either.

"Ducky, you know you're too young for him, right?"

Serena let out a small defeated sigh. "Mum says that," she mumbled, disgruntled.

"I like him too, but as a friend. This is just a friends' dinner," Sukhi said, patting Serena's back in comfort.

"Oh please, stop talking to me like as if I'm a child."

"What?"

"I know exactly what you do, Sukhi. Maybe if you stop acting like a slut you won't have a problem finding yourself a decent and self-respecting guy."

"I beg your pardon." Sukhi was shocked to hear what was being said from her thirteen-year-old sister's mouth.

"I remember what you used to get up to, before you got kidnapped."

"I don't know what you mean."

"You used to bring those men back and screw them."

Sukhi was alarmed; she had never brought men to the house. In fact she had always been rather picky with the men she had dated, and even then she had always made it difficult for them to get to the sex stage.

"You've got it wrong, Serena. I never brought anyone back here and I've always been selective with the men I've dated previously."

"Don't act all innocent."

Sukhi began to feel infuriated with the accusations that had been laid at her.

"Serena. I haven't done anything of the sort."

"Well who else could it be?" snarled her younger sister.

Karen?

Karen had always been a black-haired beauty herself, but the thought of her having affairs with different men was not in her character.

It couldn't be Karen? She wouldn't do that to her father, she loved him.

Sukhi looked at her younger sister with deep concern, worried that what she might have witnessed was Karen having affairs with different men. The thought of it being Karen was inconceivable.

"Don't think I haven't told the doctor either, he knows you're a slut. So I can only think he wants you for one reason."

"Shut your mouth, Serena. Don't you dare speak to me like that, especially as I do so much for you."

Serena was close to bursting into tears, but she held herself together before running out of the room in haste. The atmosphere was intense, cold and had turned extremely sour; the mere contemplation of being accused of such acts had sickened Sukhi's stomach. Too many thoughts braised her mind, and caused her to behave irrationally; she couldn't control her feelings, and this began to become an overbearing burden on her. Her immediate instinct was to call Ash.

She grabbed her cell phone from her bag, and searched for the doctor's number. As she found his card, in a manic state she furiously pressed the buttons on her cell phone's key pad.

"Good Afternoon, Dr Meller how can I hel—"

"Ash, I need to speak with you immediately."

"Sukhi… by God, what the hell is the matter?" He could sense the panic in her voice, how she was shaking furiously and almost close to tears from the day's events that had happened the moment he had left her.

"I need you immediately," she panicked.

"Do you want me to come over there now?"

"Just come, pick me up and take me away from here." Tears welded down her face, but he could tell she was upset as she kept sniffing every five seconds.

"I'll be over there in fifteen minutes. Don't worry, I'm coming for you." He hung up the phone.

Sukhi had riled herself up, her temper was flaring with rage. She screamed loudly whilst throwing the lampshade onto the floor, breaking the china collectables that had hung close to the fireplace. The earth-shattering noise had brought Chess running into the room.

"By God, my dear, what is going on?"

"Has Karen been having affairs with men?" Her eyes were blood shot and intense, it almost frightened Chess to see Sukhi in such a state.

"By God. I hope not."

"Who has Serena seen then, bringing strange men back to the house?"

"If it is that ruddy woman, I'll kill her."

"Chess, you are always in the house, how can you not know?"

"Not always, Miss. I do 'ave to do errands for the 'ousehold, you know."

Sukhi took a minute to compose and calm herself down. What confused her most was why Serena had got it into her mind that it was Sukhi. Karen looked nothing like Sukhi, except for having the wavy luscious black hair.

"This makes no sense."

"Well to be honest, it would make sense, Miss, if she were bringing strange men, wouldn't it?"

"No?"

"Your father, he isn't the most affectionate of men."

Sukhi saw how Chess's face fell, and small tears begun to crawl down her face.

"I remember 'ow much your mother suffered for some time."

"What do you mean?"

"Your mother and father were very much in love, but it was young love. When it was time for your father to take over, 'e didn't make the time for 'er, nor could 'e. That ruddy family of 'is was ruining everything for 'im and 'er. That's why she became depressed and dependent on those pills."

"How did she die?"

Chess' usual red cheeks had turned cold and ice pale. It almost seemed like the memory that she had kept a secret over the years had haunted her.

"I've kept so many secrets for this family, just to keep it together," she confessed.

"Chess, you have to tell me what happened to her."

"Okay, I will, Miss."

Chapter 11

A storm 'ad brewed in the atmosphere, rain poured down causing terror amongst the 'ousehold. A tall figure glided through the rain, completely drenched, she was panicking and scared. She banged on the front door, I ran fast as I could to the door to see who it was, and it was your dear mother. She 'ad tears strolling down 'er eyes, and she was panicking. 'Er 'ands were blackened from what look like mud, 'er face was dreary and pale. She whimpered as I embraced 'er. I knew she was sick, 'er illness always took its toll on 'er, but instinctively there was something different in the way she 'eld onto me for dear life.

"By God ma'am, what 'as 'appened?"

"Chess, I did something terrible," she cried, still 'olding onto my apron for comfort.

"A family. I didn't mean to… I don't know what happened… It was a terrible accident, I didn't mean to hurt anyone." She was still wailing into my cloak, it was clear she 'adn't been taking 'er medication properly by the way 'er body was quaking in fear. I knew it must 'ave been something terrible.

I 'eld 'er tightly about the shoulders, only to comfort the poor ma'am. I allowed 'er to take a seat on the couch and prepared a few chocolates and tea for 'er. She was out of all sorts, crying away.

"Tell me what 'appened."

"What's the use? My husband will hate me. He'll take Sukhi away from me."

"No dearest, of course 'e won't."

'Er long black hair was drenched and I knew if she didn't rest by the fire, she would catch a nasty cold. I put the fire on, 'oping it would warm 'er up and ensure that she wouldn't get sick. She stopped panicking eventually, and calmed 'erself down. 'Er tears turned into small quiet sobs. I gave 'er the pills she was meant to take, to reduce 'er anxiety. After ten minutes I knew the pills 'ad taken their effect as she went solemnly quiet and gazed into thin air, lost in deep thought.

"What 'appened ma'am?" I asked, 'oping it wasn't something terrible.

"I didn't mean to start the fire, it was an accident."

"What fire?"

"The house was on fire, the husband, the wife and their little boy were in the house, the boy got out. The father went back in to get back to his screaming wife, but he never did."

"What 'appened?"

"I killed them, the fire and the heat was ever blazing. I can still feel it pressed against my skin." *She looked at 'er skin as if it were tainted by blood and started to scratch at it in 'atred of 'erself. She wailed loudly in despair.*

You would think she was saying this 'eartlessly, but I knew better than anyone it was 'er medication that 'ad kicked in. The irrational guilt overwhelmed 'er and I could see from 'er actions she was in despair of losing everything, losing 'er Sukhi.

"I thought it was her house."

"Whose dear?" She 'ad just confessed to a crime, and I was

probably the first person to know. I cared for 'er and thought to tell David, knowing 'e would be able to cover it up as 'e 'ad so much power over London.

"That woman. Karen."

I'd known for some time that 'is family were purposefully pushing Karen towards him. I think what made it worse was 'ow 'e would attend events and parties and look as if 'e were dating 'er. That family forbid 'im to take Sima to anything.

"What?" Sukhi was in shock. "You've kept this a secret from me, for twenty-two years."

"I am sorry, Miss, but your father and I thought it would be best."

Sukhi noticed how Chess fumbled her fingers and could see how the frown lines appeared on her forehead.

"Do not worry, Chess, I could never be upset with you."

"Your parents I'm sure loved each other, but your father could be so stupid sometimes. It's what caused them to 'ave so many problems in the end."

"How so?"

"They argued, all the time, which was why I let 'er indulge in the drugs, Miss. It seemed to make 'er 'appier not existing in the current reality your father gave 'er, and I did whatever I could to protect 'er. In doing so I 'ad to keep it a secret from you."

"The family though, what happened to the family in that fire?"

"The mother and father died that night; the son

was adopted by a different family, from what I know the boy did well and travelled quite far."

"Do you remember the name of that family?"

"No dear, but you father does."

The doorbell had rung; Sukhi knew it was the doctor coming to retrieve her from her hell house. Karen had gone to answer the door.

"Chess, before I go, is there anything else that you need to tell me?"

"Miss, I know you want me to tell you everything, but I think it might be best you asked your father."

"I've been hearing that a lot lately, but we all know my father is like a vault."

"'E loves you despite whatever 'e's done," said Chess.

As Sukhi walked out of the drawing room, she saw Karen speaking to the doctor, too close for comfort. It hadn't occurred to her to become more aware of Karen and her actions, but now she was alert she was beginning to see the cracks in her stepmother's perfection.

"You want her instead…" she thought she heard Karen say. As her steps became more prominent down the corridor, the doctor and Karen looked up.

"Ah. Sukhi dearest," she said with a small smile on her face. "The doctor is here to see you. Apparently you called him."

"Yes I did," she said with austereness in her voice. She looked at the doctor whose face looked worried. Karen was confused and taken back with Sukhi's sudden sharp tone.

"Shall we leave?" he said, holding his arm out to Sukhi, who accepted his offer and waved her hand to dismiss Karen.

Karen's face had turned pale and unimpressed. Sukhi slammed the door behind her and walked out with the doctor to his car.

"Now Sukhi, what has happened in order for you to make me panic and come to get you?"

Sukhi sighed for a moment. "I'll talk, whilst you drive."

They both entered the car and started to drive out of her long driveway, a sigh of relief echoed from her mouth.

"How could I find out so much information in one day? That's the question that I really should be fixated on."

"What do you mean?"

"Don't go all therapist on me and call me crazy."

The doctor smiled with his wicked, charming smile; it occurred to her how demonically good-looking he was whilst racing away in his sports car along with his rugged yet slick appeal.

"I think my stepmother has been having affairs," said Sukhi.

"I wouldn't put it past her."

Sukhi at first was a little shocked by the response from the doctor who was watching the road whilst driving his Aston.

"What do you mean?"

"She has told me about her affairs, and I believe she had made an advance on me which I declined respectfully."

"Really?"

"Yes."

"Why didn't you tell my father?"

"Patient confidentiality."

"Why do you continue giving her sessions, if she's tried to make an advance at you?"

"Because it is my job to do so; it's what I am paid to do, however, I now record all her sessions, just in case I need to use her own words against her, but she has recently begun to dislike me quite a bit."

"Why is that?"

"Perhaps my keen interest in you has invoked a lot of jealousy," he said in a complacent tone, as he drove with reckless haste. It was compelling excitement growing deep within her. The doctor was smart and intelligent, and it seemed he had managed to outwit the likes of her dysfunctional family.

"Would you mind me asking what you have analysed about my family?"

"Do you really want to know?" he asked with the devilish glint of enthusiasm in his eyes.

Sukhi nodded, preparing herself for the worst.

"Your stepmother is a manipulative, sly and overactive sex fiend. She dislikes you but doesn't dare to say it. She sees you as her competition, probably because you have more affection from your father than she ever will. She finds herself compelled to seek affection elsewhere, ideally eligible suitors that take an interest in you."

Sukhi felt her stomach sink; she thought her relationship with Karen was fine, but it sounded as if she had her own personal vendetta against Sukhi.

"I feel sick, can you slow down...? She has never seemed that way but I'm only beginning to see light of it now... It must have been her that Serena had seen with other men she brought into the house."

The doctor braked to slow down the car, aware Sukhi had turned ghost white from hearing his analysis of Karen.

"Yes, Serena told me that you were the one bringing strange men into the house. I asked how she knew and what she saw. She admitted to me she could only recognise you from the clothes you were wearing. Adding this up I slowly began to realise that your stepmother had taken the liberty to wear your clothes as a disguise during her indiscretions."

"How fucked up can my stepmother be? And poor Serena."

"Your stepmother needs validation of being worthy from others, so she deliberately does what she needs to in order to feel satisfied that the opposite sex adore her. Competition isn't acceptable in her eyes; her hatred towards you can only mean she sees you as competition, which has brought about the small conclusion to this out-of-the-ordinary situation."

"You think my stepmother has had a hand in my kidnapping?"

"Yes, that is exactly what I think… Thinking about it logically, she wanted you out of the picture."

Has Karen had me fooled all along? Did she pretend to get along with me all this time?

The doctor continued the thrilling drive; they drove far and extremely fast.

"Poor Serena," she sighed. "I had the audacity to shout at her as well."

"She's thoroughly spoilt and that's because of you. I think she also has a jealous tendency towards you."

"That's because of you!"

"No, I think there's a lot more than me to feel that way about someone… and I reckon your father is to blame for that."

It hadn't occurred to her that the doctor would be releasing such confidential information about her family. It was deemed unprofessional in the medical world, yet the doctor was keen to put his entire career on the line for her.

"Why have you told me all of this?"

The doctor had driven into a viewpoint overlooking her entire town. He stopped the car, switched off the engine and sighed.

"I don't know, the way your family treats you is appalling, and no wonder you cling on to your housekeeper. I believe she may be the only one who cares for you… It's also no wonder you fell in love with your kidnapper."

"Yes, but the information you just told me is private; you're putting your entire career on the line."

The doctor looked at the view of the town; it was beautiful watching the sunset. He turned and stared at Sukhi, whose face although pale was still candescently radiant in beauty.

"How can you be so good from a family that is selfish and self-absorbed? Your father does neglect the other family members atrociously, including you. Your stepmother is vain and relies on demoralising affection, and your younger sister is becoming just like her."

Sukhi seemed dumbfounded by the critical analysis and information on her family. Had she been so naïve and stupid not to realise her family had set out their own agendas? Here she was kicking herself for being so egotistical and self-centred for wanting to find the kidnapper. The man she believed she had fallen irrevocably in love with.

"You defended a kidnapper who treated you abominably; so far you've protected his identity without revealing any sort of information to the police. You showed compassion and feelings towards your housekeeper. I can see that you care for Serena, as if she were your own... These are qualities that none of your other family members possess."

"You're making me sound angelic," she whispered. "But you don't understand, I've had my own hidden agenda."

"To find your kidnapper..." he said, annoyed.

"Well I had given up, you told me to give up."

There was an awkward silence between the two.

"Why do you want him?"

Sukhi sighed, having pondered that question many times in her head. She couldn't make heads or tails of it, but she knew one thing.

"Because he's human like the rest of us, I think he was hurt… but I do believe he found some short-lived happiness whilst he was with me. There's evil in this world, but he was not one of them."

"How can you be so sure? Everything you described were signs of a psychopath."

"He isn't, I just know it," she said defensively. "If I told you we are tied together in an unfulfilled fate, you'd think I'm crazy."

The doctor looked at her, piercing his rakish beautiful eyes into her; it wasn't his analytical approach but one of sympathy. He breathed in heavily before turning to face her properly.

"Is there anything else you needed me for?" he asked.

"I found out my mother was the cause of an accident that killed a family." She took a deep breath, as her heart raced harder. "She accidentally set a house on fire, killing two members and leaving a little boy an orphan."

The doctor shifted his hand through his hair; his calm demeanour suddenly turned restless.

"How do you know it was an accident?"

"She thought it was Karen's house. Karen at the time was thrown into my father's life by his horrid family and I think she became paranoid."

Sukhi sighed, realising that there were far more cracks in the perfection of her family.

"Are you okay?" he asked, placing the palm of his hand on her soft cheek; a small electrical charge went through, shocking Sukhi.

It was clear by the vacant expression on her face that she was upset, the hideous nature made her feel appalled to be part of such a family.

"Well the conspiracy behind my stepmother's intention to kill me is unsolved."

Wait, that must mean she knows who the kidnapper was.

"That's a theory. I am no detective but after years of studying human psychology, it would be clear to me your stepmother is a primary suspect."

"Didn't even know she hated me that much."

He sighed, playing with the steering wheel with one of his hands. Everything he had told her was just making her more upset by the minute, judging by the small tears that had begun to flow down her cheeks. He pressed his thumb against her cheek, wiping away a droplet. Her cheeks were soft and delectable; he took small pleasure from caressing them with his thumb.

She peered up to look at him, noticing how the lines on his forehead had formed. His touch was warm and comforting, she breathed in, taking in the cologne that exuberated within the car.

He clasped the hand around her face, eyeing the radiant glow that shone from her. She moved into him, quaking under his grip. His eyes were dark and intense and she melted within his grasp. He had full control over her and without effort she felt herself submitting to him.

"You're so beautiful," he groaned, as he pulled her

in, inches away from pressing his lips against her. His touch had heightened all senses around her; she was succumbing to his every need. He kissed her, an ignited spark struck between the two of them, the pit of her stomach leaped up with excitement; it had seemed ages since she felt that jolt lunge from within but she liked it. She kissed him back, this time wanting more for him, but this felt like something she knew before.

He pulled away, leaving her a little disorientated and waning for more.

"I think that's enough," he commanded. "You don't need more complications, I apologise."

"No need to apologise, I quite liked it," she blushed; the rush of heat swept through her body, burning for him to touch her again.

"Of course you did," he chuckled to himself.

Sukhi frowned, a little confused, she hadn't felt that strange urgency to pine for more since the kidnapper.

"I wasn't expecting that," she stated. "Last time I felt like that was when I was with…"

The doctor looked at her and understood she was referring to the kidnapper. His face dropped; he had hoped that she would forget him, but it seemed all his efforts were in vain, especially as he had made it his primary goal to divert her full attention off the kidnapper.

"I hope you will leave him in the past."

"I know." She bit her lip, contemplating whether she should forget such an overbearing yet perfect man. He gave pleasure that was so beautiful and devouring the thought of leaving it behind was heartbreaking.

"I should really take you back."

"No, please don't," she snapped, feeling the pining urgency to not go back. "Can you not take me back to yours?" He realised she wasn't willing to face the wrath of her family. He had just revealed to her that most of them disliked her and for no reason other than jealousy, hatred and their own selfish gains.

The doctor's face dropped in shock. "Erm, is that wise?" he asked, but took notice of how Sukhi was fumbling with her fingers and the look of uncertainty dwelling through her eyes.

"I'm not even sure where to call home."

"What do you mean?"

"If by all accounts you are right, with Chess leaving tomorrow... I'm not sure I even feel safe in that household."

Sukhi cowered in the seat next to him, closing her hands around her face. Instant pressure instigated within her mind; she didn't feel safe.

A warm hand pressed against her back. "Okay, I'll take you back to mine... but you must inform your father or at least Chess that you're with me."

"You know I'm not a teenager," she protested, annoyed he would make such a condescending demand.

"I know, but all the same... They will send huge search parties for you."

Sukhi huffed whilst rummaging through her pockets to find her cell phone. She dialled home, hoping Chess would pick up. Unfortunately it was not the case, it happened to be Serena.

"Serena?"

"Oh it's you, what do you want?"

"Stop being such a pain and pass it to Chess now."

"Yes, but you're with him… aren't you?"

"I will not ask you again. Pass the phone to Chess."

Eventually the phone was taken off her younger sister's hands, and a stronger voice came through. Sukhi knew instantly it was Chess.

"Hi Chess, I know you're leaving tomorrow, but I want you to know that I love you."

"You aren't coming back here, are ya Miss?"

"Please let Dad know I'm safe."

"I will Miss, but ya know Karen saw you with that young doctor."

"Then tell him I'm with him, and I won't be coming back tonight."

"Okay Miss. To be fair my sweet'art I rather you weren't ere."

It was like she knew my safety would be in peril now that she was leaving.

"Whatever you do, please be safe, Chess. I love you."

Sukhi knew that she would miss Chess and would never get the chance to see her again, her lifelong friend and the closest person she could call a mother.

In her heart she knew Chess didn't want her to come back, she'd rather she was safe with Ash. Home was never going to be the same again and with Karen being the primary suspect, it was clear that it wasn't going to be safe either.

Her instinct was telling her to stay with Ash, for some reason being with him in that small moment made her feel safe and secure.

The doctor sighed and revved the engine to his Aston; it was a beautiful roaring sound of a lion that echoed through the windows. He started to drive onto the road, using his same perfect agility to manoeuvre around traffic and other cars.

Eventually he pulled up to a private road, and entered a long drive. The pebbles to the drive made a rustling noise beneath them. As they approached a long building, featuring its own security guard, she knew instantly the doctor had made a fortune.

"Are you a therapist for other families?"

"Of course, but your family somehow takes priority over them."

She fumbled her fingers in her lap. "I suppose my father pays you well."

"He does, I won't deny that… but Dr Blease asked me to take special care of you."

He parked his car in an underground parking garage where he was allocated his own private space. She got herself out of the car and walked by his side as he led her to a lift. There was a small awkward silence. As he slid his arm around her shoulders, she felt a rush of heat sweep right through her body. It was warm and gentle and comforting enough to ease her nerves. As they approached the floor, he led her to a door and opened it up for her to enter.

She walked in with shy steps, feeling uneasy with the new surroundings. His walls were tall and white and opened up to a large room that had a huge sofa facing a large flat-screen TV. He had small portraits of art representing something political and endearing on the walls. As she walked further into his apartment, he had a large L-shaped kitchen that had utensils hanging above the electric cooker. The stairs led to two doors, one she assumed to be the bathroom, the other the bedroom. She instantly blushed at the thought of the doctor lying naked in a bedroom with her. The thought was provoking and arousing. She wondered if acting upon it would be the first step to moving on, and pondered if this would help her forget the kidnapper who had encapsulated her mind for so long. She had endured something of a perfect kiss with Ash and now all her desires and attention had attuned to him.

"Would you like a drink?" asked the doctor, as he poured himself a large glass of wine.

"Yes, please," she replied with a smile.

He opened his hand, presenting his couch for her to take a seat on. There was a small fireplace built within the wall, and he remotely switched it on. She took a seat on his couch and made herself feel comfortable; she couldn't help staring at his apartment with awe. It looked like a remarkable penthouse suite.

He walked over, offering her the glass of wine she

had requested; he was not his normal professional well-presented self, he instead looked far more laid back and approachable. His hair was messy and shaggy, his rugged face was beautifully appealing to her needs. She eyed the two doors that were closed above the stairs and blushed again.

"What did Dr Blease tell you about me?" she asked, sipping a taste of medium sweet wine.

"He told me many things about you, right from when you were a child." The doctor smiled, twirling a small strand of hair that laced around the angle of her face with his finger.

"Did he tell you bad things about me?"

"No, on the contrary, he was happy to see that you had managed to not become a replica of your parents... He wondered if that might've had something to do with Chess being involved with most of your upbringing."

"Perhaps... I don't remember much of my childhood, but most of it was spent with Chess. What else did he mention?"

"He told me you were special and the person he was most concerned about within the family."

"Oh, I didn't realise." Sukhi smiled.

"Ah. We haven't sorted sleeping arrangements; well you can stay in the bedroom whilst I'll take the couch," he stated, placing his glass of wine on the coffee table in front of him.

"Oh, I don't want to impose."

"No, not at all... I'll go change the bedding upstairs for you." The doctor rose from his seat and ran up the stairs. Sukhi felt the need to down her glass of wine. The fruit-tasting wine had warmed the cockles of her icy heart and instantly she felt lightheaded and at ease. For the most part she felt even more confident.

"I have the bedroom ready for you." The doctor ran down the stairwell to meet her by the couch. "Wow, you finished your glass very quickly."

Sukhi laughed as she poured herself another one. "Nightcap before heading off."

That stiff air of tension was between them again, but she could tell the doctor was seemingly patient with her; he hadn't touched her without consent and was calm in all mannerisms. He continued to twist his finger through a strand of her hair.

"Are you okay, Sukhi?" he asked, looking at her with his usual concerned face.

"Do you ever feel lost?" she asked. "Like you aren't sure where you belong?"

His face fell, he frowned a little which baffled Sukhi. "Sometimes, but I'm beginning to see otherwise."

She couldn't help but feel as if he was referring to her, but the thought of her moving on drew back memories of her kidnapper. She was hesitant. "I think I'm going to head off to bed."

She rose from the couch; the doctor rose himself too and took two steps closer to her. He was facing her head on, reeling in the lustful aura that exuberated from her. She bit her lip, knowing he was expecting her to kiss him. She leaned in a little, waiting for his gentle lips to caress hers. This was not what she received; instead he embraced her shoulders with his hands and pulled her in for a soft kiss on the forehead. At first Sukhi thought it was a little patronising and it formed a small frown instead of a smile.

"I was expecting at least a smile from you, Missy."

Her frown creased more lines on her forehead, showing her disapproval of his small action.

"Go to bed now," he ordered, tapping her bum for her to be on her way. She gaped in shock at his condescending demeanour, but his cheeky smile melted away the lines on her forehead.

She ran up the stairs and walked into his bedroom. It was a large boxed room with its own flat-screen TV on the wall. He had a large white bookcase up against the wall, it contained a vast number of his medical books. It was a beautifully made-up modern room, it was clear he must have had an interior designer come to decorate his household. A man of his calibre would never have had the time to decorate his own household to a high standard.

She sat on the bed, which was made up with black satin silk sheets; it was indeed a perfectly sultry bed. She could only imagine the numerous women he must have slept with rolling around in his large bed. The thought of it made her stomach turn a little and to some degree she had become jealous at the thought of it.

Rain poured against the window pane, thumping down hard against the glass. She tossed and turned, wondering if coming here was a mistake. She lay down, lost in her thoughts, wondering if the kidnapper was out there still coming for her. Would he forgive her if she had moved on? The doctor was a nice enough man, and proved to be a perfect gentleman with impeccable mannerisms.

"Please forgive me," she muttered to herself, as she stripped down to her knickers and bra, and placed herself within the satin silk black sheets. *Why? He never came for you… Ash would be a better man for you and you know it.*

The rain had made it difficult for her to fall into a deep sleep, instead it had made her restless; it pounded harder against the window pane, causing its own loud panting noises. Soon enough it had begun to hail with a loud clash of thunder following. She sighed, realising it was impossible for her to try and have a good night's sleep. It had barely been half an hour, and the restlessness of feeling unsafe had caused anxiety to build up. She threw the silk satin sheet off her body, and decided to go down and see Ash. She wanted him to be beside her, just so she could feel *safe*.

As she opened the door, she could see him lying on the couch with one arm around his head. The muscular formation was showing perfect cuts, he looked presently angelic. The desire to touch his perfect abs drew an incredulous desire deep within her. She tip-toed down the stairs and knew she was only wearing her underwear; she had no shame, because all she could think of was wanting his warm body next to hers.

His eyes opened as she approached the bottom of the stairs; he stared, astounded at the attire Sukhi had chosen to bestow on him, for she was hardly wearing anything befitting. The rain began to crash down, causing ferocious noise of destruction within his apartment; a flash of bright light struck for a few seconds which was then followed by a loud clash of thunder. The atmosphere had turned intense. She swayed a little, fumbling her fingers before shifting a piece of her hair behind her ear.

His facial expression hadn't changed; he was still looking at her with a small frown.

"Sorry, I erm… was hoping you might come stay with me." She fretted and couldn't look directly at him in the eye. He raised an eyebrow, impressed with his view.

"Not to have sex," she blushed.

He raised himself from the couch and sighed; he ran his large hand through his dark thick luscious hair. "So you're scared of lightning, are you?"

"No. I just…"

Another flash of lightning struck the midnight sky, causing a larger threatening clash of thunder to roar around them. Sukhi jumped in fright as the lights suddenly went out.

"Are you afraid, Sukhi?" he asked in his gentle manner.

"A little, I've never liked thunder," she answered, feeling extremely embarrassed that a twenty-six year old was still afraid of thunder. Darkness surrounded them, dancing dark shadows as the continuous threads of lightning struck. A warm hand glided about her waist, and a vast amount of heat pressed up behind her.

"Come then, let's go." He shifted his hand from her waist to her hand, and led her up the stairs.

She wasn't expecting anything; in fact, all she wanted was his company and to just feel safe and secure.

As they both entered his bedroom, he walked over to the other side and placed himself within the bed. At first Sukhi was a little nervous, but she put her fear aside by repeating to herself to control her amorous desire for him; she didn't want to do anything with Ash that may screw things up. She sat on the other side of him, placing her body down onto the mattress, unable to move as she turned her back on him. She heard him chuckle to himself as she turned away.

"Why do you need me again?" he asked, lying on his back with one arm about his head, which invariably showed off his perfect musculature with full capacity.

"I just don't like the weather at the moment," she mumbled to herself.

"I see," and with a full sweep he moved his arm off, and pulled the back of her waist close to him. She didn't push him away or flinch at the touch of him. Instead she breathed heavily, reeling in the comfort of his body and aura. Her lips twitched with a small glitch of happiness.

"So you like spooning," he whispered into her ear.

She nodded with a degree of delight as his voice trailed down her spine causing sensational shivers throughout her body.

"Ash, is there a reason why you haven't given any

form of inclination towards me before?"

"You're my patient, I wasn't going to take advantage of you... Besides, you're still vulnerable and I personally believe you haven't recovered from Stockholm Syndrome."

"How do you know? I think I have."

Ash laughed. "You're still thinking about him."

"What? How... how do you know?" she mumbled to herself.

"I'm a leading psychiatrist; it's my job to read people," he chuckled. This annoyed her a little, but she shrugged it off and enjoyed the warm embrace she was held in.

"Stop reading me then," she groaned, as she pulled herself into the warm silk satin quilt, whilst pushing the back of her body against his warm embrace.

"It's a little hard not to... Why do you care so much for him?"

Sukhi's guilt warped its way back into her mind.

"He made a promise he would come and get me."

The arm around her waist tightened, as she noticed he was listening. This was it, the truth had to come out eventually, there was no point hiding it anymore.

"I'll tell you... because I think you're right, I do need to move on."

"Go on," he insisted, now fully focused on her. Sukhi could feel his eyes burning into her, which only made her nervous.

"The day he let me go..."

Chapter 12

The binds were about my wrists, it hurt needless to say but the pain inflicted caused me such pleasure. My limbs were aching from being suspended within the air, as were the small tie burns that were beginning to bruise my wrists. I didn't care; the procrastinating suspense from being withheld from the sheer joy and pleasure of having him inside of me was overbearing torture. The air was thick and warm, but the gloomy walls mystified the looming darkness that surrounded me. A large hand trailed down the side of my body, I was open, bearing all my naked flesh to him. By now he knew how my body worked and all he cared about was pleasuring me. He knew pleasing me meant infliction of pain, and he knew I had come to be his perfect candidate.

The executioner's mask over his face allowed him to do many things with his mouth. He kissed my inner thigh, causing sensational thrills. His fingers splayed against me, causing my body to arch and become wet beneath, this made him increase the intensity by sucking my flesh with sweet violence. I cried out with immense pleasure, beckoning him to do more. I'd completely submitted myself to his every need. His moist tongue sucked the clit, I was streaming wet with ecstasy... only he could please me. My mind had made its decision; I wanted him and no one else.

He rose up, he knew I had succumbed to the pleasure he had given me, and he took hold of my hips, situating himself perfectly in between my legs. He was ready to mount inside of me but that was not how he liked to do things. No.

He loved teasing me, tracing his large firm cock around the entry, causing me to cave in, inducing me to become wetter. Only when I was warm and good enough for him would he enter me. He thrust his vast member inside forcefully, pounding hard against me below. I screamed with every thump, his large hand taking control around my neck, squeezing it to suffocate me. This only increased my burning excitement; my entire body was at a different height as I was suspended in the air by bounds.

He moved his hand from my throat to around my mouth, where I voluntarily sucked his thumb, swirling my tongue around and clucking it hard to entice him more. The large thrusts were sadistic pushes of lust. I craved and yearned for more of his sinister hunger for devouring pain. I bit his thumb, provoking him to retract it in haste and forcefully hit me across the face hard. There was a distinctive sting across my cheek; the feelings of fear built up within me, but it only compelled me to succumb to his very tortured passion for manic desire.

"Take me," I moaned, desperate were my pleas, but he was cruel and callous and wouldn't let me give in so easily. I loved his cold, heartless and selfish being when it came to vengeful, vicious sex. He dominated me and gave in to the darkness of his nature with welcoming arms.

His groans were distinctive but I knew I was pleasing him just the way he liked it. I could feel him expanding with every forceful thrust that was now pacing harder and faster. I was squeezing every ounce of him within me; then a needful cry out from him and he released everything inside of me. The warm sensational flow burst inside and it was pure exultation as I cried out. All muscles that were tense and had worked into a state were now limp and lame.

The moment of bliss had passed, and my kidnapper released me from my binds, allowing me to return to the floor. My legs had been suspended in the air for a while and my knees buckled. He came down to the floor beside me, embracing me into his warm chest, kissing the nape of my neck, melting my body naturally into his.

"You know I have to let you go, Sukhi," he whispered into my ear.

I remember my gut sinking deep within; I didn't want to leave... not now. How could he want me to leave? Was he sick and tired of me already? Was I not good enough for him? I frowned in complete contempt, pushing him away from the embrace stubbornly.

"No, I don't want to go," I protested. "I refuse, I won't go."

He sighed in my ear, he wasn't angry with me. Clearly he knew I had formed an attachment and wanted nothing but to stay with him.

"You have to, you can't stay down here." His voice was silky and dark, the essence of sinister heaviness that sent tingles down my spine. "I had a plan of revenge, Sukhi, and things have gone pear-shaped since this began."

"So what? You're just going to let me go?"

"I promise you once my vendetta has been paid, I will come for you."

"How will I know it's you?"

"Don't worry; I will make it known to you… but first I need to settle a few things."

I felt like the one person who had salvaged me from my hell had betrayed me. I was a selfish being, and having him put me in my place made me feel like I was a better person. He was never a bad man, I believed there was good in him and I desperately wanted to help him. I wanted to do whatever it took to please him, help him sort his vendetta. I sighed, realising what I needed to do.

"You'll need to beat me up."

"No. I won't do that," he said angrily in the dark, thick sultry voice that was overpowering.

"You have to, if I'm found without any evidence of physical torture, there will be a serious amount of questions from the police. You'll need to beat me up and make me look like I was raped."

"Are you crazy?"

"No, but I know what they will expect… You'll need to hit me so I can appear to be a victim, otherwise they'll interrogate me, crucifying every word that will come out of my mouth just to find you… and I won't let them find you," I said in earnest. I had made it clear that my loyalty was to him and only him. To this day it still is.

"Hit me."

In those few hours he did just that, he beat me to a pulp. Bruised me unrecognisably, it was a pleasant turn, and every so often he would kiss me, attempting to ease the beatings he was giving. I could see from the way his body was reacting he was not happy with what I was forcing him to do. Occasionally tears would roll from my eyes, but everything he did was necessary. Once I was content with how I looked I told him to drug me with hallucinogens, that way I wouldn't be able to retrace my tracks back to him. My father would have me under serious amounts of heavy protection and I would have police tracking my every move.

"I promise to come for you," were the last remaining words I remembered from him; it almost seemed like a distant memory I could hardly recall, the drugs at that point were seriously kicking in."

***

"He promised he would come, and he hasn't." Tear drops began to stroll down her soft cheeks, her marks of affection towards a different man were clear and this had caused some discomfort towards the doctor, who could only sigh at her distress.

"You were protecting him all this time," said the doctor whose face had turned back into his normal, professional, concerned look. "That explains your stubborn attitude in the beginning of our sessions."

Sukhi couldn't help feeling betrayed; tears strolled down from her eyes. Perhaps the kidnapper had lied to her and he had no intention of finding her.

"He never came," she sighed, as she allowed tears to stroll down her face. The doctor could see she was upset.

"You do need to forget him," he insisted. "He's an idiot for not coming back for you."

Sukhi turned to face to the doctor; he was without a doubt elusive and ruggedly handsome. His chiselled features and rough stubble made his appeal perfect.

His muscular arms were ripped to perfection, but it was his intense eyes that caught hers. He melted straight into her, making her feel vulnerable.

Those features.

He stroked her hair as she lay there in front of him; she looked up at him, defenceless and weak. Her guard was down and he knew it. He moved in slowly, hovering close to her lips, she moved into kiss his soft delectable lips; they were warm and moist and his kiss was gentle and sweet. She melted deeply into his warm muscular arms, as he pushed himself hard over her. She could feel him become hard down below, and a strange urgency overwhelmed her.

That touch.

"No. I shouldn't do this," he said, moving away from her, huffing in discontentment. "You aren't ready, and I won't take advantage of you."

Sukhi was taken aback by his immediate reaction. She collected herself together, annoyed and upset that he had gone to such lengths only to reject her.

"You're the one telling me to move on," she replied, frowning at his sudden retraction.

"You still have feelings for him though and that's why I shouldn't." His comforting demeanour had changed.

Sukhi huffed before turning her back against him; there was a moment of silence between them, before he relaxed and turned to press himself against her, wrapping his arm around her waist. She was safe and that was all she needed to fall asleep throughout the night.

***

Sukhi awoke from the blinding light that infiltrated through the blinds; it stung at first but she desperately tried to turn over and pull the quilt over.

"Wake up, sleepy head," said a smooth voice from the door; it was clear the doctor had risen early morning to get ready. She felt the bed sink down beside her, he had sat where she was sleeping and he was watching her wedge herself warmly within the covers.

"Did you sleep well?" he asked, stroking the top part of her hair that had formed into bed head.

"Yes, but why did you wake up so early?" she said, wrapping herself in the warm satin quilt, almost refusing to get herself ready for the day.

"I think I have to take you back home, before your father starts to worry about you."

She flung the quilt off her face begrudgingly.

"Please, he barely knows he has a family," she scoffed, as she turned over to one side.

"Still, I need to take you back, before your father calls the police on me and I'm out of a job."

"Can I just spend the day here?" she asked, as she yawned and stretched herself in his bed. He smiled at her with a look of admiration.

"You need to let someone know. I have a few appointments as well this morning, so I'll be back around twelve."

"Okay, can I sleep in?"

"Yes of course, just make sure to call your dad."

Sukhi rolled her eyes. "You're very condescending, you treat me like I'm a teenager."

He chuckled to himself, "That's because you behave like one."

Sukhi rolled over, to retrieve her phone from the bedside table; the doctor was watching her face. She was a natural beauty, she never needed make-up as her skin was always clear. Her bed head, though, had clearly lost control. The doctor stared at her, admiring her figure and face.

"Hi Dad."

"Sukhi, what time are you coming home today?"

"I don't think I really want to come home just yet."

"Are you still with the doctor? Chess told me last night you were with him."

"Yes." She laughed; she noticed by the corner of

her eye that the doctor was eyeing her every move with delight.

"So you like him then?" he laughed.

"Yes… I do."

"Okay darling, take all the time you want to stay there, but does that mean he has cancelled his session with Karen?"

Fuck, he has to see her. No doubt she would be sly and attempt to make a move on him, now he has overtly shown his affection towards me.

"Could you ask her to cancel it?" she asked with an angelic voice.

"Hang on, let me ask… Karen sweetheart, would you mind if you cancelled your session with the doctor today?"

"Did *he* just cancel? He knows I've been through a lot this week," she whimpered. Sukhi could hear her stepmother pretending to be coy which only made her blood boil.

"No, Sukhi is actually asking if you wouldn't mind." Sukhi could hear her father's tone and knew that Karen had no choice in the matter.

"Very well, please tell Sukhi to come back home safely." She could hear the melancholy in Karen's voice, no wonder she hated Sukhi, as the doctor had rightly said.

"Will you be coming back home today?" her father asked.

"We'll see, I'll give you a call later."

"Okay, well just drop me a message and let me

know if you are."

Her father hung up.

There was a small silence between her and the doctor, who was still admiring her with a smile.

"So you cancelled one of my patients, did you?" he asked, tweaking a wider smile on the edge of his lip.

"She doesn't really need your help... There's nothing wrong with her," said Sukhi, sponging her face into a pillow.

"If she's a threat to you, then yes I think she does need my help." His face had become a little sober. "I take my work very seriously."

"Well that's good, but I don't think my stepmother deserves your attention."

"Ah, so you're worried she might get her claws into me," he smirked.

"Perhaps," said Sukhi with a small frown on her forehead.

"Well she tried before I showed any interest in you, and she failed. I don't think you have anything to be worried about; I know how to take care of myself."

Sukhi huffed, wound up with his answer. She didn't want him to have anything to do with her stepmother, especially if she was the type of woman to know how to dig her claws into someone like Ash, regardless of how intelligent and smart he may have been.

"I will be back at 11 then, seeing as you cancelled your stepmother. Breakfast is in the fridge downstairs."

With that, the doctor picked himself up, assembled himself to his normal professional apparel, picked up his briefcase that was by the side of the door and left without another word.

Sukhi was left to lie in her bed; she breathed in, taking in all his masculine essence that had been left behind. Her mind drifted back to the nights with the kidnapper, she was giving up on him, and guilt was bit by bit being overridden by the mere passionate thoughts of herself with Ash.

Her mobile began to vibrate, she quickly picked it up and noticed it was Jonathan.

"Hi Jonathan, what is it?"

"Hi Sukhi," said a sorrowful voice from the other side of the line. "I was hoping to apologise for my behaviour last time."

Sukhi didn't say anything; she remembered how he had threatened her and called her selfish and self-centred, just because she rejected him.

"I know you didn't feel anything when we kissed."

"This is awkward; I'm not sure it is a good idea that we speak," she said.

"Wait. What?" he protested with earnest in his voice.

"Jonathan, I'm going to make it very clear to you, I don't like you in that way and never will. So stop this now."

"Okay, but can we not at least be friends?" he asked.

"I don't think so; you don't like it when you don't get your way."

"Fine, you're right. But I didn't think it meant you'd stop being friends with me."

"You need to give me time then," she barked, desperately aching to get off her cell phone. He had sickened her, but it was only because of her desire to be rid of him in her life.

"Okay, I will, but Sukhi please don't go out with your doctor."

"What? He is none of *your* business."

"Sukhi, something about him doesn't make sense."

"Goodbye Jonathan."

With that, she hung up the phone; she knew Jonathan was jealous but his persistent behaviour was annoying and trying her nerves. Why could he not realise that there were no feelings there from the beginning? She was forced to try to move on and she didn't want to. *But now I may actually have a chance to be happy, happy with someone who understands me better than I understood myself.*

She rose from the bed and decided to take a shower and get ready. His bathroom was the latest edition and the highest technology. It was clear Ash had done very well for himself and had taken care of himself in all aspects. Indeed he had his own mood shower with lights of all sorts. At first it confused Sukhi, but eventually she worked it out.

She walked down the stairs, feeling plush heat press against her skin as she walked into the sun. She smiled; the place was a safe haven somewhere she could readily escape to. Peace was all around her; a small water fountain was a feature beside a wall, with orchard flowers surrounding it. It was peaceful living, something she had always wanted in life, but due to her father's constant business and social media lifestyle, she was always left in the spotlight.

Something I desperately want to escape from.

She decided to attempt to make tea but somehow the equipment Ash had was too high tech, in the end she ended up making a small flood, which she desperately tried to clear up but only made more of a mess.

Oh Fuck. Forget it then.

She sat on the couch and began to watch television; the news seemed to be the first option.

"Daughter of David Rai seems to have found a new beau in her doctor, Dr Meller. The two were spotted in the…"

Fucking media. Can't they find someone else to hound?

Sukhi instantly jumped in fright as the phone rang, it caught her off-guard as the loud ring seemed to encapsulate the entire living room. It went straight to voicemail that was on loudspeaker.

"Hi Ash, it's your mother…"

Shit.

"Your father and I love you, and miss you terribly. Please come home soon."

Of course, Ash is a workaholic.

"You told us you were practicing in California… Why did you go to England? And you are with that girl? Your father and I are concerned about your welfare and why you thought it was okay to lie to us... Please call me when you get this." The strong Northern American accent that came through could only be Ash's mother.

Well my celebrity status clearly does me no justice. But then why would Ash lie to her about where he worked?

The door unlocked, it was eleven o' clock already.

"Hey Sukhi, I finished relatively early."

Sukhi stared at him, confused and baffled as to why he would lie to his mother about his whereabouts.

"Your mother called," she said with a glare. "California?"

"Ah, yes, she would be annoyed about that," he said, still smiling. "My mother wanted me to be mentored by Dr Black... He has one of the best medical practices in California. However, I wanted to be mentored by Dr Blease as his thesis and methods of human psychology seemed far more constructive and effective."

"So you lied about it?"

"Look, when your parents pay for college and everything else in your life, there's an obligation to want to make them happy."

That makes sense.

"I wanted to be mentored here under Dr Blease, and she didn't like it... so I kept it secret from her... Speaking of which, how on earth did she find out?"

"Let me show you." She took the remote control

and switched on the news. Images of the doctor and Sukhi were all over the media, with reporters giving their views and opinions.

"Why the heck would my mother be up at six in the morning? She lives in Pittsburgh. I tell you that woman is getting crazier by the minute."

Sukhi sighed, her face and complexion dimmed.

"What's the matter?" said the doctor, stroking the side of her cheek.

"That's why I just want to leave this place. I feel like I could have my own life to live, rather than be in this constant spotlight where the entire world knows my business."

"If that's what you wish for, go and do it."

"I don't know."

"One day you could, you never know."

"Maybe, but it's very unlikely."

The doctor nodded, staring at her, analysing every angle of her saddened face.

"If I didn't know any better, you've always wanted to escape the clutches of your family."

Small tears began to stroll down her face. She remembered how much she used to dream of travelling the world, but all dreams were shattered the moment she was forced to come back to reality.

"The moment I returned from my kidnapper, I thought I was never going to escape this life."

"I suppose your father likes to keep you supervised, but the media are relentless."

"Exactly… the only good that came out of the kidnapping was I got to escape for a small space of time."

The doctor eyed her and noticed this was the most vulnerable she had been. Her eyes fluttered as she wiped away her tears. Her brave front was no stranger to him. He saw her true colours and admired her strength and desire for a life worth living.

"This may seem strange, but I feel more in a prison in my current situation than I ever did with the kidnapper."

"Maybe that's why you grew feelings for him."

"No, that was on my own accord, I believe. He never forced me to do anything."

The doctor gave his usual lax smile. "I'm beginning to grow jealous of this man."

She looked up at him with a beautiful hazy glow about her that was spellbinding; he admittedly grew nervous with the desirous stare she had bestowed on him. "You should, he was one of a kind."

He stroked a piece of her hair away from her face, before leaning into kiss her soft lips; they were luscious and moist. Full of warmth and the hope of happiness filled within them. She began pulling his body against hers, thrusting his body in between her legs to feel her close to him.

"You are hard to resist," he muttered in between stuttered kisses.

"Then don't resist," she spoke back in between breaths.

"I have to, for your own good." He frowned,

pulling away from her. Sukhi was taken aback by the sudden push again. He had rejected her once more against her wishes.

"Trust me, Sukhi, this is for your own good. I just… I want you for myself. I don't want you to belong to anyone but me."

"Oh, and you won't because of my feelings for the kidnapper?" Her face fell to disgrace.

"Don't be ashamed, I'm not judging you… I would just like to have you for myself. Is that not fair to ask?"

She nodded, realising she knew exactly what the doctor had meant.

***

The whole day passed whilst the doctor and Sukhi spent the rest of the hours cooking food and watching movies together in his apartment. It had been the perfect day, a day where she had relaxed and managed to stay away from the spotlight. Her life was calm and quiet, and being wrapped within the doctor's arms made her feel safe. Something she hadn't felt since she had been with the kidnapper. Eventually her day had ended and she had to leave and go back home. She called Clive to come and pick her up with the limo.

Clive drove up to her driveway after passing intensive security to get to the gates. She paid the cab and walked towards her door. She noticed how Karen had stepped up and opened the door before she could even ring the bell.

"So you've finally come home." Her eyebrow was

raised and her face glowered at Sukhi.

Sukhi glared back, pushing her stepmother aside. But before Sukhi could take a step further, Karen grabbed her by the shoulder.

"You listen to me, you little bitch. Don't you dare tell your father. He'll put me and Serena out on the streets."

Sukhi fought her stepmother back, by pushing one step in front of her.

"It's because of Serena I haven't told my father about your indiscretions, and if I were you... I'd start acting like a mother, because Serena has witnessed you."

"What?" said Karen, shocked by the words of accusation that Sukhi was throwing at her.

"You disgust me. But I'll put up with you," and with that Sukhi walked away in haste, up the stairs and into her bedroom. The desire to have Chess around for confidence was long gone, for she was on her way back to her home. As she ran and fell onto her soft bed her mind went off into a complex thought process. An overwhelming desire to investigate her mother's accident brought on a feverous temptation to ransack her father's office.

A small knock came about the door; she could tell by the light tap it was her little sister. The last time they had spoken, venom had come through her words.

"Go away," said Sukhi, but the blight didn't listen; she opened the door and slid in.

"Suks," said a small timid voice by the door; Sukhi looked up and saw her younger sister looking sorrowful. "I'm sorry for all the things I said to you."

It was clear Serena had been crying for a long time, judging by the large puffy bags that had formed around her eyes.

"I don't think I've ever said anything bad or wrong to you." Sukhi sighed with contempt.

"You haven't, you've been the best older sister any girl could ask for."

Sukhi melted her frown from her forehead, which was acknowledgement that Serena had won her sister back.

"Oh. You know I can't be angry with you. Come here, Ducky."

Serna ran, jumping onto the bed, warmly embracing her elder sister. Sukhi knew, however, from the lack of tightness, that there was more than just their fight that was bothering her.

"Something else is up?" said Sukhi.

"It was Mum, wasn't it?" Serena's face had turned pale white.

Clearly her sister had overheard the conversation between Karen and herself. It wasn't what Sukhi had intended, but guilt began to run through Sukhi. Her sister was beginning to realise that her mother's indiscretions were leading to a failed marriage and a failed family.

"I'm sorry too, you should not have heard that."

"If you want to run away, can I come with you?" said Serena, staring up at her with tearful eyes.

"Of course, where shall we go?" said Sukhi,

hugging her.

"China, Thailand… perhaps we can both stay with Chess," said Serena. "Why haven't we gone yet?"

"Do you honestly think Dad will let us go?"

There was a small silence; Serena slowly tightened her hand around her sister's jumper, sensing something wasn't right.

"If you do go, please take me with you." Serena was not herself, Sukhi could tell.

"Okay, I promise," said Sukhi. "What's going on with you?"

"I'm not sure, but I do sense something bad might happen."

Sukhi kissed her sister's head and embraced her more to try comfort her.

"Don't worry… I won't let anything happen to you."

Chapter 13

Sukhi was woken by her phone ringing next to her. She grumbled, annoyed her perfect sleep was rudely imposed on by the constant vibration of her phone.

It was Jonathan, much to her displeasure.

"You woke me up. Are you being serious?"

"You were with the doctor, and I told you not to get close to him."

Sukhi was not only frustrated with Jonathan for waking her up early in the morning, she was also livid by the tone of his voice.

"Okay, I'm going to hang up, because this is ridiculous."

"Look, I'm sorry… you've clearly got feelings for him."

"I don't think I need to repeat myself, but that's none of your business." Sukhi's tone was even sharper.

"You're right, I'm sorry… but I've found out some information…"

"Look, honestly Jonathan… no more. I've had

enough. Goodbye."

Sukhi wished she had never led him on in any way, as now he wouldn't leave her alone.

And with that she hung up.

She had wondered if Jonathan would just give up on her, his motives and consistent overbearing willingness were beginning to annoy her, strain her nerves even. As she had been rudely awoken by her cell ringing, she decided to get ready to seize the day. She grabbed her grey jumper dress and wore it with her black tights. She scrunched her hair into a messy bun and ran down the stairs.

She decided she was brave enough to confront her father. She took a few breaths before entering his private office to collect herself. She opened the door and slid in; it was clear her father hadn't slept well, large dark circles surrounded his eyes and coffee stains marked his shirt.

"Hello darling," he said, as he rustled through his papers, not even glancing up to take a look at her. "What can I do for you?"

"Dad, I need to ask you something and I need you to be honest with me." Her voice was shaking a little. She knew bringing up her mother, her real mother, was a sensitive issue. The entire situation made him look like a villain, but she hoped she was wrong.

"What is the matter?" He finally looked up at her with concern and noticed by the frown lines on her forehead that she had something serious to say.

"I need you tell me something about Mum, my real mother," she said voluntarily, sitting in the seat opposite to face him.

He folded the paper he was holding and placed it neatly on the pile he had collated on his right-hand side of his desk. He leaned back in his chesterfield chair and eyed her carefully.

"What exactly do you want to know about your mother?" he asked, knowing his daughter had been up to some investigative research of her own, otherwise she would not have raised such a question in the first place.

"The accident you covered up?"

"And how did you find out about that?" her father asked.

"So it was true, there was an accident you had covered up."

"Who told you?"

"Dad, just tell me what happened." Sukhi remained calm and in control of the situation. She knew that by remaining focused and unemotional she would have a better response from her father, especially about sensitive topics like her mother.

"I'm no longer a child… I just need to know the truth," she pleaded.

"No. Dammit, I won't." Her father had lost his temper. It was clear that talking about Sukhi's mother caused him a lot of pain and anguish; weakness appeared all over the lines on his face that were easily readable to Sukhi.

"Dad, I just want to know the truth about Mum, or at least what happened to the family." Her voice remained ever so calm.

"Why do you want to know such information?"

"Dad, what happened?"

Sukhi wasn't letting go of the issue, her tenacity and consistent badgering would always let her have her way, and her father wasn't able to fight back or fend her off.

"There was an accident, a fire was set off and the family was killed. The young boy survived, but I ensured he was put into a good orphanage, and in a few months he was adopted by a family."

"How did you cover it up?"

"I said it was an accident, a gas cooker was left on, and a fire started."

"But Mum started it, thinking it was Karen's house? She ended up killing a family by accident. You ruined the family by consorting with Karen, and Mum had to pay for it dearly. What kind of man would do that to his wife?"

He sighed, closing his eyes for a moment.

"Let me start from the beginning. I married your mother and I loved her, more than anything. I defied my family and was willing to give up my wealth, name and title, just to be with her. But like all Rai members, I had to take my father's place once my brother died. I was aware of my family mistreating your mother, but I kept her safe and assured her that nothing in the world would tear me apart from her."

Sukhi remained still, soaking in every word her father as saying. "But she didn't die from cancer, did she?"

"She didn't die from cancer, like I told you. She was

murdered in the rehabilitation centre I put her in."

"So all this time you've lied to me, about everything, and the thing you called a rehabilitation centre was more like an asylum," said Sukhi whose blood began to boil, venomous hatred fuelled through her.

"Sukhi, I did everything to protect her."

"No Dad, you did it to protect yourself. You don't actually care for me, or for Serena. How could you put the woman you were 'supposed' to be in love with, in a rehabilitation centre?"

"To keep her safe from my family." He sighed. "They certainly aren't the most forgiving family and scandals as such would've caused a huge problem for them."

"So that family, who have treated me with such contempt since I was born, you protected?"

Her father was speechless.

"Dad, I'm going to leave and there is nothing you can do about it."

"No, Sukhi… Wait…"

"No, I've come to understand that you're a liar and a coward, and I don't want to have anything to do with this family." Sukhi rose from the seat, angered and upset by the lies and sheer mistreatment her mother had. She stormed outside his office, banging the large oak doors behind and causing a small quake within the hallway.

"Sukhi," said a voice from down the corridor. It was Serena, whose eyes began to wield tears. "Why are you leaving?"

She could tell Serena had been listening in to her conversation with their father. Sukhi braced her tears back.

"No, Ducky…"

"You said you were going to leave?"

Sukhi sighed for a moment. "No, not yet at least, I still need to get to the bottom of certain things."

"You mean that family that died?"

"You heard that," said Sukhi, cursing herself in her mind for allowing her sister to overhear their conversation. "God dammit, Ducky."

"I know where Dad's secret safe is."

"Dad has a safe?" said Sukhi, slightly shocked by her sister's revelation.

"Yes, it's hidden behind the book 'The Wind and the Willows' in the library… I accidentally came across a few years back."

"You have to show me," said Sukhi.

"Of course I will, but you have to promise me that you won't leave me behind."

Sukhi knew that Serena wanted to go wherever she went, but this was a promise Sukhi couldn't make, knowing all too well that Karen would hit the roof and her father would go on search parties to hunt them down.

"I'll see what I can do, you know Karen won't let you leave and stay with me."

"Please, we both know she never has the final say. It's Dad you need to ask."

Even that would be more difficult.

"Sukhi," yelled a shrill voice from the front door. It wasn't courteous or nice as it normally was. In fact it was filled with disappointment.

Karen.

"You and Mum aren't on good terms anymore," said Serena.

Sukhi could see how Serena was upset with how the family was deteriorating right in front of her eyes. It was clear she had been crying over the past few days over the truths and realities of her dysfunctional family.

"No Ducky, we just see things differently now, but it doesn't change the fact that we both love you."

Sukhi stroked her sister on the head in an attempt to comfort her. "Go upstairs, I'll come up and explain in a moment."

Sukhi walked towards the door, and noticed how Jonathan was standing there talking to her stepmother. It seemed a little strange to see them standing quite close, but Sukhi had only recently became aware of Karen's true nature, and it was slowly becoming more apparent.

"I was hoping to reach you," said Jonathan in earnest.

"I was hoping you wouldn't," she snapped.

"You left me no option but to come here."

"Jonathan, I don't understand *WHY* you bother." Sukhi frowned with full impatience.

"Maybe because I care about you." Jonathan's face

was full or sorrow and regret.

"No. Just please leave me alone. If you don't, I'll have my father put a restraining order on you."

Jonathan looked stunned by her comment; he looked at her stepmother who merely shrugged her shoulders, whilst gulping more of her drink.

"She's been too busy with *her* doctor," said Karen, who took a large gulp out of her glass of straight vodka.

"You really like him, don't you?" He was shaking in what looked like anger.

"Jonathan it's really none of your business." She found herself wound up by his presence. She was grateful for all the help he had provided for her before. His constant pressure to have her as more than a friend had become annoying. Maybe she was considered a tease; she had felt bad that she might have led him on, but it was only on the advice her doctor had given her at the time.

"I don't think he's good enough for you, Sukhi."

"Oh please, just give up already. I have nothing to say to you… therefore I request that you leave my house immediately."

"I know what you're looking for… actually I know who you're looking for."

Sukhi's heart dropped instantly.

Could he possibly know who? Or was he just saying that.

She paused and side glanced at Karen, who was listening into the conversation. Her sour face was one of pure venomous delight, any information to bring the downfall of her step-daughter was enough to make her smile. She could see that she wanted to know this 'what' or 'who' Jonathan was referring to.

"I don't know what you are talking about," said Sukhi, covering her tracks. "Now get out."

Sukhi turned her back on Jonathan, and walked up the stairs with huge strops in her stride, as she glanced to ensure that he was leaving the house. Clearly this was a cold war between herself and Karen, the two of them could feel the intensity of hatred fuelling between them. Jonathan walked out of the door with a slam.

***

Damn that girl. She's fucking pushing me away.

The cell phone rang whilst he was walking out. Work.

"MI5 Agent Smith," he replied to the ringing tone.

"Smith, what happened with the girl? Is she still refusing to spend time with you?"

"Yes, because that damn doctor has got in the way."

"No he hasn't, he's doing your job better than you."

"But…"

"I asked you to do one thing, Smith. Get close to the girl and find out what she's hiding."

Jonathan remained vigilant but it was clear he was becoming frustrated and made to feel like an idiot.

"If you want to get back in my good books, you better find a way to get close to that damn girl; you're a double agent for a reason."

"Look, I don't know what you want me to do; she's bloody stubborn."

"Do whatever you need to do. Fuck her if you need to. Get information."

With that the chief hung up. Here he had to play the fool, something that would make him the butt of the joke in the MI5.

At first when he was assigned by the chief to go undercover as a mate for Mr Rai's daughter, he had never really found her in the forest, a regular jogger had. However, MI5 had made him pretend to be that particular jogger.

He remembered all the MI5 agents who had been briefed on the kidnapping case of Sukhi Rai were gutted when he was given the opportunity.

"Ain't she a looker," remarked one of the agents.

"I think the only person who is responsible enough to keep it together and professional is Agent Smith," said Chief Wiggins. "He's proven to me that he is a hard worker and sharper than all of you idiots."

"Yes, that's 'cause he's Agent Dickhead," laughed another agent. The entire team were laughing, except for Jonathan. Of course he took his job seriously, he was the perfect agent on any job, and he remembered how he didn't see this one as a particular challenge.

It wasn't a hard one to figure out; the problem was collecting enough information to allocate the whereabouts of her kidnapper. Sukhi was protecting him and that had become clear to him the moment she started to search for things. He had connected all the dots from the beginning. Things had turned sour, it became very clear that his questions had become a nuisance to her, and she did not find him appealing enough to melt her. He clenched his fist.

"Who does that little bitch think she is?"

Now she was turning him out, at the most crucial point of the investigation. He needed to get Sukhi to start talking, otherwise his entire career was on the line.

Fuck. The doctor's messing up the entire investigation. Unless the doctor's removed from the picture, there's no way I can take charge of this investigation, The chief knows I'm not making any progress, and if he knows that I'm not making progress, then 'they' know.

"The son of a bitch," he murmured to himself.

"Ah. Jonathan, how are you today?" It was the devil himself. Smiling with his rakishly perfect smile, Jonathan couldn't help but feel a pang of jealousy form in the pit of his stomach.

"Fine, doctor." His tone was cold, severe and harsh.

"Ah, I see." His smile faded as he acknowledged the well-known tone of jealousy. He had encountered many men like Jonathan before, who always seemingly despised his natural allure for the opposite sex. The doctor carried on walking towards the house, whilst Jonathan scathingly scorned at him with pure hatred.

Sukhi opened the door, embracing him with pure joy and excitement. For a small moment Jonathan felt remorse build up within him, as he glimpsed at the small bonded happiness between the doctor and Sukhi.

Watching the two of them made his blood boil, the doctor was ruining his chances for a promotion and there was no way he could let that happen. His selfishness empowered him to do whatever it took to remove the doctor from the scene, regardless of who got hurt in the end.

Chapter 14

Sukhi lay on the couch in complete bliss, enjoying the doctor stroking her hair; she felt at ease when she consumed her thoughts of freedom that lay ahead of her. The world was full of adventures, which was something she had yearned for her entire life. The doctor kept her smiling which was something she never thought would happen, but putting her entire trust in him made her feel taken care of.

"I want to know what's going through that mind of yours," he said, moving his hands from her hair to stroke her soft cheeks.

"Guess you'll never know," she replied, teasing him.

He kissed her on the forehead.

"So what's your next plan?" he asked her. She felt the warmth of his body exuberate next to hers.

"I'll be heading out of town soon, just to have a breather if anything."

"That will be good for you," he whispered into her ear.

"Yes, I'd hope so. Why don't you come with me?"

She paused for a moment and thought of the prospect of having a divine future with him. "In fact, why don't we go travelling around the world together? See new places and meet new people? How exciting would that be?"

He stared at her with complete adoration in his eyes. The prospect of adventure and a new life sparkled between the two of them. A world of no fear or anxiety, a world filled with endless opportunities. But soon her smile faded and Ash knew there was something wrong.

"What's wrong?" he asked, pushing a piece of hair away from her face.

"Nothing... I just..."

Her actual intention was to find out about the boy who was orphaned at a young age by her mother. Curiosity had got the better of her, and her guilty conscience was to ensure that the boy had been well taken care of by a good family. Despite her father's word, it wasn't enough to satisfy her. She knew all too well that her father was a selfish and career-minded man who cared little for his family, let alone others.

"Sukhi, just be careful."

"What do you mean?"

"I can sense the tension in the household, especially with you and Karen. Just be careful. I don't want anything to happen to you."

"I've decided that I'll be leaving here soon. I told my father."

His face began to falter; she knew that he was a little gutted by the news of her moving. He had grown to love taking care of her, became protective of her and harnessed the power of understanding her thoughts and perceptions on matters.

"I know that will be a good move for you. You'll be out of the spotlight." Despite his enthusiasm she could tell behind his eyes he was upset.

She bit her lip.

"You know I can't help myself when you do that." His lips trailed down to the nape of her neck, sending small tingles down her spine that melted all barriers in her body.

Her fire-like spirit was enough to burn through him and cause rivalling passions and sensations that caused his mind to go ballistic at the mere sight of her.

"Yes, and finally I might get the peace and quiet I need to write my book," she said whilst her fingers began to fumble through his thick shaggy hair. She felt his body, that was pressed against hers, stiffen.

That body.

She looked up at him, gazing at his chiselled features that were angelically decorated with stubble. She radiated a beaming smile, glowing charm that had overwhelmed many people in the past.

"I don't think I ever told you this, but I do like you quite a lot…I never thought I would be able to let go of the kidn—"

His face fell, she remembered the last time she had liked someone. It was when she was with a man who had wanted to kill her from the beginning. She frowned, realising the notion of it just seemed ridiculous. It was as if she had been blinded by lust over her kidnapper, and she was finally seeing the light to the end of the tunnel.

"He's still in your head?" asked the doctor in his usual calm voice.

"No, it feels like he's a distant memory... He never came back to me and you are right, I need to move on." Her face fell, and he could see that she was upset that she had been misled into believing she was in love.

He caressed her forehead and she felt at ease around him. He leaned into her, breathing in her essence. He closed in towards her for proximity; she felt the heat build up between them. He stroked the side of her face whilst pining into her eyes with intensity. She felt herself becoming weak within his grasp. He kissed her sweet-smelling neck, moving across her jawline until he reached her soft lips. She moaned, as she moved her hand about his neck and through his luscious thick black hair. She coaxed her tongue into his, desiring for him to do more to her. This time he was more needful than he usually was, it was sweet yet passionate. He pushed himself onto her and she graciously accepted him to coax more of her.

"Ash," she moaned, it seemed a little strange that she wasn't referring to him as her doctor, but it was a wonderful feeling to say his name as if he were hers.

He groaned as he pushed himself closer to her, racing his fingers around her delectable body. He deepened his kiss, but it was clear to Sukhi that he was holding himself back, restraining himself. It must have been the years of servitude to healthcare that had inflicted such restraint, for she could not understand why he was holding back to something that now belonged *to him*.

"Don't hold back," she whispered, pulling his jumper off and over his head. She could feel his urgency that was inflicting pain on him.

"Sukhi, No… I really shouln… Oh God." Before he could say another word, her hand had moved over across his extremely aroused member, massaging it with pure burning lust. His eyes turned strangely into something menacing, something that aroused her inside. He reached down, hastily pulling the buttons off her shirt; she panted, pining for him to be deep within her.

That touch, the feeling…

She knew she had unleashed his animalistic instinct within; his hands were strong and in full control, his lustful burning desire ambushed her with haste. She widened her legs to allow him inside of her. He reverently lifted her skirt, pulling down her knickers. He pushed her down with force and placed his fingers over her clitoris, before pushing his fingers deep inside of her where she was wet.

"You're so wet," he groaned. He rhythmically moved his large fingers inside, hard and fast.

That feeling.

She moaned louder, clawed her fingers deep into his back. He wailed at the ecstatic pain she had inflicted. This didn't stop him; in fact it only antagonised him to want to do more to her.

"Don't stop," she whispered. He placed his finger over her mouth. She voluntarily sucked it with enticement, rolling her tongue around to provoke the beast within him.

He pushed himself up from his arms; his perfectly angelic muscular back arched, leaving Sukhi in awe over him. The desire within her down below began to ache, pining for him to penetrate her. She pulled off the buckle from his trousers, pulling them off with ease and gently trying to coax him down onto her.

"Are you sure?" he asked her, looking at her with uncertainty.

She looked up at him, for a moment she paused, wondering if she was ready. The small gleam of hope and desire that shone through his eyes was enough to put her conflicted mind at ease.

"Yes," she smiled up at him. She pulled his face closer to hers and kissed him with pure love. He took it as permission to go further, but it was clear to Sukhi from the small frown that appeared on his forehead that he was conflicted and unsure himself.

"Suks, I'm not sure if you're ready. As your doctor I wouldn't think this is advisable... You're st—"

"Shh," she said in her smooth, silky, calm voice. It was soothing and more than just an invitation to let him in. Her instinct was telling her to let go; she hadn't felt the urge to have someone close to her since the kidnapper. It seemed like the doctor had broken down all barriers and walls.

He kissed her, tasting the sweet, delectable, plump lips. He could tell she was smiling as he stroked her soft cheeks, smiling himself as he brushed past them with him lips.

"They're so soft." He licked his lips before kissing them.

He pulled himself up and raised her legs in between his arms. As he slowly penetrated within her, he felt her entire body tense in his grip as she moaned with pleasure, biting her lip with pure delight. He loved knowing he could please her and saw her smile with happiness, a fulfilment and sustaining happiness.

This wasn't the same pleasure she had encountered before with the kidnapper, it was something different, joyful pleasure in a sweeter sense. *Love?* She felt nothing but completely enraptured and was encapsulated in his warming embrace. She was finally moving on with someone she trusted, someone she had grown to have feelings for and had already fallen in love with.

But what if it's him?

He pushed deeper and harder, she craved him as her body arched for him. She was warm and incredibly enticing, which only brought him to push into her more, causing her to cry out in ecstasy. He traced his hands around the nape of her neck before cupping his hands around her breast.

She had wondered many times whether her body would repulse to some other man touching her, but she was finding her body willingly give herself into him. It was strange for she only thought there would have been one man in the world that would have made her feel like that. Here she was giving it all up to a man who was her confidant, who had become her best friend and was now her lover.

She pushed herself up, positioning herself seated within his lap, leaving him still penetrated within her. She rummaged her hands through his long dark hair, pulling it with eagerness; he groaned profoundly, pushing himself deeper within. She had wrapped her thighs around his waist and rhythmically intensified the closeness; he seemed like he was in a trance of ecstasy, pushing his fingers deep around her waist whilst he suckled on her breasts, compelling her to push more with enticement.

He pulled away to look at her sweet face that was going through ultimate pleasure. Their eyes locked for a moment and the atmosphere changed, a strong force deep within lunged at her.

That smell?

Suddenly she felt her legs give way and her entire body become weak. His eyes were rakishly dark and intense, she felt him pierce them straight into her, making her nervous and giddy as unrivalled feelings built. She couldn't understand why he had the power to overwhelm her and make her feel the way she did.

She pulled her body back, allowing him to take control, praising her contoured body within his grasp. The pining for passion and craving to have him touch her had been fulfilled; he had met her demands and exceeded her expectations and satisfaction. He had built up and rigorously and pushed harder, she cried out in ecstasy and with a final blow he gave in, filling her with warm pleasurable fluid that calmed and soothed her inside.

***

The feeling was all too similar, every touch and sensation. *What if he was the kidnapper?* But she needed to be sure... his accent now was the only indicator that he wouldn't be.

The two of them lay next to each other; she felt his warm arm embrace her about the waist. It almost seemed too perfect for her to comprehend. Sukhi had her eyes closed but she could sense that he was watching her with admiration as he stroked away strands of hair about her face and then moved onto caressing her soft cheeks.

"What is your greatest fear?" she asked him. It was a random question, but it was one way to fill the empty silence between them.

She heard him laugh. "Failure."

She opened her eyes to gaze at him; his perfect and content face matched hers.

"In order to succeed, one must never have the illusion of failure," she said, glowing at him. "Chess taught me that."

"That's a very clever saying… What about you?"

She lowered her gaze from him, ashamed to think of her fear.

"Getting hurt… by you."

He pulled her in closer to him, cradling her in his strong muscular arms.

"That is one fear you can put aside, I could never hurt you." He smiled. "You, on the other hand, have it in your power to hurt me."

"What?" said Sukhi in disbelief. "That's not true."

"Really?" he said with a raised eyebrow.

"Why do I feel like I know you?" she asked. "There was a moment when…" Sukhi caught Ash's eye and realised by his expression he was a little amused with where she was going, so she stopped mid-sentence. "Tell me about your hobbies instead."

Ash continued to stare at her. "Erm, I guess I like to keep fit, I used to like gardening, sports, food. What about you?"

"I love to write and on occasion I like painting and playing the piano... but tell me more about you. Can you tell me about your previous relationships?"

"Erm... have you turned into *my* therapist?" He laughed. Sukhi blushed, realising she must have sounded like she was interrogating him. It wasn't that she was; she found it fascinating to get to know someone, understanding the true human behind the facade of work.

"Sorry, I just wanted to know more about you."

He grinned. "It's fine. I've had girlfriends before, but I tend to get bored very quickly and easily."

"Oh, I see, and as a therapist which part of your history made you unable to commit to a girl?"

"What?" He looked at her, shocked by her sudden abrupt analysis.

"Well, isn't that what it is? You have commitment issues?"

"Yes, you could say that, I don't know... women have never been my priority."

So what am I?

Sukhi frowned at the doctor's remark, wondering if she might have been anything different. A small voice in her mind forced her to doubt his intentions.

The doctor stared at her, noticing his comment

had caused a hurt reaction.

"I didn't mean to upset you," he remarked.

"You didn't." Her voice had become quiet.

His face remained complacent. "I have upset you."

He lowered his face and kissed her again, reeling in her soft essence and sweet delectable lips. She felt herself slowly ease into him, but doubt encouraged her to be smart and keep her wits about her. He was a man with commitment issues; Sukhi could not imagine her situation turning for the worst.

"I promised you, I wouldn't hurt you," he said to her in hushed tones, shifting the small strands of hair away from her face.

"Is that supposed to be comforting?" she asked.

"What would you like from this, Sukhi?"

Sukhi sighed and turned away from; he kept her close by ensuring his arms were firm around her waist. But as she lay there she couldn't help wondering if she might have been better off with no man in her life.

"Nothing," she replied. "Or at least I am not sure yet." She was lying to herself. She knew very well what she wanted; she wanted to move away to country far away and have him come away with her. She wanted to make a fresh start with him, leaving her family and life in the past.

"Doesn't seem like you aren't sure, seems like you know exactly what you want."

"That is presumptuous of you." She rose up from beside him and leaned over to pick up the clothes she had thrown to the floor from her session earlier. He swooped in to pick her up from the waist.

"You are upset, I knew it... You want me to move away with you," he said, swiftly grabbing her and reeling her body back next to him. His lax smile melted her within his grasp. She squealed with laughter and played as he whisked her back into him, she fought him back but his overpowering muscular strength allowed him to win the small fight. He trapped her within his arms, not allowing her to move or escape.

"I want a new life and yes, I suppose I had wished for you to start one with me." He thought she spoke like an angel.

He kissed her on her forehead. "You know I spent hours being your therapist. Do you honestly think I don't know what's running through your head?"

"It might be nice if you stayed out of my head." She giggled.

"No, I'll never leave your head."

Sukhi couldn't help wondering about her doctor's true intentions, but her guilty conscience about the orphaned boy forced her to focus her attentions elsewhere. *What if he is the little boy?* She thought.

"Ash, you know I'll be out of town for a while."

There was a pause, but looking at her he knew what she needed. Perhaps it was second nature to him to understand women and their minds, but for some reason he had locked into Sukhi's mind and heart. He knew things before she even knew it herself, but that was the power he had over people, and that included Sukhi.

"I know." She could sense by his tone that he was a little unhappy with her decision to go out of town, but regardless remained understanding. "Take your time. Do what you need to."

She smiled at him and kissed him. "Thank you."

The doctor rose from beside her and began to redress himself, Sukhi began to do the same. As the doctor bid her goodbye and left her, she couldn't help feeling a sense of loss sweep right through her. She had grown to have stronger feelings for him than she had anticipated, but she couldn't shake the feeling as if she had known him her entire life. It was a strange feeling that overwhelmed her senses and thoughts. *Is he the kidnapper?*

The thought of immersing herself in a relationship with a man who had commitment issues worried her, however, was she any different? The two of them were not so dissimilar. Would he hurt her? Did he really care for her?

She sighed, wondering if what she was doing with Ash was smart.

"I suppose you and the doctor are together now," asked her sister who was primly leaning up against the door.

Oh dear, of course she isn't happy with me.

"Ducky, men are complicated, it's best not to develop anything for them until you are at least twenty-one years old."

Serena rolled her eyes. "You sound like Dad… Anyway that's not important, have you not gone to see Dad's secret safe?"

Oh god. How did I forget? I've been so distracted.

"No, I forgot, would you show me?"

"I'm not surprised, you've been spending a lot of time with Ash and he's been in your head a lot too. I can tell." Her little sister rolled her eyes but pulled Sukhi towards the library.

As the two of them headed down, Sukhi felt Serena's hand grip harder.

"What's the matter, Ducky?"

Serena's face was one of concern and worry; she knew something was burdening her.

"I have a bad feeling you'll be leaving us soon."

Sukhi sighed, knowing she would be lying to her younger sister if she were to say that she wasn't.

"Ducky, I will need to leave soon and Dad will have to let me go."

"But you said… you would talk to Dad." It was clear she was upset.

"Ducky…"

"Stop calling me that. You have to stop treating me like a child… I'm your sister for God's sake."

Sukhi suddenly looked a little startled by her sister's outburst, but she could tell she was trying to make a point, and rather than make fun of her she just turned to hug her.

"I just love you Serena, more than you think." Sukhi kissed her sister on the forehead and held her close. Serena seemed to calm down within her grasp and hugged her.

As they approached the library they closed the door carefully behind them, ensuring that no one was around to see them. Serena ran to the book located in the far-right corner of the large bookcase. It almost seemed like a maze with the amount of books stacked on the shelves. Serena, however, knew where she was going and pulled the book. A small sector of the bookcase opened to reveal a steel safe.

"Have any idea what the code might be?" asked Sukhi, but her younger sister shrugged.

"I hoped you might know," she said.

Sukhi attempted her birthday, but the dial failed. She then tried Serena's birthday but that failed too. She knew it wouldn't be Karen; her father wouldn't have put her first over Sukhi or Serena.

"I wonder if it might be…"

Sukhi dialled in her birth mother's birthday, the safe clicked and opened. Sukhi smiled with bustles of excitement bubbling within her. She knew her father would have kept secret files that could have ruined the family. However, this was not on Sukhi's agenda, she wanted to know more about the fire and what had happened to the orphaned boy. She pulled out six files, five of them had something to do with his business and valuable stocks and shares but one was dated twenty-two years ago and had been labelled 'The Saachi case'. As she opened it, she knew it was about the family that had died in the fire.

"Have you found what you were looking for?" asked her younger sister with hope she had been helpful.

"Yes, I believe so. Thank you, Ducky, this is

exactly what I needed."

Serena beamed with glee. "You better hurry up and close everything before Mum sees."

Sukhi shut the safe and locked it before closing the bookcase, ensuring it looked as if it hadn't been tampered with. She took the Saachi case files away with her, reassured she had enough information needed to find the young boy.

"I wonder why you're looking for that young boy; I'm assuming you must think he might have been the kidn—" Serena stopped speaking, aware that the words could have upset Sukhi.

"Serena, it's very complicated."

"I know you've been looking for him and I think you're wondering if that orphaned boy was the kidnapper." Sukhi lowered her eyes. "Why are you trying to find him?"

It might be Ash, but then it might not be… I need to be sure and see if this is the link, but what if it isn't. What If it leads to a dead end?

"I'm not…" said Sukhi, but even she began to doubt herself. Was this as an excuse to keep trying to find her kidnapper?

Serena walked away, knowing all too well her sister was lying to her. Sukhi couldn't reveal her motives or her true intentions. Had she fooled herself into believing she felt guilty for her mother and father's actions. Or did she hope that the orphaned boy was the kidnapper? Was she still searching for him?

As Sukhi ran up the stairs she felt her heart throb. She was beginning to feel worried about her predicament. Was she still trying to find the kidnapper? Had her relationship with Ash gone too far for her to turn back? Should she have left everything in the past?

As she opened the case file, she noticed how the files contained information and photos of the incident. The picture of Mr and Mrs Saachi turned her stomach; the mother looked young and beautiful, whilst the father looked firm but handsome. Her heart sunk harder than she had ever imagined. *Strangely a lot like… How could my father hide such an incident?*

Of course her father would keep it from the world. His deceased wife had caused the problem and protecting his family name was more important. As she pulled the case file apart a picture of a small boy fell out of one of the pockets. It caught her attention. He was a dashing boy, with dark gleaming eyes; his face, however, was filled with sorrow and dismay. He was innocent and young, and it was clear from sorrow filled eyes his world had been taken away from him.

Aaron Saachi
Aged 6, - Ms Patty's Orphanage
Houndsgate Terrace.

Good tempered young boy, extremely intelligent
Hobbies: Gardening, Football, Tennis,

It can't be… but you have to know for sure.

Sukhi's stomach fell into a deep pit. What if the kidnapper was Ash all along?

The page was ripped, and no further information was found. The address was a good start for her investigation; the good thing was the orphanage was only in town, it was an opportunity to finally find out the truth of what happened to the little boy. A bustling urge from within her pushed her to find out.

"Sukhi, whatever you do, please don't be stupid." Serena's face had become glum.

"I know it is difficult for you to understand, but I must find out the truth."

"No. You aren't looking for the truth, you're looking for *him*. He's a dangerous man that kidnapped you."

"Serena. I told you, you're too young to understand, and I'm not looking for him."

"Do you honestly think you can fool me?" Serena's face had turned bright red with anger, and she stormed out of the room, slamming the door behind her. Sukhi sighed, she had no time to chase and settle her feuds with her younger sister. She pulled her phone out and had speed-dialled her bodyguard to prepare the car for her. She sighed, staring at the photo of the parents that were killed. It had begun to haunt her, the endless thoughts of how her father could have ruined this poor young boy's life.

"Ma'am, the car is ready for you," said Clive. Sukhi nodded her head in acknowledgment and prepared herself to leave with her bodyguard.

Chapter 15

Sukhi stared out the window from the car; Clive was carefully driving around the back streets to ensure no paparazzi were out to get her.

Is the kidnapper... Ash?

He pulled up to a small dilapidated building with large playgrounds around the front. Children were screaming and playing. It seemed like a happy place, despite the derelict building. Long vines twisted their way around the stony building. Sukhi opened the door and walked towards the gate of the orphanage. Some of the children didn't bother to stop their playground games, but others glanced up at her with bewilderment. As she walked into the building she noticed how the walls were decorated with children's paintings and drawings.

The entire place looked quite charming and prim to a good standard. Sukhi approached the receptionist who was staring at her behind large brown frames and with her large green eyes. Her hair was neatly tied into a large bun, and her clothes were unflattering and large.

"How may I help you?" she asked Sukhi.

"I'm trying to look up a family member who was placed here many years ago. Do you know who would be the best person to speak to?"

The receptionist scrutinised her face, assessing her statement to see if she were telling the truth.

"Who exactly are you looking for?"

"His name is Aaron Saachi, it was many years ago and probably before your time here," said Sukhi, without trying to appear as if she were lying.

The receptionist dropped her pen, her hand started to shake. She removed her round glasses from her face and stood up to face Sukhi.

"Ms Patty won't give you any information in regards to orphans who have been adopted and moved on to other families."

She knew him.

"Ms Patty will know you aren't family."

"How do you know him?"

The receptionist ignored her question. "Meet me at the cafe around the corner, the La Resion."

Sukhi nodded with acknowledgement.

A small tubby woman came running down the stairs. "Hello, I'm sorry to keep you waiting, how can we help you here at Ms Patty's orphanage."

It was clear the large woman was Ms Patty.

"Oh," said Sukhi, trying to create some misdirection. "My name is Sukhi Rai and I'm here to—"

"I know who you are. You're the daughter of David Rai." The woman beamed at her, clearly there was a motive due to her status.

"Yes, my father would like to make a donation, and ensure the facilities for this establishment are improved for the children."

"Oh, ma'am that would be wonderful, would you like me to take you on a tour?"

"Ah, no. I'm going to have to leave and see my father right now. But thank you, I will keep you take your contact details and be in touch shortly."

Ms Patty was unconvinced.

"You can cut the act, what are you really here for, Miss Rai?"

Sukhi knew she was terrible at lying. "I'm looking for a child that came here years ago, his name was Aaron Saachi."

The large woman sighed, her warm smile faded, she scrutinised a massive frown at the receptionist.

"Come with me, and you too," she indicated towards her receptionist.

The large woman waddled her way to her office. Sukhi followed her, unsure of what to make of the discontented responses she had received from mentioning the name.

The large woman closed the door behind her; the office was small but had a warm environment with pictures of herself with children and government officials. It appeared to have a friendly appeal, despite the cracked walls that were disguised by pictures children had drawn.

"If you don't mind me asking, why are you looking for Aaron Saachi?"

"If you really must know, I found a file and it appears my father placed this child here."

"Indeed he did, but it was many years ago. And we know that it was *your* mother that killed his parents."

Sukhi's face fell, guilt turned her stomach inside out. She felt sick.

"You didn't tell the press?"

"Of course not, your father is a patron to our orphanage."

"I just need to know where this boy went and if he went to a good family."

"He did and from what I heard he has done very well from himself."

Sukhi sighed.

"I just want an address to see this for myself," said Sukhi.

"You know this child, is no longer a child. He is a grown man."

"I am fully aware of this, but I don't think I could ever forgive my father until I see him with my own eyes."

Ms Patty eyed her carefully, scrutinising every angle of her face to see the true agenda.

"Unfortunately it is policy; we cannot disclose any information and that includes you, Lucy. Don't think I don't know what your intention was."

"Ms Patty, you know Aaron wasn't entirely normal

and I think Miss Rai has a right to know."

Ms Patty became red in the face; it was clear she was becoming angry with her dallying half-wit receptionist.

"Miss Rai, whilst Aaron was in our care he showed clear signs of dislike towards your father. This is clearly to do with your father wiping out the fact his parents ever existed. It was not fair to Aaron, but what extent do men with power go to cover up their wife's mishaps, eh?"

"So this boy, Aaron, knew that his parents' death was not an accident?"

"Of course he knew."

"How?"

"I don't know."

Sukhi acknowledged the fact her presence was unwanted and she was clearly disliked by Ms Patty. "I can reassure you I'm nothing like my father or mother."

"There is nothing I can do to help you, and I believe you have overstayed your visit here. That is all. You may leave. Lucy may escort you out of the building."

Sukhi nodded and raised herself from the chair, Lucy followed.

"I apologise, Miss Rai, for not being able to help," said Lucy, walking beside her. As Lucy reached the front door to allow Sukhi out, she quickly grabbed hold of hands.

"I do wish you the best."

She unfolded her hands and shoved a scrunched-up piece of paper into her hand. "In all your endeavours." She smiled with sincerity, but the firm grip Lucy had on her hands was trying to tell her something.

Sukhi mouthed a 'thank you' to Lucy who nodded at her, notifying her of their mutual understanding.

Sukhi walked towards her car where Clive was standing by, ready to open the door on her behalf. Sukhi swooped into the car whilst opening the piece of paper, which contained the address of Aaron's home. He was not adopted by a poor family, that was for sure. Judging by the address she knew he lived in a remote area in Pittsburgh, Pennsylvania.

America. Could he be?

Sukhi suddenly stopped dead in her tracks; her stomach began to churn whilst her head couldn't stop spinning. Could Ash be the kidnapper?

She needed to convince her father she could fly off to the USA or come up with some other alibi. She took her phone and dialled Ash.

"Hey Ash." Her voice had become shaky. "I need to tell... you, erm, something."

"Sure, what's up?" he said.

"I'm going to the USA for... a, a, a few days, and I need you to cover for me."

"I see... and why are you going?" She could tell he had become a little suspicious.

Sukhi paused for a moment, trying desperately to think of an excuse that he would fall for without thinking she was up to something.

"There is a world-renowned spa in Pitts… Washington."

"I see, okay, well have fun." He hung up. It was abrupt. He was her therapist; he knew she was lying. She needed to leave as soon as possible, if he was the kidnapper he would be coming after her.

"Where are we going, ma'am?" asked Clive.

"Back home, and then straight to the airport. I need the first flight out to Pittsburgh."

If he is the kidnapper, why could he not just tell her? Did he not trust her? Why would he make her go through all the agonising stories? Push her away even… It didn't make sense for Ash to be the kidnapper, but now all the arrows had begun to point to him.

Chapter 16

The flight was long and tedious; Sukhi's anxiousness and nerves kept her awake for the entire flight. She hadn't concocted a plan as to how she would approach the family, but she had to make up something to explain her presence.

The very idea of a kidnapper invariably being someone she'd fallen in love with, how could that be even be possible?

"We will be landing in approximately ten minutes. Cabin crew, take your seats."

The announcement was clear and concise. Only moments now and soon she would land and she would go directly with her personal driver to the address she was given. What would she say to the little boy's family? How could she explain her unexpected visit? How could anything she do rectify her father's mistakes? *What if this young man was the kidnapper? What if the man was Ash? All the arrows were pointing to him.* She instantly felt nervous.

Thoughts raced through her mind and she panicked, causing her to feel nauseous and a little faint.

She dived into her pre-ordered limousine that was waiting for her on the other side and sighed, feeling the constraints of her exhausting lifestyle take its toll on her.

"Where you off to?" asked her personal driver, with his thick authentic accent.

She handed over the crumpled piece of paper that she had been nervously fondling over the entire flight.

"To this address, please."

"I'll go through some back streets, might be a bit quicker."

Sukhi sighed for a moment, unable to think straight as her nerves were getting the better of her. After twenty minutes the driver eventually slowed down at a large driveway that was gated. Her eyes widened at the size of the estate; the house was large and perfectly situated within a forest, purple vines stemmed their way up the house. It had a long pebbled driveway, with a fountain foundation on the lawn.

Her nerves heightened; she felt herself fumbling her hands around her lap.

"Ma'am, this is the house," said the driver. "Would you like me to open the door for you?"

She sighed. "No thank you, I can take it from here. Please wait until I finish. I shouldn't be too long."

As she stepped out of the limo, she noticed how well kept everything was. It was almost too perfect to be true. She walked towards the gate, reaching for the call button.

"Who are you? And what do you want?" The voice through the speaker was whiny and unfriendly, Sukhi stood back wondering if what she was doing was the right thing.

"Oh, for Pete's sake. Let her in," said a female voice. There was a small amount of kafuffle before the speaker went silent and a tonal buzz rang, allowing the gates to open.

She walked through, feeling her stomach pit grow nervous with each step. What was her reason for coming? This was not going to be easy to explain. The boy was no longer a small boy but a man now, what could be her reason for checking in on him after so many years? *To see if he was your kidnapper maybe?*

She approached the front door that was opened by a tight black-suited man with a prominent austere face. It was clear he was the butler of the house, and didn't look too pleased by her arrival.

Sukhi tried to speak, no words came out of her mouth but by then two children rushed right by her. It was clear they were playing, but stopped dead in their tracks when they caught a glimpse of her standing by the doorway. The two round faces were that of a boy and girl, both had dark shaggy hair but had astounding blue eyes that complemented their brown skin.

"Who are you? You look awfully familiar," said the young boy.

"She's the girl all over the news," chirped the girl beside him in a very loud whisper.

"Mia. Jamie. Can you both go to your rooms?" The voice behind was without a doubt their mother; she smiled at her two children very lovingly, but turned an austere gaze upon Sukhi.

"Yes Mum," they said in unison, before running up the stairs.

Sukhi thought to introduce herself. "Sorry, my name is—"

The woman's lips curled. "I know who you are… Follow me," she said, walking through her large marbled corridor. Sukhi was afraid to echo even two words; the woman may have had a glowing face for a mother, but was fearful as anything else. Sukhi was used to the cold reception people gave to her, so she shrugged and hoped this wouldn't turn into something ugly. She opened the door to a large lounge area that was nicely decorated with a deco theme. The marble floor was perfectly matched with the dusky pink sofas, and the interior design was marvelled with carefully thought-out mirrors and ornaments.

"Take a seat," she offered, closing the door behind her after Sukhi had entered.

Sukhi walked towards the chaise-longue that was perfectly situated opposite a far larger sofa that the stern woman had come to sit on.

"So you're Sukhi Rai?" the woman asked. Her eyes pierced into Sukhi, scrutinising her every move. Sukhi sat frozen, unable to think of what to say. "I have to say, I don't trust girls like you."

Sukhi remained frozen in her seat.

"You're practically famous after your kidnapping scenario… and now you're here. I wonder to what is it I owe the pleasure?" The woman was cold, severe and harsh. Sukhi could feel each word cut into her like the edge of a knife.

"Ha-have I offended you, ma'am?" Sukhi stuttered.

The cold woman snorted. "No… no need for civilities… you can just call me Nikita. Your presence hasn't offended me yet."

Sukhi gulped.

"I… I… wanted to ask about your son?"

"My son." She laughed. "Don't you know him already?" The stern woman had poured herself a glass of whiskey from a decanter in front of them. "I had expected your visit a little different, I suppose."

Had the orphanage informed the woman of her arrival?

"Did Ms Patty's orphanage contact you beforehand?"

The woman's smiles of laughter stopped dead in their tracks.

"I meant to inquire about Aaron Saachi? Someone informed me he had moved to this address, presumably when he was adopted."

The woman looked carefully at Sukhi, this time a little alarmed.

"Is this a sick joke?" Her accusing tone was enough to make the atmosphere cold and disconcerting.

"No, of course not." Sukhi had become alarmed by the reaction the stern woman was giving.

"Are you to say, you don't know who I am?" said the woman, frowning.

Sukhi's eyes widened, a swarm of anxiety had built and was beginning to overflow. Was she Ash's mother?

"No, I don't… should I know?"

The woman's stern face fell into dismay, she seemed confused and somewhat uncertain with the situation. She grabbed her drinking glass and gulped down the remains of her neat whiskey.

"Please, ask me whatever it is you want to know."

"Aaron Saachi, do you know much about his past?"

"You mean before *we* adopted him? His parents had tragically passed away in an accidental fire. That's about it."

"I see, well I know what actually happened. I cannot condone what my father did to his family, nor can I forgive him. I just recently found out, you see—"

"Found out what exactly?" asked the woman.

Sukhi fell quiet, debating as to whether she should inform her of the incident.

"My… mother who is now deceased was the cause of the accident, and my father covered it up. I can understand my presence here is unwanted, but for my own sake and my own peace of mind, I just wanted to know if the young boy that was adopted was safe and was well taken care of."

The woman's face became whiter than snow. "Oh, by God, I feel faint," she uttered.

"I seriously didn't mean to offend you. If you could just tell me he is okay, then that will be enough to put my mind at ease. I can't pardon my parents' offenses and to be honest I can't forgive them either."

"He is fine," she said weakly. "You may go now,

I'll ask the butler to escort you out."

Sukhi nodded, rising from her seat ready to leave, but a sudden thought occurred to her.

"What did you mean by me not knowing who you are?" she asked. "Was the boy renamed Ash?"

The woman's eyes widened. "Oh dear God."

It is... isn't it?

"Wait, you know something, you aren't telling me, was the boy renamed Ash?"

"Honestly, I think you should leave," said the woman.

Sukhi managed to find some courage. "No wait. You aren't telling me something... How am I supposed to know you?"

"Jeffrey. Can you please escort this lady out of our house?" Her tone had turned into ice again.

Sukhi's eyes glimpsed at a certificate that was hung neatly in the corner of the room along with other décor. As she squinted to get a better look, she noticed a familiar name. A surname she knew very well. Her stomach dropped deep into a sinking hole whilst her face became pale with fright.

Meller.

Chapter 17

Worst nightmare. Ash was the boy all along. How humiliating. Why would he lie to me? Why did he push me? Oh my goodness, all the things I revealed to him. She blushed. *He's been the kidnapper all the time. How dare he not tell me. His accent, how did he manage to change that the entire time he was with me?*

Sukhi found herself flushed and panting in the backseat of her limo.

"Where we off to, ma'am?" asked the driver, unaware of the amount of shock that was going through her mind.

"Take me to my hotel please, The Ritz – Carlton."

"Yes, ma'am."

As the limo was moving, a series of hot flushes surpassed through her. Her mind was beginning to burn. Ash Meller was the young boy named Aaron Saachi?

Why? How? Was this planned along?

The limo eventually reached the hotel, yet Sukhi felt herself restless and unable to pull herself together.

How could she face Ash? How embarrassing. She had admitted she was in love with him. In love with him before even knowing who he was. She was revealing all her feelings to him all along. *The shame, and the audacity, the unscrupulous and venomous snake. Who did he think he was? The liar.*

He could have just told her from the beginning, but he put her through a living nightmare of making her confess. Sukhi rushed to the reception and requested to check in as soon as possible. The young receptionist could only frown at Sukhi, who seemed quite frantic in her discontentment.

Once Sukhi was checked in, she rushed to the lift that would take her to her room. Her mind had become erratic with non-stop chatter. She had opened up to her doctor, revealed her deepest and darkest secrets to him. *If he was the kidnapper...* She blushed. *I told him everything, he knows I'm in love with him. That bastard.*

She reached her floor and walked down the narrow corridor, she tried to compare the sex she had with her doctor and the one she had with the kidnapper. A thought, his touch; the perfect angelic curves in their backs were exactly the same. Her body naturally flowed with both of them... her body was even trying to tell her he was the same man. The chiselled features, the kiss. *Was I blind? How I could I be so stupid?*

Worst of all, her doctor had diagnosed himself as a psychopath. Why would he?

As she entered the room and turned on the lights, she noticed a dark slender figure sitting on a chair, his dark eyes were fixated on her. *Ash.*

"I worked out you were coming to Pittsburgh, when you accidentally let it slip."

"How did you get in here?"

"Picking up a master key from the cleaner is not hard."

He paused. Sukhi knew instantly he was boring his sinister appeal by intensifying his dark stare. Sukhi was lost for words.

"So you met my mother, a little bit earlier than I had anticipated." His thick American accent had begun to change into the slow, deep voice that reflected that of the kidnapper. Her body went into a frozen state.

"Ah, it is not hard to change a voice, you just need to breathe and slow down your voice to bring about a completely different voice."

"Why?" was all Sukhi could say. "I don't even know who you are anymore. You lied to me."

His smiled twisted into something she never thought him capable of, it was something quite menacing but Sukhi wasn't afraid of him. In fact she wanted him more, her body was craving him more than she knew. Sukhi could feel her heart becoming heavier as she dreaded the worst and couldn't understand how or why she was ambivalent.

I need him.

"Sukhi, this wasn't about you."

"How did you know the fire was not an accident?"

"Because two prominent members of your family paid me a visit and told me what exactly happened, but in light of this news I was not allowed to tell anyone. If I did they would ensure my life would be of squalor. If I was silent, I would have a good life."

"Who? My father?"

"No, but two members of your 'Rai' family."

"So your revenge was to kill my father?"

"No, it was to bring down your family... bring them to justice... even if it meant killing you."

Sukhi felt her heart heave and break into pieces, was everything a lie? Was she just a pawn in his game?

"But then you came into the picture... and... everything became... clouded."

Sukhi was torn, her heart was screaming to just kiss him now she knew he was the kidnapper all along, but he was a psychopath. She felt like he manipulated her into thinking she was in love with him.

"You could have told me it was *you*. Why did you lie to me?" Her face frowned and overwhelming tears strolled down her cheeks. "You tried to make me move on. Did you not care about me at all? I waited for you... you fucking asshole. I needed you and—"

"I was there all along," he interrupted her coolly. His dark silky voice sent tingles down her spine.

"But you lied to me—"

"I had the intention of hurting your father... through you."

He got up from his chair and walked over to Sukhi slowly.

"Stop, stay away from me." She panicked, unable to know how she would react if he were to get closer. She was in love with him, but he had wanted to kill her. *How much bad luck can one girl face?*

It hurt her, yet she couldn't repress her feelings of love when in reality she should have been thinking of her survival and escaping from his clutches.

"I could have killed you on many occasions," he continued.

She began to walk backwards slowly, knowing she should try to escape from him, but only to find herself backed up against the wall. Ash, realising her motive, rushed to slam her hard against the wall and pin her down to face him. He was blocking her and there was no way of escaping; he was too strong for her.

"How dare you, I hate you," she yelled at him, beating her fists against his chest. "Fuck you, let me go," she screamed. He wouldn't move, instead he just stared deep into her eyes, making her uneasy.

Sukhi, in full blown anger, slapped him hard across the face.

Silence fell in the room, both were in some confusing rage and without hesitation, Sukhi grabbed Ash and roughly kissed his lips with urgency. He could feel her raging anger, and set himself to dominate her, knowing it was the only way to tame her fire and wild nature.

"Fuck you," she whispered, knowing that the more she antagonised him and beat him with words, the harder it would be for him to control the beast he had inside. He pushed her down, trying to ascertain control, but her legs and arms were flailing to fight him. She took her hand and scratched his chest. He growled, and Sukhi knew she was getting under his skin. *But I want to.*

"You'll pay for that," he said, taking his hand and slapping her hard across the face. She licked the corner of her lips and bit down on her lower lip. In turn he changed into a wild animal; seeing that small glimpse of her fire changed him into a ravaging beast. He took his strong hand and held her down by her throat, choking her. He spread her legs with force with his other hand, using his own body strength to hold her down to keep her legs wide as he forced his fingers straight into her. She cried out with indescribable pleasure, taking in the pain of his force and urgency.

She hit his face again, only enticing him to become the menace he was and push her legs up and around his neck. He thrashed off her blouse violently, so he could have access to suck on her breasts. She moaned, clawing her hands down the perfectly angelic curves of his back, forcing him to suck harder on her. The passion was intense and the need to possess her was detrimental.

He unbuckled his trousers, then moved his hands up her thigh to push her skirt to the waist. Sukhi knew his intention, and the anticipation of him entering her was driving her body to eccentric heights.

"Turn over," he said in his dark voice.

Sukhi did as she was told. He took the tie about his neck and noosed it around her neck as a leash. She smiled again, arching her back in allowing him to have full view of everything. He couldn't help touching her supple skin that was soft and smelled sweet. Her very essence was driving him to breaking point.

She could hear him take his belt off the trousers, hearing the clanks of the metal piece clasp in his grip. The anticipation of what might happen frightened her but excited her at the same time; he pulled onto his tie to wring her neck upwards, she moaned.

Without warning, he took his leather belt and whipped her hard across her flesh.

"Argh," she cried out in pain.

The thrash itself was painfully brutal, the tingling sensation after soon turned into a soft burn. She became more aroused by the action and had become increasingly wet.

"Count," he ordered her.

"One," she stifled, but before she could recollect herself he had thrashed her with another one.

"Two... Three... Four... Five."

Her body dropped, and she had succumbed to the pain, and he knew it. He threw his belt to a side, and realised tears had strolled down her cheeks. He placed his fingers around her clitoris and realised she was dripping wet; astounded, he flipped her entire body and attempted to hush her tears.

"Do you feel safe?" he growled at her; it was clear he was showing no mercy towards her, but Sukhi would not have it any other way. She grabbed a fistful of his hair and yanked herself onto him; he forced his member inside of her, seeing her wail and cry out in sheer pleasure.

"Yes," she replied.

"You belong to me," he groaned. "Say it."

"I belong to you," she moaned in a provocative voice.

She was filled with too much ecstasy; she could only reciprocate by nodding ever so slightly as she cried out with every penetration. She arched her back as he pulled her up onto him in a seated position. Finding some ground, he used his hips to thrust inside of her. He was not going gentle on her, quite the opposite. She grabbed hold of him and ran her fingers through his hair, gripping onto him for dear life as she approached her climax. He thrust into her harder and faster, not allowing her to have any moment to rest. She was screaming too loud so he had to stifle her with his hand, forcing her to stay quiet. With a sudden large thrust, she cried out and had finished.

Ash rose above her. "Suck me," he demanded. She looked up at him with confused eyes, he wouldn't have any of it, he slapped her hard across the face. "Suck me."

He yanked her hair, ensuring her mouth was open wide. She teased him by licking her lips and staring at him with pure menacing devotion. He moaned as her large, almond-shaped, dark eyes bewitched him.

She laced her fingers delectably around his large cock, tracing them lightly up and down with playful teasing. She licked the tip with her tongue, sending light sensations through him.

"You drive me crazy, you know that?" His voice was dark and filled with lust.

She licked his cock aggressively from the shaft to

the tip, then took on the full cock into her mouth. It was warm and moist, and with her tongue she massaged him, only giving him more gratification. She paced herself before deep throating him hard. His sounds grew even louder, as she felt the entire moistness encapsulate his cock. She moved rhythmically fast, whilst still caressing him with her tongue.

"That's it." Sukhi could feel things clench up and she knew he was going to release. "I want you to swallow," he demanded.

She smiled, that devilish smile that drove him wild. But he was impatient and before she could even continue, he grabbed her face and fucked her mouth hard, hitting her gag reflex many times, but she embraced it, for all she wanted to do was please him.

He released into her mouth, but as there was so much it had overfilled and dripped down the sides of her lips. She took a gulp and swallowed his entirety, the overfill she used her fingers to trace back his cum to her lips and tasted it with delight.

"You're so bad," he stated, still in some state of euphoria. She rose herself and stood naked in front of him.

She leaned close to his ear, "Now you are mine," she whispered.

"Don't play with me," he said.

"I just did," she responded.

He looked at her with his deep swooning eyes and smiled. He glanced below to admire her beautiful, slim body, that was graced for his vision. In haste, he picked her up with ease and cradled her in his arms, whilst walking to the bedroom. He held her firmly within his grasp and her body naturally caved into him. As they approached the bed, he placed her gently down, cocooning her into him.

"You know I'll never let anything happen to you," he said, stroking her head; she nodded as she lay into him on the bed. She leaned her head into his chest as he wrapped his strong arms about her waist, her body instantly felt at ease.

"I had my own fuelling hatred towards your father, it was nothing personal against you. I was convinced by someone that the best form of vengeance would be to destroy the one thing someone loved the most… In this case, your father loved you the most."

He can't still think it would be okay to kill my own father, could he?

"The entire operation was planned, I was intent on hurting your father the same way he had hurt me, but when I first saw you I knew I would struggle…"

***

"My step-father was an ex-CIA agent, and someone who I trusted my entire life with. Knowing I was keeping a secret that was underlyingly ruining my life, I opened up to him. He realised the injustice your family had inflicted on me and probably many other families; he trained me with a set of specialised skills no normal person would know.

"He had trained me to become a killer, one without feeling or care, to avenge my parents was my life's mission. To bring down the Rai dynasty was my aim.

"I knew from day one, the fire was no accident. You saw my surname was Saachi but did you know my actual full name was Saachi-Reiler?"

"You mean you're related to the famous oil tycoonist in the 1800s, James-Jackson Reiler?"

"They very one. Did you know that our families were the 1% of the population that control all the world's wealth and power…? Well once upon a time my family did…but your family seized full control of the Reiler establishment."

"How did you change your name on all the files?"

"Your father did, out of guilt no doubt. I think he was afraid of your family coming after me, so he ensured there was no trace of the Reiler name to reclaim any entitlement."

Sukhi's heart sunk, as much as she wanted to deny her family's part she knew very well they were capable of many things.

"So you did want to kill me?" asked Sukhi whose face became sorrowful. "I daresay I probably deserve it for everything my family did to you. How were you planning to bring down my entire family through my father?"

"I cannot tell you, but there are others… who I am working with."

"So your plan was to kidnap me and kill me, and bring down my family that way?"

"No, I just had a personal vendetta against your father… I did want to just kill you, not kidnap you… but I couldn't."

"What changed?"

"Growing up, I thought I knew everything about you. I saw you as the spoilt little rich girl the media had portrayed you to be, but when I moved to England and begun to spy on you and on your daily routine… things begun to change."

***

I watched her… every feeling in me revolted. It was her eyes, they were just so bewitching, and the hint of sadness behind them had made me weak. My whole life's training couldn't go down the drain, it couldn't and wouldn't happen.

Watching her only made things harder; it was part of the job criteria to analyse the victim's movements and daily routines. This was to have a better understanding of their survival instinct. However, watching her only made me feel sad; she was not the girl the media had portrayed her to be. She was a loving sister with a kind and caring nature, it was clear her protective instinct was quite high concerning her sister.

It was obvious she and the father had a fairly good relationship. At times he was quite dismissive but the twenty-something girl was far better and smarter at handling him then the rest of the family.

The stepmother was someone that gave me great discomfort; her sinister portrayal of deception, worst of all was the entire family soaked it up, except for that tubby housekeeper of theirs.

I remember encountering her asleep one night, noticing a diary that was kept on the side table close to the window. Rest assured she was fast asleep, so I could slip my hand through and reach out for the diary.

"Dear Diary,

My father and I were battling again, he won't let me go travelling around the world. Somewhere far and distant.

Doesn't he realise I'm not happy here? The media just write stupid lies about me every day. Like the other day when I walked out with my friend Sam from a club, oh I forgot to mention he happens to be gay. Yet the media portray him as 'my new beau'. I've never had a beau. Men are only interested in me for the wrong reasons.

It would be nice just to meet someone who would see me as me rather than see my father's title and superior standing. Perhaps in South East Asia, like Thailand. I could start a new life over, meet someone who wouldn't see me as David Rai's daughter. I've had enough of this life, can't I just leave this place? Oh God, why do I cry…? I know there are more people in this world that deserve more help than me, but I'm so miserable. Please God, please help me escape this life."

It was clear some of the pages were botched from tears. This girl wanted an escape from this life, and by the look of things people wanted her dead. Perhaps I could help her; perhaps I could take her away and make her mine. She would never have to be miserable.

Wait. You need to kill her…

But you can't.

***

"By the end of it, I decided not to kill you but within days of making that decision a request was made on the darknet."

"What is the darknet?"

"It is an underground computer network with restricted access that is chiefly for illegal peer-to-peer file sharing, but also a place for people to sell their services and request for certain drugs and all sorts of other things…"

"Right, so what happened?"

"A request to have you killed for $100,000,000 came up and the moment that happened. I knew I had to save you... so I kidnapped you."

***

I watched her closely every day, ensuring nothing would happen to her, but she was not safe in the public eye. Nor with her family, who would want such a sweet girl dead for that kind of money?

Why the fuck am I giving up everything to save this girl? What has she got over me?

"Well you have me now," stated Sukhi, resting in his arms.

"I needed to own you, you can only belong to me," he said angrily to himself.

"Shall I tell you something?" she said, looking at him with her large hazy brown eyes. "You were the only person who gave me freedom and a sense of belonging somewhere, does that seem strange?"

He smiled at her, feeling comforted with some sort of peace that she belonged to him and only him.

"I'm glad you came for me," she said.

He placed her in his firm grasp. He kissed her neck from the back sliding down to her collarbone. He inhaled her sweet scent of pomegranate and vanilla.

"You still want to kill my father, don't you?"

He sighed and paused for a moment, nestling into her aura.

"No, things changed when your father revealed the

full truth behind the fire and the death of my parents. He didn't want to protect himself and he dearly loved your mother, but he was not protecting her either, he wanted to protect *you.*"

"What? My father couldn't care less if I were dead or alive."

"Not entirely true, Sukhi, he behaves the way he does to protect you. He knows a lot of men would do anything to bring him to his knees. By showing a disconnection to the public, it was his way of protecting you."

"I don't believe you, that's ridiculous."

"Then explain why his share of the Rai fortune goes to you instead of any other member in the household. Your stepmother and younger sister receive nothing."

Sukhi remained silent.

"He admitted to me that during the time you were kidnapped he cried every night, praying for you to be alive and he blamed himself. To show composure whilst giving a statement to the public about the fearful loss of his daughter was the hardest thing he ever had to do."

"Why did you forgive him so?"

"I guess we both had one thing in common, we both loved you."

"I guess I was your downfall," she whispered.

Sukhi sighed, turning to the side and kissing his arm whilst gripping his hand even tighter.

"Sukhi, you aren't safe… I believe whoever was

trying to have you killed, is still after you... and whoever wanted you killed certainly didn't want to leave a trail behind."

Sukhi paused, realising how things had gone from bad to worse, there was an unseen person wanting her dead, and the thought of it scared her.

"I'm sorry," she said in dismay.

"What for?"

"Because I'm making you suffer."

"Perhaps, but then I have you all to myself." He turned to his side and faced her with a small grin, looking at her straight in the eye whilst stroking her soft, pillow-like cheeks.

"Do you think it's my stepmother?"

"I believe she has some part to play in it, but she's not the instigator behind it..." His tone had become serious and less comforting.

The doctor had got himself into a deadly game of cat and mouse, and Sukhi couldn't help feel that it was all her fault. Her associations and family had led to the misery of this particular individual who meant the whole world to her.

"I can't believe I've put you through so much." Sukhi nuzzled into his chest as if to hide in shame. Small tears flowed down her cheeks, it seemed to have drilled into her that normalcy was something she could never have; here she was destroying a man's life.

"Don't say that."

"Can't we just go away together? Run away to a far-off country."

"Running away doesn't solve our problems."

He sighed, she knew that meant he was to finish what had started.

"No, we have to continue as we are… Once this is all finished, I promise you we can leave this place and go wherever you wish."

"But that doesn't explain why you pushed me into going out with Jonathan."

He smiled at her, as if he knew all along what he was doing and she was a puppet on his strings.

"That, my dear, it's called a man's game." He laughed at her.

"What the heck does that mean?"

"It means I was making myself unavailable to you."

"You mean… a… I can't believe you…" She huffed in annoyance, but curled up even further into him.

"You are cute."

"Don't try to change the subject."

He laughed at her whilst admiring her flawless face and perfectly contoured body in his arms. Sukhi lay there on his strong chest, holding him. As her mind started to ponder, her eyes drifted into a blissful sleep. The thought of leaving this place with Ash was her dream come true. The underlying question that kept arising in her mind was, was it right to accept that he was not sane himself? Being a proficient intellect and a highly trained killer of some kind made him an extremely dangerous individual.

Chapter 18

Ash and Sukhi took the first flight back home the next day. As usual they were flocked by the media, but instinctively Ash protected her from her surroundings.

"I hate this," she whispered to him on her flight.

"I know, just hang in there, kid. We'll have this sorted soon," he said, whilst stroking her hair.

"Ash, do you think I could come and stay with you? I think I'd feel safer if I was with you," she said, nestling her head into his shoulder.

"I think I'd feel better if you did as well," he said.

"I can have someone pack my things and bring them over."

"You want to come today?" he asked.

"Yes, as soon as possible, I don't want to stay another minute in that house."

It did seem right that he should keep her safe, at least until they found out who exactly was behind instigating Sukhi's murder.

As soon as they got off the plane, Sukhi's mobile began to ring.

"Hello Sukhi, this is Detective Darryl."

"Oh, hello Detective."

"You gave me a symbol to investigate and I have some information regarding it. It's actually a symbol for an elite group with only select members, I'm assuming your father must be a member. I have some information. Shall I come around to yours? I can be at your house in a few hours."

"Ah…ok, yes I'll be home soon then."

"Ok, see you around then."

Sukhi hung up the phone and sighed.

"Ash, would you mind if we went back to mine for a bit? The detective will be coming to see me."

"Sure, do you want me around?"

"Yes, I don't want to me be left alone."

***

By the time they had got to Sukhi's mansion the entire household was in a frantic state.

"WHO THE HELL WOULD DO THAT? WHY IS SHE GETTING EVERYTHING?" screamed Karen.

"BECAUSE SHE IS THE ELDEST!"

Sukhi heard the sound of a vase crashing onto the floor, every piece that shattered on the floor echoed throughout the entire house.

"THAT WAS EXPENSIVE, KAREN!"

"Oh Suks, you're back," Serena sighed in relief. "Mum's lost it."

It was clear Karen had lost the plot by throwing vases and special artefacts around the hallway. It was a screaming match in her father's office, and Sukhi knew that Serena had become worried and was gripping on to Sukhi's arm.

"What the hell is wrong with you, Karen?" Her father had never raised his voice to such levels.

"You only want to give everything to your selfish daughter. How can you not leave anything for Serena or me?" she yelled.

"Oh," was the only word Sukhi could mutter. She knew herself what Karen must have been thinking. Knowing of her stepmother's affairs, Sukhi would have no inclination to take care of her *if* something were to ever happen to her father.

"It's only right that everything goes to my eldest. Besides, Sukhi would never turn you or Serena out."

"That's what you think... That girl is spiteful. After everything I did, she couldn't care less if I were dead or alive."

Why not explain your affairs to him instead of blaming it on me?

Ash stood beside her.

"I would feel bad taking you away today, especially as your sister needs you," he whispered.

Sukhi glanced at Serena who was slowly beginning to cry.

"I think you're right."

"I'll take my leave. I'll be back in the morning for your appointment," said Ash to Serena, who falsified a hard smile across her face to show her enthusiasm for seeing her doctor.

He quickly pecked a small kiss on Sukhi's cheek and left without another word.

"C'mon, let's sort this out," said Sukhi, still holding Serena's hand within her firm grasp.

As they entered the office, the room fell silent. David's eyes fell onto Sukhi.

"Ah, you're back Sukhi… How was your trip?"

"Good," she replied.

She noticed how her stepmother had backed herself into a corner, whilst Serena looked at her father with large watery eyes. He sighed when his gaze fell onto her.

"I'm sorry I was yelling," he said to her. Serena, however, was unable to answer or say anything so she stepped aside and hid behind Sukhi.

"Couldn't help overhearing your lovely conversation, Dad," said Sukhi, with her voice of authority. "Just so you know, I wouldn't leave Serena out in the cold."

"And Karen?" he asked.

Silence distilled itself in the room.

"Ah, so something has happened between you two. Hence Karen has started this rant." He smiled to himself, realising the entire domestic quarrel was based between the two main ladies in the household. Sukhi sat on the seat opposite, pulling Serena to sit on the arm of the chair.

The atmosphere had become quite stale, and Karen hated the fact it had become a Sukhi and David match against her. Her odds of winning anything were slim, as they were both known for being quick and sharp-minded.

"Are you going to pull up a chair, my dear?" Karen's face turned white, she pulled herself onto a separate chair to also face her husband.

"Let's try to resolve this, shall we?" he said, smiling at his whole family that sat before him. Karen squirmed in her seat, whilst Sukhi sat deliberately facing away from her.

"You two used to get along, so what has changed all of a sudden?"

"I'll let Karen explain that one."

"See what I mean? Spiteful," said Karen.

"Clearly, Karen, you have done something which has offended my Sukhi, so care to explain what that is?"

"Of course. She is *your* Sukhi, *your precious Sukhi*. Serena and I will always come second," hissed Karen.

"Now stop," yelled David.

"I don't have to explain myself, I want a divorce. And I want my share of the years I spent with you… and I'll take Serena with me."

Sukhi looked at her in shock.

The little wretched bitch just wants my father's money. After all the shit she put my mother through, who does she think she is?

Sukhi turned to face her father, but noticed he was still smiling with a rather complacent look on his face.

"Serena dearest, please go upstairs. Your mother needs to have an adult conversation with Daddy."

Serena whose face had gone from tearful to pure fright, nodded and walked out of the door without another word.

"Karen dearest, are you sure you want a divorce?" he asked her.

Sukhi sat still in her chair, not sure if she should break her silence about the affairs. She remembered Ash informing her it was possible someone linked to her stepmother wanted her dead.

"Well if I'm not getting anything later, I'll take my cut now."

"You little bitch. You just wanted his money..." said Sukhi in haste, unable to contain herself with her stepmother throwing insults directly at her father. "After everything you put my mother through."

"Wait, Sukhi. Firstly my dear, if you were to divorce me you wouldn't receive a penny, secondly you will not have custody of Serena."

"What?" she said. "No, I have my rights over my claim."

"True, however I have enough evidence of your infidelity and alcohol abuse that will prove how incapable you are of being a respectable wife and a loving mother, including video footage of you insulting your own youngest daughter."

"How the...? It was you... wasn't it?" she accused Sukhi. "You told him from the beginning."

"I did nothing of the sort, only reason I never said anything was for Serena's sake," Sukhi shouted back in defence. Glancing towards her father, she could see from the smirk that had crept on his face, he had his own dirty tricks up his sleeve.

"Chess…" he said coolly. "She kept hidden cameras all over the house, something I failed to mention to you and Sukhi… She did it a long way back when Sukhi was merely a child."

That brilliant Chess.

Sukhi looked stunned and impressed by her father's intelligence to keep things under wraps. This is how he kept an eye on his family. The cunning old fox was always one step ahead of the game.

But why would he stay married to her, knowing she was having constant affairs?

"You can't be serious, that's an invasion of privacy, that is just plain neurotic," said Karen.

"Actually that is considered normal," said Sukhi. "As he is one of the most prestigious businessmen in our city he must have top security, even within the household."

Sukhi smiled, realising her demons with her stepmother had been vanquished, and she no longer had to hide secrets from her own father.

"Karen dearest, those cameras were installed before you even met me, therefore you would not win in court if you were to play that trump card either." His voice was cool again.

Sukhi couldn't help feel as if Karen's secret was no longer a weight on her shoulders. Her sense of pride for her father shone on her face.

"So Karen, would you like a divorce?" asked her father, whose wicked smile only made Karen more red in the face.

Karen turned into a menace, she stormed out of control from her seat.

"Oh, before you think you can take Serena away, I'll have you arrested for kidnapping," said her father with a slick edge to his voice.

With that, she stormed out of the office screaming down the hallway and breaking more valuable ornaments in her path.

"You knew all along?" asked Sukhi.

"Of my wife's indiscretions, of course I did," he said in a matter-of-fact tone.

"Why didn't you just divorce her?"

He sighed, paused and looked at Sukhi. "For the same reason you wouldn't tell me when you found out the truth about her indiscretions."

Serena.

"It pains me to say it, but I never did love her... She was someone my family wanted me to marry... so you could say it was a marriage of convenience."

Sukhi nodded in acknowledgement, proud in that moment knowing her father was beyond intelligent and two steps ahead in everything. At the same time he cared about his own family as the doctor had informed her.

"Sukhi, I need to tell you something about your mother... I never cheated or had an affair with Karen whilst I was married to her."

"What happened?"

"My family never made her life easy… I tried my hardest to protect her but she was pushed too far I guess."

"But the fire? And the family that died… Why did you throw her into an asylum?"

"I never threw her in there, she requested herself that she wanted to go for rehabilitation, to protect you from her."

"Why?"

"That accident… made her afraid of herself… unsure of what she was capable of doing."

"Dad… why did you not just tell me the truth?"

"Honestly… because I wanted you to remember her for all the good things she was… She was an angel that loved you and I loved her more than anything in this world, regardless of what you may think of me, Sukhi… She was the light of my life."

"I had no idea how much you loved her."

"It's because it pains me to speak of her… and it scares me sometimes how you remind me so much of her."

Sukhi was in awe, never had her father opened up to her like he did in that very moment. For the first time, in a very long time, he showed he was human.

"I love you Dad… I never tell you but I do."

A smile appeared on his lips, one that was of sincerity and enough to kindle the frozen heart of any soul. A humane smile without fault that filled Sukhi with warmth and a knowingness that she was loved very much.

"Dad, I need to tell you something," started Sukhi.

"Sure, what is it?"

"I think there is someone out to kill me, and I don't feel safe here so I want to move in with Ash." She bit her lip, squinting her face in hope her father wouldn't lose it.

"What! No! There is no place safer then here... If we are referring to the kidnapper we will catch him."

"No Dad, just... I can't explain."

Sukhi paused, realising she could not reveal to her father who the kidnapper was. If he found out it was Ash all along, he would get the wrong idea and forbid them ever being together.

"You just feel safer with Ash?"

"Yes..." She smiled. "Why were you so accepting of us being together?"

She noticed a small smile creep up onto his wickedly dashing face.

"I am your father, a man who can stand up for my daughter against any Rai member, is worthy in my eyes."

Sukhi looked confused for a moment, but then remembered the moment Ash had stood up to Great Aunt Vera.

"Wild Orchid... is that right?" he asked with a smile.

"Yes... that's what he called me."

"He is right."

There seems to be a small understanding between the two of them and just in that moment, she took in what seemed like a genuine warm smile from her father, who couldn't look more pleased or happier for his daughter.

"I think Karen would be happier if I was not living here anymore anyway."

"She's been throwing herself at the doctor since he started here. I knew he was a good one when he kept throwing her off."

The two of them laughed, and in an instant she felt at ease. As if in that moment she had shared a true father and daughter moment.

"Do you like him, Sukhi?" he asked, now watching her with more concern. "I could not bear to lose you to someone who was not worthy of you. He is a good man, and I can see that."

"Yes Dad, I like him... I like him a lot."

"So do I," he said. "I know he will keep you safe."

He lowered his head and with a smile, she knew from the years of growing up that was code language for her to take her leave of him so he could continue his work. She rose from her seat and glided out of the office.

"Be careful of that crazy woman throwing things in the hallway," he added. Another small stifled laughter echoed from both of them just as she closed the door behind her.

The old man is brilliant and smart.

***

The doorbell rang and Sukhi ran down the staircase to open it; she knew it was Detective Darryl and he had information regarding the symbol she had given him.

"Hello my dear, how are you feeling?"

"Better, thank you. Would you like to come to the study?"

"Of course."

They walked through the hallways and approached the study; she opened the large oak doors and welcomed the detective into a seat of his own.

"Would you like any tea or coffee? Mind you, we don't have our housekeeper anymore and I don't know how to make either to be honest," she said, slightly embarrassed by the fact she couldn't do a simple chore.

"Oh, don't worry about me, I would like you to take a look into these files."

Sukhi opened the file and saw what looked like large school photos of gentlemen standing on stone steps with long navy cloaks and golden staffs. There was an extensive list of around fifty surnames, only eight were crossed off.

Samuel J Ernest

William Cavendish

Bernard J Horrace

Nathan Austen

Adam Hastings
Frederick Boule
James-Jackson Reiler
Davos Dartagnian.

A named sprung out to her, one that was mentioned not too long ago from Ash.

"Detective, tell me everything you know about this elite group."

The detective's face fell, he became somewhat shifty and a little reluctant to reveal much information which was unusual.

"All I can tell you, is that these people are part of a group called the Agorati, the people crossed off are all ex-members who left the group."

"And…"

"'Pecuniate obediunt omnia, this means money masters all things."

"Oh…"

"That is all I know… The best person to ask would be your father, as he is a solid member of this group, in fact your family are the founders of this group."

Sukhi saw the detective's face fall and knew there was more than what he was letting on.

"I just came to give you these files, it is up to you to speak to your father."

Chapter 19

Sukhi ran through all the files throughout the night, it had worried her that there really was not much information regarding this group, and the fact that one of the ex-members' names was in fact Ash's family.

Whilst packing, she decided to go to her father, first thing in the morning to ask about the Agorati group.

"Hi Dad, would you mind if I asked you something?"

"Good morning Sukhi, yes, please take a seat," he said, placing his mug of coffee down on the table.

"Since Chess left, these coffees have been tasting awful," he laughed.

"What is the Agorati Group?"

"Oh, it's just one of those gentleman members' clubs, nothing important. Why?"

Sukhi looked up at him with earnest, and shook her head with disappointment. As if she knew he were lying.

"These ex-members, why was Reiler on it?"

Her father looked down at the file and sighed, he sat down in his master chesterfield chair, and looked up at her with a small look of despair.

"Explain everything to me Dad, no more lies."

"It's complicated, but we are an elite group that control the world's population, and we do it by keeping the world's wealth amongst ourselves, but we do it as it has become unsustainable for the world's population to survive on what's left of the world's resources."

"What exactly are you trying to say, that we control the world? How is that even possible?"

"Reducing democracy amongst the people, Shaping Ideology, Designing our Economy accordingly, Running the Regulators, Contro—"

"Wait, Dad, are you admitting that we kill people?"

"Every major event that has happened, that will happen, has been controlled by us…the French Revolution, World War II and World War I."

"Kill people? To make this world sustainable…?"

"No, that is not how it sounds… we need to protect this planet and we have to reduce the population to 500 million, otherwise there is no way we can survive."

"Survive who… you…"

"It's not like that…"

"Dad, where is your compassion for humanity? The people all have the right to live… not just us…"

Soft tears began to stroll down her cheeks, she could not believe her family could be part of a grander scheme of things, how was she kept in the dark for so long?

"I HAD NO CHOICE… I don't agree with their methods…but our God damn family founded the group… I just play my part."

"What do you mean, you had no choice Dad? Everyone has a choice!"

"When your uncle died, I was the one to take over. I did not want to… but I suddenly had to step up into my brother's shoes. Do you think I wanted that? Do you think I genuinely wanted that burden?"

"Well quit, do the right thing! Quit. Give up all our money… and make a difference to people's lives in this world."

"I can't do that, we have five families with the Rai name in different parts of Europe, we don't just quit, we can't."

Sukhi had soft tears flowing down her cheeks, she began to realise that her entire family were villains from day one. If they had orchestrated major events in the world, there was nothing that could be done to bring down her own family, for they ruled the world.

"Dad, I know there is a good man in you… so make a difference."

***

"You're leaving? Can you not take me with you?" asked Serena, who sat on her sister's bed watching Sukhi pack her clothes and belongings to take to Ash's the next day.

"I wish I could, but considering the fragile circumstances with Dad and your mum I can't just yet," she replied with sadness in her voice.

"You said you wouldn't leave me." Serena knew that with Sukhi gone, the entire household would turn into a war trench, and she would be caught in the crossfire.

"Dad, will take care of you… and I'm not really gone. I'm just moving out for a small while."

"Dad barely knows I exist, and Mum…" She paused, not knowing what to say next. Serena was attached to her mother and Sukhi knew it. Having eavesdropped on the conversation outside her father's office must not have been easy.

"Regardless of whatever Karen has done, she still loves you," said Sukhi, trying to reassure her sister.

"That's easy for you to say, I had no idea my mother was just a gold digger. Do I even belong here?"

Sukhi froze in her tracks, her sister was beginning to think exactly how she used to feel about herself. She remembered how hurt she would feel and upset she would get when the media would slander her and make up falsified stories about her and men. Eventually she learnt to suck it up and lash back at them, which was never a good thing as it made her image even worse.

"Listen to me, regardless of what the world says about you, stay true to yourself. You do belong here, no matter what people tell you. Regardless of whatever happens you will always have a home and a place with me."

"Aunt Vera and Uncle Jacob are trying to convince

Dad to take me to Vienna with them."

"Oh, why is that?"

"For a lady's education. One needs to behave properly in public and not behave like their older sister, floundering about with different men." Serena's impression of Aunt Vera was quite amusing.

"Well I never liked them, so they can bugger off with their pre-historic views about women's behaviour."

Sukhi attempted to try to make Serena smile, but her attempt was in vain.

"I just feel like since Chess left, our entire family has fallen to pieces."

"I feel like that too, but eventually all the family secrets were meant to come out, Ducky… Just promise me you'll take care of Dad whilst I'm away," said Sukhi, stroking her sister's head.

Serena nodded yet her face was full of dismay as she realised she would not have her older sister around. It was clear the family had been broken for some time; it was just a matter of time before the cracks began to show. In this situation nothing more could be done.

"The doctor will be picking you up."

"Yes he is."

"Do you love him?"

Sukhi paused for a moment and thought to herself.

"I've contemplated what we are for quite some time… I genuinely believe I'm in love with him and I believe he is something far more important to me than I would've ever imagined."

"How do you know, if he's the one?" said Ducky, confused by her sister's expression.

"It's a gut feeling, an intuition, almost like you've known that person your entire life when in reality you've known little about them. He's not a box ticker but a kindred spirit and you can recognise them through their eyes. He's the only man who has truly made me feel like I belong somewhere."

Serena sighed, hopping off her bed and heading towards the door.

"Was he your kidnapper?" Sukhi stopped dead in her tracks and didn't answer. "You were in love with your kidnapper, weren't you?" she continued. Sukhi nodded. "Then I'm happy for you," she said, smiling at her sister with a gleam before leaving. "I hope to find someone, just like you did, without the kidnapping perhaps."

"You will, I have no doubt," said Sukhi, smiling back at her sister, who closed the door behind her.

Sukhi continued to pack her things, and became lost in thought. She had slowly come to realise that Karen was no mastermind, nor could she ever have sought the demise of her, and it was because they both loved Serena.

Serena was the pillar in the family that kept everyone together. Little did she know it; *she certainly does belong.*

Either way, leaving and staying with Ash was the safest thing she could do right now. Who would've thought the kidnapper was him all along and all he did was try to keep her safe. In his very sick and twisted way, but why would that matter? In those days of being kidnapped she had loved every minute she spent with him. Perhaps not at first, but the moment they had shared intimacy on a different level, that had made her feel like she'd lost all *control*. In a strange way that had suited her, for once she had felt like she had been taken care of and wanted for a different reason and purpose.

There was a knock on the door.

"Come in." Sukhi turned to see if it was her sister again, but it was Karen. "Oh, it's you."

There was an icy feel in the room, which sent shivers down Sukhi's spine.

"I wanted to apologise, and I'm glad that you will be starting a new life with Dr Meller." Her voice was hostile, but Sukhi chose to ignore her insincere sentiment.

She continued to pack her things, she didn't know why but the very presence of Karen made her fill with rage and anger.

"I know you don't want to hear from me anymore..."

"That's not it, I want to have nothing to do with you." Sukhi was harsh, but Karen deserved it. "How can you be so fucked in the head? What exactly did my father do to you?"

Karen began to cry. "You don't understand what it's like to be me."

Her sobs were pathetic, but as usual Sukhi, being the one to never hold a grudge, attempted to hear her whimpers.

"He always put you first, even over your own mother… You were the light of his life and Serena and I were nothing."

"What was so wrong with your life? Seriously, what was so bad? He gave you everything you wanted, the big house, the clothes. You did one good thing and that was bringing Serena into this world. But you're a selfish, self-centred bitch."

"I was envious of your age and beauty, most importantly the love your father had for you was nothing I could ever ascertain, no matter how hard I tried."

"That's why I think you're pathetic."

"I think I became envious of you when men started to notice you. Naturally I hated it because I was always the one who was admired by men."

"Well, I'm glad I'm not you… I never sought men's attentions, I just wanted to belong somewhere and not be judged by my appearance and be accepted for who I was."

"I just wanted comfort and I wanted to be loved by all the men that admired you."

"Can you not hear yourself? Do you know how ridiculous you sound right now?"

"I know," she cried. "I became envious of my step-daughter and I'm terribly sorry."

Sukhi had finished packing, altogether eight suitcases containing her clothes and shoes and twenty boxes containing personal items, paints, and bathroom necessities. She sighed in relief, feeling as if a huge weight had been lifted off her shoulders. She didn't mean to think of her family as a burden, but the latest revelations had taken their toll on her.

"I'm leaving in the morning, and I need to finish up a few things."

Karen was unable to bring herself to look Sukhi directly in the eye. She turned around and left her bedroom.

Ash had arrived to pick up Sukhi; along with his arrival was a moving van.

Her father had already left for the office and therefore was unable to bid her goodbye. Her stepmother wallowed away in the library drinking neat whiskey from a Linley whiskey glass. Serena on the other hand was the only member with stifling smiles and watery eyes. She was trying her best to put a front for her sister, but it was proving to be quite difficult as the watery eyes were close to breaking into full-fledged tears.

Sukhi was ready to leave and embark on her new life with Ash. The moving van was packed and Sukhi was ready to leave in Ash's Aston Martin. Serena bolted faster than she had ever done before to hug her sister and wish her well. Ash could see the attachment between the two sisters was terribly strong, as he had witnessed when he had laid eyes on Sukhi; a feeling of nostalgia rushed through him.

"Don't worry Serena, I won't keep your sister away from you," he said, throwing his charming smile that seems to have its oozing effect on all women and young girls.

"You can always come visit us, just get Clive to

drop you over," said Sukhi.

Serena's embrace tightened.

After the final goodbyes Sukhi found herself heading off to her new life with Ash.

"Ash, may I ask you something?" she muttered.

"Of course."

"You know the skills your father taught you, that he learnt from the CIA?"

"Yes."

"Were they easy to learn?"

Ash smiled at her, bemused. "No, of course not, but why do you ask?"

"I was just curious," she said. "May I ask you another question?"

"If you must..."

"I don't think Karen could organise for me to be killed, but I'm wondering, who could it be?"

"I'm still trying to work that out, and whoever it is, I'm going to kill them." Ash's face dropped in horror, his face became pale. "Sukhi, what if it's your family?"

"We just said it wasn't Karen."

"I didn't mean your immediate family, I meant your foreign family; the ones that are distantly related to you through your father."

"You mean... I know they dislike me, but I would never think they would want me dead."

"Think about it Sukhi, they want the fortune to go to your younger sister because Karen is from a family of wealth and stature and your mother was a waitress. They never liked you or your mother."

"Oh God… Dad would never let… But…"

"I think we shouldn't eliminate them as suspects. I had thought someone close to your father… but now I'm beginning to think it could very well be your own family."

The car was approaching his apartment complex and he came to a halt.

"Let's discuss when we are inside."

He opened the gates with a click of a button; the car and the moving van that had been following them drove up to the front of his garage.

The drive may have been short but the move was long and proved to be tiring as well, running up and down flights of stairs to have boxes and suitcases moved into the apartment. After three hours of what seemed to be a long workout, the couple retreated into the bedroom, as they both fell onto the bed. Ash moved his arm around Sukhi's waist, pulling her in. All tension and anxiety released from her.

"How will we ever find out?" she asked him.

"Even worse, how will we ever prove it is them? They are a family of some Agorati group that want to kill the human race… They basically own everything in the world, and not even the justice system in the UK could protect you."

"So you found out about the Agorati group?"

"Worse, my family were the founders of such a group… The crimes and atrocities they've committed to save the world's resources…"

"So you've worked it all out?"

"I'm still finding it difficult to comprehend."

"So if your family could commit such atrocities against humanity, why wouldn't they want you dead?"

There was a small silence between them and there was some small truth behind the matter. The elders always disliked her, just for being the daughter of a waitress. Her cousins always used to beat and tease her on family outings, and she would always find solace hiding in places no one could ever find her. Why wouldn't they want her dead? After all, she was always dead to them in the first place.

"What can we do?" said Sukhi.

"Money is power, Sukhi, your family have a lot of it."

"And…"

"We bring down the establishment, hold a revolution and bring power back to the people."

"And how do you propose we do that?"

"If our forefathers built it… we can bring it down."

Perhaps Ash was right.

Sukhi moulded herself into his arm and lay on his chest, stretching herself comfortably. She was exhausted from the day. Ash, however, was restless, the thought of her very own family coming after her made him feel sick inside. Truth was, how could he protect her from them? Especially if something happened to her father. Where was the one place in the world where the Rai family members could not get to her?

Chapter 20

Ash stirred until he woke up to the delicious smell of dinner; his primal instincts flared. As he rose himself from his bed only to find Sukhi gone, he knew she was in the kitchen from the clattering about of saucepans. He smiled, realising he wasn't going to be alone anymore and his life would turn upside down. He walked down his stairs in his mezzanine flat only to find Sukhi covered in sauces and looking a terrible fright. She had a few red burn marks around her arm, and it was clear she had cut her fingers a few times from not being able to cut vegetables properly.

"You can't cook, can you?"

"I'm trying," she yelled. It was clear she was frustrated with herself.

He opened what looked like a chicken hotpot. For someone who couldn't cook it smelled delicious.

"This looks good," he remarked.

"Let's hope it tastes good."

Ash smiled, he decided to leave Sukhi and the kitchen to themselves. He knew Sukhi was attempting some kind of concoction that was to please him. However, it seemed to be causing her some distress, due to her lack of cooking knowledge. He chuckled to himself and walked over to his remote to switch on the TV.

There was a huge clatter and the sound of shattering plates in the kitchen. *BANG*.

"Oh dear," he remarked to himself.

"Assshhhhh." An innocent voice echoed through the door. He knew what was coming. He approached only to find the kitchen had turned into a cooking graveyard. Yet amongst the entire mess was a dopey angelic face looking up at him with puppy-like eyes. "I'm sorry." Her facial expression was one of helpless guilt.

"Ha. You look awful."

Her sappy face suddenly turned into a stubborn frown. "I was trying to do something nice for you."

Ash was in hysterics, he walked over to her so he could place his arms around her for comfort, but he couldn't bring himself to stop laughing. He placed his head on top of hers and as stubborn as she was, she wrestled with him, attempting to get out of his grip. She gave up as she felt his warmth enclose around her body with a soothing touch. There was a moment of silence.

"This feels normal, doesn't it?" he asked.

She sighed, realising there was no normality in their circumstances or situation, but a moment where the two of them shared normality suddenly seemed like bliss. She wanted this. She couldn't imagine a happier time than right now, despite it being such a small moment.

If only we could stay like this forever. I could be so content in just having a normal life.

"If this is what normal feels like, then I don't ever want to let go of it," she muttered into his chest.

"I don't want to let go either," he murmured. "But you're a far cry from normal. Come, let's get a takeaway, I think that might be a better option," he said, smiling down at her with his beautiful smile.

"What are you trying to say about my cooking?" she frowned.

"That I don't want to be poisoned."

She gazed up at him with admiration and kissed him quickly on the lips.

He gestured her to the sitting room where they both became comfortable on his couch. She leaned into his chest whilst he swiftly picked up his phone to order some food.

Sukhi wondered off into her own trail of thoughts. "Ash, why me?" she asked quietly. He raised an eyebrow looking at her with disbelief.

"Why not you?" he responded. She knew he was deterring himself from answering her question.

"I can't cook, I'm pretty awful at most things... I have a terrible reputation, according to the media."

He sighed. "True, you are a bit useless," he said. She frowned whilst punching him on the shoulder but that had no effect on him. He grabbed her by the waist, tickling her whilst nuzzling his face into her neck.

"Get off."

He finally had her clasped in his grip where she couldn't escape. Instantly she felt the warmth of his body penetrate through onto her.

"Why you?" he whispered in her ear as she stopped under his grip and sighed. It was clear she had surrendered despite her useless efforts to get out of his grasp. "Perhaps because of your rarity. You're unique, extremely fiery and profoundly the most curious thing I have found."

"Oh." Her face turned red. "I don't think I was expecting that."

His lips curled into a smile, and she kissed him more, reeling in the essence of his sweet breath; it melted her body every time. It was like he had some form of control over her, and she loved every minute of it.

"Plus, you're a pain in the ass."

"Heeey." She smacked him on his arm, but that had no effect. He laughed at her, playfully messing around with her and giving her a hard time. It was just sheer joy, and she hadn't felt so much happiness build up inside of her like that. She wanted this to last forever, but she knew better than anyone else that was not going to happen.

"I can't let anyone else have you; you must always be mine," he said, gripping his hands around her face. "I won't let anyone or anything harm you, do you understand?"

It was her kidnapper, the one she loved more than anything in the world; the forceful strength that would normally scare most people, only aroused her.

"I love you," she said, kissing the palm of his hand and glancing up at him with tender eyes.

"I know, you crazy thing." He kissed her with all sorts of passion, making her entire body tremble. The build-up was becoming heated and they were close to taking their clothes off and running into a session before the doorbell rang.

"Takeaway," he said in a huff. He pulled himself off her and straightened his dishevelled self. He went to the door to collect the delivery.

***

The two of them sat there eating together.

"Is this what couples do?" she asked him, whilst scoffing her vegetable paneer.

"Sit down, watch TV, eat Indian... I think so. I've never really had a girlfriend, as I said I only dated them."

"Oh, I see... Well you better eat loads then," she said.

"Why?" he asked.

"Because someone is going to need a lot of energy tonight," she smiled.

His eyes widened but a smiled cracked up on his lips.

"Well, if I have to, then I must oblige."

As she had finished her vegetable paneer, she ran to the bathroom to brush her teeth and slipped into her lacy silk chemise to surprise Ash. Her stomach filled with warm butterflies and she felt excited and nervous at the same time.

As she finished changing and dashed on a little make-up, she crept outside the door and walked down the stairs, Ash caught her at the corner of his eye and double turned at his view. His eyes were fixed, he dropped the food he was eating onto the floor and rushed towards her.

"You're so bad, you wouldn't even let me finish my meal," he said.

"Well you wouldn't want me if I was such a good girl." She smiled before racing up to him and jumping on him, hoisting her legs around his waist. He caught her with ease and gleamed with devilish excitement.

"You're right, I do love it when you're naughty." He hoisted her over his shoulder and spanked her bottom lightly. She giggled, excited over the anticipation of what was to happen.

But then the phone rang, Ash rolled his eyes, a little annoyed by the disturbance. He reached out to pick up the call, but Sukhi wouldn't let him.

"Leave it," she requested, "I've been naughty so…" The phone went onto answer phone and a voice on the other side came out.

"Sukhi," said a small voice on the answer phone.

Serena.

Chapter 21

"Suks, Mum and Dad are in trouble." It was clear from the message that Serena was hiding as she was whispering. Everything came to a complete stop, Sukhi jumped off Ash and rushed to the phone in urgency.

"Hello, Serena?"

"Sukhi, please come home," she said, clearly distraught.

"It's only been a day, what's happened?"

"Mum, she's lost it... please come home," and with that the dial tone went dead.

Sukhi stood there, unable to comprehend what was happening.

"Ash... something doesn't feel right."

"What do you mean?"

"Firstly, Serena never whispers down the phone, and she never hangs up on me like that."

Ash's eyes widened. Her face was ghostly white and the thought of someone hurting her sister or father made her blood run cold. "If that stupid family…" Sukhi became sick with anger and horror and the thought of something bad happening to her family.

"Breathe, Sukhi, let's go there now, but you need to remain calm," he commanded and she instantly released all anger. "It could be a trap."

Sukhi's breathing became irregular.

"You don't look good." He placed a hand on her shoulder as if to comfort her, but there was no comfort. Her house was still guarded by police, how could her family possibly be in trouble? "I'm sure everything will be fine," he said.

But those words were empty, Sukhi knew Serena better than anyone else; it sounded like she was in trouble, perhaps hiding in her small cabinet.

"I just have a terrible feeling."

Ash whisked Sukhi into the car, and drove off towards her place. As they approached the area Sukhi lived in, police were all about the streets. There was meant to be a peaceful protest but things had taken a turn for the worst and the city had become anarchy.

Eyes gleamed on Ash's remarkable Aston Martin, but without a second thought and before the people could have a chance to attack the car, he had swiftly reversed and decided to take a back route to the mansion.

"What is going on?" asked Sukhi.

"Protest between a marginalised population, i.e. the poor against the rich."

Sukhi paused for a moment, remembering what her father had said to her, when she had questioned him about the Agorati.

"How do you know this back route?"

"I don't, my sat-nav is showing me," he said, manoeuvring extremely fast down the narrow lanes. "How else do you think I managed to spy on you naked?" he said.

"If that's a joke, it was a pretty lame one to say at such a time."

"Calm down."

Within twenty minutes he had arrived back at the mansion. There was no security around the premises, and there were no lights on in any of the rooms. Of course her father would have pressed the immediate lockdown with all the mayhem that was being caused on the street.

"Sukhi, follow me." Ash grabbed her arm and pulled her down the cobbled path that led to her basement. A large steel door was in place but by all accounts there was no other way of getting in.

"Mr Rai…" he yelled, but there was no sound from inside.

"Dad," Sukhi yelled, trying to help. She knocked on the door, but nothing moved.

"I don't think he can hear us."

Ash stood still and looked up, he noticed above the door was a security camera looking directly at them.

"He can't hear us, but he can see us." He glanced at the camera, ushering Sukhi to look into the lens.

The door opened.

Ash and Sukhi ran in, locking the steel door behind them to ensure no one would come in from behind. With unprecedented riots taking over the streets, Mr Rai's house would be prime location for an attack.

Sukhi felt a cold shudder sent down her spine. The atmosphere was quiet. Too quiet.

"Ash, something doesn't feel right." She gripped onto his arm tightly, terror built up inside of her and she couldn't calm her nerves.

But you have to be brave, and find your sister.

"I'm sure it's fine," he said, leading the way to find their way up the staircase to the main house.

As they reached the door that led to the main house, the entire house was encapsulated in darkness. Sukhi heard voices in the study; she tried to charge into the room but Ash grabbed her hand and looked at her with a cautioned glance.

"Listen, let me go find your sister. Whatever you do, stay quiet and don't move," he ordered.

Ash hurried away, sneaking up the stairs to go find Serena. Sukhi knew she had to stay put, but her curiosity got the better of her and she needed to know what was happening in the study.

She crept up towards the doors, only to hear a familiar voice.

"It's the truth… which only led me to believe he has a personal vendetta against you…" It was a cold, cruel voice.

"No. You are lying," shouted Sukhi's father, who was clearly distraught by some news. David was fighting back.

What the fuck is going on?

"I also think your eldest daughter is aware of his true identity and has decided to play to his tune, by making her a viable threat to you, sir."

Jonathan.

"That piece of shit," growled Sukhi, who was staring at him with daggers though the small cracks of the door. Sukhi squirmed at the mere glimpse of him, every feeling revolted inside of her.

"I won't believe you."

Sukhi pressed up further to the door to hear the conversation better, but the hinge was unbalanced and Sukhi pressed down too far. *Thud.* Sukhi fell through, crashing onto the floor into the study only to find Jonathan, Karen and her father staring at her idly.

Jonathan grabbed his gun and aimed it directly at Sukhi.

"Put that God damn gun down… Sukhi, please come here," her father requested, but Sukhi didn't move.

"Sir, I would not advise that," said Jonathan, who was still pointing the gun straight at Sukhi.

"I'm not moving anywhere, Dad."

"Sukhi, Ash isn't who you think he is," beckoned her father, but her feet wouldn't move; she stared straight into Jonathan's eyes.

"Dad, I know," she yelled, still watching Jonathan carefully, whose face was mixed with small confusion.

"Sukhi, Ash was your kidnapper," screamed Karen.

"I know who Ash is and I'm not moving," Sukhi shouted back.

Jonathan's face dropped as he lowered the gun from pointing directly at Sukhi. She became less tense as the gun lowered, but her eyes were still fixed on Jonathan. There was something wrong and she knew it by the dark glint in his eyes. His lips curled into something more sinister. Jonathan's perfected face began to falter; his pleasant demeanour had taken a cold turn.

"So it's you," Sukhi said, realising that the person who was always out to get her was Jonathan.

With manic laughter Jonathan turned his gun ninety degrees, now aiming at David.

"No." There were screams of terror and Sukhi saw how her father, sitting helplessly, didn't have enough time to move out of the way.

A loud bang echoed and the room fell silent, whilst a soft ringing pierced through the ears. Silence, shock, stillness.

The chair fell back and David fell to the ground motionless. Blood curdled over the antique carpet, staining it like spilt red wine.

Sukhi's blood turned cold as she witnessed her father being shot.

It was Jonathan all along. That son of a bitch.

"Isn't this tragic?" said Jonathan, with his dark sarcastic humour.

"Jonathan, how could you? You're an MI5 agent," screamed Karen who fell to her knees, crying.

"Spoilt little bitch," said Jonathan, as he took aim at Sukhi. "We could have it all, Karen. Just let me finish her and the inheritance all goes to you."

"No, that's where you're wrong. It goes to Serena, and even then her finances would be tendered for by the Rai family until she was eighteen, you sick bastard."

"Karen, I did this for us."

Sukhi seemed confused for a moment, she had thought Jonathan's interests were always in her, but it seemed he was quite taken by her stepmother.

"You had an affair with him?" said Sukhi.

"You fucking piece of shit," Jonathan continued, glaring at Sukhi. "You're just a confused slut, who thinks she can walk over whoever she likes. Not anymore."

"I don't understand, you saved me from the forest," she yelled back at him. "I trusted you."

"Ha. Clearly not enough... Also it wasn't me who found you in the forest, if I did, I would have killed you then and there... I was an agent in the MI5 pretending to be the person who rescued you."

"You *were* an agent?" asked Karen, who seemed baffled.

"Yes well, I lost my career thanks to this little bitch," said Jonathan, laughing.

Jonathan was the evil menace.

Karen suddenly crawled to block him.

"That's enough, Jonathan," she said. "No more." Karen had now stepped in, trying to redeem herself by protecting what was left of her family.

"You can't be serious. I've done all of this for us… so we can be together." His expression changed, but Sukhi could only find his despicable nature antagonising. He was disgusting and an absolute villain.

"Not at the expense of my family." Karen was tearful and for a change Sukhi felt grateful towards Karen.

"Don't you see what we can do? I'm an ex-MI5 agent, the cops will never suspect me. I have it recorded on tape, Sukhi admitting she knew about Ash being the kidnapper. This is all the evidence we need to be together."

"No, I don't want that," shouted Karen.

"You'll come to your senses, once this has finished," he said, holding her head in both his hands with affection. It was clear from his behaviour they had been involved in some lustful affair for quite some time.

Karen pushed him away. "You're insane," she cried.

"Am I?" he asked, but his eyes had turned dark and lustful. "Everything I did was for us. You complained about your step-daughter and her ravenous beauty. You hated the fact she would inherit everything. I had set up everything tonight perfectly just for *us* to be together."

"*Us?* There is no us," stated Karen, her eyes had become swollen from the tears, but Jonathan cared for nothing.

"Do you want to know the whole twisted tale of how 'Dr Meller' came into the picture? I find it hilarious actually."

Jonathan was no longer good-natured, he was the definition of a psycho whose obsession with Karen had turned their life upside down.

"Let's rewind time shall we, a six-year-old boy had lost his family in a fire… From then he vowed to take revenge on the one person who had covered up such an injustice. He spent his life learning skills only CIA agents would know from his step-father. Ash, whose hate for your family had only grown, but in a twist of fate his mind changed upon meeting the young beautiful Sukhi."

"Call the police, Sukhi," said Karen, but before she could grab her phone, Jonathan laughed.

"They won't come, that manic in the streets tonight will keep them at bay."

Sukhi growled, realising Jonathan had planned everything. This was a trap.

"Tell me Sukhi, what exactly did you do to allure the great Dr Meller? Did you bat your big eyelashes, or did you whore yourself out to him?"

Sukhi's face was red, anger and hatred was fuelling her veins.

"Well, either way you wrapped him around your little finger. It was clear from the moment Sukhi had started to look for her kidnapper that something had happened. She showed no signs of trauma or even looking like a victim." His smile had become more alarmingly menacing. "It was clear you had formed a relationship with that man."

"You know what Jonathan, I don't fucking care. Thing is, you can kill me and you still won't get what you want," she sneered. "So go ahead and kill me."

"Tell me, where is your perfect little Ash now?"

Jonathan took aim at Sukhi's forehead, preparing to fire his next shot.

"Doesn't look like you two will have the happy ending you both wanted." His smile was sinister, but before he could pull the trigger, Karen lunged forward, blocking his view of Sukhi.

Ash had found Serena and told her to stay outside the study and to find a hiding spot in the kitchen. He crept in, hiding behind the sofa, out of Jonathan's view.

It seemed like Karen had a soothing effect on his manic and deranged personality.

"Don't you see, Karen, if we get rid them all, we can be together." Karen's face was red and puffy from the tears that had flown down her cheeks; she was trying to calm down her own hysteria whilst trying to reason with a psychopath.

"Yes, I understand but there has to be another way," she said. "We could run away together." Her voice was shaking in fear and it was clear from the slow tears that burned down her face, she knew that one wrong move would be fatal for her.

"We must kill them all," he said in lustful hatred. "Remember when you came to me, and told me the very first time we got together how much you needed me? How much you hated your life? We can start a new one."

It was clear Jonathan was one of the men Karen had seduced, but in a cruel twist he had fallen hard for her and became obsessed.

"They are my family, and my daughter loves Sukhi so you cannot kill her." She tried to calm him down and force him to put the gun down. In those moments the temple creases in his brows began to mend, she was effectively his remedy.

"You're right, they are your family, which means I can never have you," said Jonathan. In his frenzy he took the gun and aimed it at Karen.

"If I can't have you, then no one can." He smiled.

BANG.

Sukhi heard a loud thud hit the floor. Karen was dead. Jonathan had shot her. There was a long silence as realisation kicked in as to what had just happened. Jonathan fell to his knees beside Karen and began to wail.

The situation had now become far more dangerous than she had anticipated. Jonathan was unstable. Sukhi glanced at her father in the chair. *He was still alive.* Her father was breathing softly and as quietly as he could, trying to remain calm and still whilst aiming to grab the gun he stored in his desk. Sukhi eyed Ash to take note of her father still being alive. Sukhi's father looked at Ash directly in the eye, as if to nod some form of acknowledgement, as Jonathan was too busy wailing beside Karen.

Sukhi began to shake uncontrollably as her heart

raced. She didn't know what to do but she crawled towards the door; her next move was to go to her sister but to her shock and horror, her sister appeared by the door. Her face was pale white, she saw her mother's blood sprawled along the antique carpet and watched as Jonathan sobbed over her lifeless body. Jonathan had caught sight of Serena entering the room, and without constraint took aim.

Sukhi tried to grab Serena by the waist and pulled her down to take cover and protect her. Sukhi could feel her breath quicken and she tightened her embrace around her sister. But it was too late, the shot fired and the atmosphere had become stagnant and quiet.

Sukhi felt her body ring, it had become numb as she feared the worse. Her grip around her sister turned rigid as if she were trying to shut out the reality. She closed her eyes in despair, unable to find a voice to scream. Her throat choked her from the tears that had now started to burn down her face and block her throat.

A hand touched her head, as she began to lose sense of feeling.

"It's okay," said her sister's voice. "He will be with you."

The body that she clenched onto harder dropped into her arms; her elegant beautiful body had become limp.

No. Not Serena.

She wailed, she cried and screamed. Unable to contain the pain that had hurled itself out at that very moment.

"No. Serena."

The blood curled down her patterned dress, the flowers wilted in a crimson red. Her body was lifeless.

"No, Ducky," said Sukhi's strained voice. "Stay with me, we'll get help." The tears strained down her face, pouring harder than ever before.

Serena's face smiled at her sister. "I love you, please don't leave me. Please stay."

"Always," said Sukhi, unable to control her grief; her heart was being stabbed a thousand times, but no pain could console her broken heart.

As Sukhi held her sister closer and in her one last breath, her body became still. The colour that had once been so rosy and fair was all gone. The small heart had stopped beating and all that was once good had disappeared. Sukhi's life shattered in an instant.

"No, please stay. Stay." She sobbed, clenching harder onto her sister's lifeless body.

Sukhi's heart was torn to pieces; she looked up at Jonathan square in the face with a blank and lifeless expression.

"Go ahead, you've taken all I care for… so take me too… Go ahead, you monster."

"Three down, and one more to go."

The tears had erased all beauty in her face, but Sukhi couldn't care. She closed her eyes, waiting for fate to take her to her sister.

Ash threw himself at Jonathan, and the gun flung into the air. Ash punched his face brutally before twisting his arm behind him and stepping into the back of his calf. Jonathan screamed in pain, but grabbed the arm of Ash and threw him over the shoulder. Jonathan threw himself down, punching Ash's face menacingly, but Ash countered him by stabbing him on the side of his abdomen with a pocket knife.

Three large bangs echoed through the room. Sukhi felt neither pain, nor felt like her circumstances had changed. She opened her eyes only to see Jonathan had been shot through the chest. He fell to the ground with a large thud.

Sukhi turned to the door and to her astonishment, it was her Uncle Jacob and Aunt Vera.

"Oh dear Vera, look at the mess," said her haughty uncle, who stood tall with his green blazer and large braces.

"I dare say we won't be able to fix those carpets. Such a shame, they were antiques from the late 1600s, rare and valuable," said Vera with her cold mannerisms, now eyeing up the murder scene. "I daresay this boy was rather a nuisance."

"Aunt Vera, Uncle Jacob... what are you doing here?" said Sukhi, she was still weak from the shock of her sister's death. There was a small relief that they had just come in the nick of time to save her from Jonathan.

"Oh dear, you look awful," said Jacob in his austere and cold tone, looking upon Sukhi as if she may have been a pauper's daughter.

"Wait... Why are you here?" she asked.

"Well, to be very honest with you, now that your

father, your stepmother and your step-sister are dead, I guess it means we're here to kill you too and unfortunately your dashing new beau," said Great Aunt Vera.

"What?" Sukhi shuffled back. "I knew you hated me, but why kill me?"

"Why? How absurd, because you are not purely bred, my dear," said Vera, whose calm demeanour had come off far more callous and cold than one might've imagined.

"Because of my mother, you want to kill me? Being your nephew's daughter, did that not mean anything to you?" She knew her outside family despised her.

Ash sidled himself upwards against the piano, tired from the fight. He spied the gun Jonathan had flung into the air, and attempted to discreetly shift his weight across to try grab it.

"Yes, I have many nephews so David was never really my favourite. Besides, we have rules, and your father decided to break them by marrying your mother. We had to work every angle to have your mother disposed of, which she made very easy the moment she set fire to the wrong house." Aunt Vera smiled.

"Then it was just a case of having someone murder your mother in a mental asylum and frame a lunatic in that hell hole," said Jacob, who was now laughing hysterically.

"Now your sister is of pure blood and naturally we would have wanted her to inherit the Rai fortune; someone who would've listened to us and not acted out of line… but I guess that fool murdered the wrong girl," said Vera, now pointing her finger at Jonathan. "I warned you Jacob, he was sloppy."

"Well we can't have the daughter of a waitress alive, can we?" said Jacob in response. "What should we do?"

"Shoot her dead. I never want to see her again," stropped Vera.

Sukhi was far more heartbroken than one could've imagined.

Jacob took aim at Sukhi's head, and once again Sukhi closed her eyes, holding her sister tight, whispering gently into her ears, "I'll be with you soon."

Ash had flung himself to the gun and took aim and shot Jacob's arm, making him fling the gun in to the air and round the corner of the room. Jacob screamed in pain.

"Well, if it isn't Sukhi's new beau," said Vera. "I must say I'm not thrilled seeing you again."

"Yeah, feeling's mutual, hag," said Ash, pointing his gun at Vera. "You will not harm her, not whilst I'm still here."

"You won't kill me," said Vera laughing.

"Give me three reasons why I shouldn't… No one harms my girl."

A dark figure arose from behind the desk, her father had found the strength to pick himself up and take aim with his hand gun and pointed it directly at Aunt Vera.

"Get away from my daughter, you bitch," said David from behind the desk.

"David, I thought you were dead," said Vera. Her face had turned pale white.

"So you're the reason my first wife is dead, and now you're trying to get rid of my daughter." He held the gun firmly in his hand, pointing straight at Vera's head.

"This is all a misunderstanding," said Vera, still laughing.

"Ash, take Sukhi now. Call Clive to take you to location B, and get the fuck out of here."

Ash looked bewildered for a moment, he glanced at David and noticed how pale he had become from the loss of blood. It was clear to Ash that David was not going to survive the end of the night.

"You won't be laughing by the time I'm finished with you, Vera."

Sukhi could see from the corner of her blurry vision her father had arisen and was holding a gun straight at Aunt Vera and Uncle Jacob.

Shots were fired and Aunt Vera and Uncle Jacob were dead.

David fell to the floor, Ash pulled himself up and rushed over to try help David.

"It's too late…you can't help me," he said almost in a whisper.

Ash desperately tried to ascertain the bleeding, but David was right, there was no way to save him, it was too late.

"Listen to me Ash… Take this…it's a USB key that has all the deeds, entitlements and inheritance for Sukhi…"

"No, you can tell her yourself, you are going to make it."

"Take care of my girl and tell her I love her and like her mother… she was the light of my life…"

David was gone.

Ash stayed still for a moment, shaking him a few times to see if he was still alive, but he wasn't. He was gone.

Ash ran over to Sukhi who was still mourning over the loss of her sister. Sukhi's eyes were sunken and lost, Ash knew she had been hurt and torn to pieces in the space of a few minutes.

"Sukhi, look at me," he said.

In circumstances like this there was nothing he could do to spare the heartache of his beloved.

"I'm so sorry," small tears welled up in his eyes as he tried to console Sukhi.

"Don't touch me," she yelled. He backed away, realising the pain had wrought into some form of loathsome hatred towards everyone around her.

She wailed louder, crying her heart out.

"Wake up!" she shook her sister's body.

The blood had now seeped through her clothing, the more she gripped on to her sister's body the more reality had set in.

Ash fell down on his knees, desperately attempting

to save the one he loved; he knew at this point, things were never to be the same again. He grabbed hold of Sukhi, trying to tear her away from her sister, but her wails only grew louder as she reluctantly let go of the small lifeless body that lay still on her lap.

He grabbed hold of her arms, willing her to shake herself out of her own turmoil. Sukhi was in a state of shock and denial; he held her close, hoping all the pain would be quelled, but it couldn't.

Sukhi's eyes dropped and she blacked out. Darkness, nothing but darkness.

Chapter 22

"Sukhi, Sukhi can you hear me?" A familiar voice rang through her ears.

It was Ash.

"Hello, my dear," said another voice; it was his mother who was hovering over her. "Perhaps she might need a fresh glass of water."

"No Mum, not yet. She still hasn't woken up fully."

"Where are we?" Sukhi was delirious.

"We're in Pittsburgh," said Ash. "But we need to leave soon."

"How… did we get here?" she asked, still waking up from a confused state.

"Your father had a private jet in the location he gave me, the only place I could think of was to bring you to my home for now."

Sukhi was still confused.

"Where are my sister and my father?"

"Sukhi, do you remember what happened to you?" said Ash, who was now concerned that Sukhi may have been experiencing a mental breakdown.

"Oh." A sinking hole deep within her plunged her into a depressive state. "They're gone, aren't they?"

"Yes, I got you here. The only place I could think that would be safe for us, for now."

"Yes no doubt, those other Rai family members will be after you," said Nikita.

"What do you mean?" asked Sukhi.

"With you still alive, they cannot take over your father's fortune, assets, or businesses," said Ash.

"I think I'm going to be sick," said Sukhi, who seemed distressed by the news.

"Mum, can you get that useless butler of yours to get her a sick bag or a bucket?" shouted Ash.

"Gerald, would you go and—"

"Yes, ma'am," said a disapproving butler.

Jaimie and Mia hovered close by around their brother.

"Is this your girlfriend?" said Mia, giggling. "Are you two going to be married?"

A cold palm went down onto Sukhi's forehead, soothing down the fever that had formed.

"Hmm... interesting," said Nikita, who eyed Sukhi's face.

But Sukhi had thrown up all over her marble flooring.

"Second thoughts, Gerald, could you grab the bucket then mop and clean the mess, and whilst you're out, could you grab a pregnancy test?"

"Mum, she's not pregnant. She's just dealing with a lot. I think I would know, I'm a doctor," said Ash, slightly frustrated by his mother.

"Call it women's intuition, but I know what a pregnancy glow is, and your girlfriend has it."

"No, that's impossible… I'm not pregnant," said Sukhi, trying to rise from the bed she was put in.

"When was your last period my dear?"

6… 7… weeks.

Sukhi fell silent.

"Oh," was all she could say.

Ash's eyes widened in shock and slight horror at the news.

"Gerald, second thoughts can you just go out and get that pregnancy test, I'll sort out the mess here."

"Yes ma'am," huffed the butler.

"Stop giving me all that sass," said Nikita. Mia and Jaimie giggled more as the butler rolled his eyes.

"Erm… right, Mum could you give me and Suks privacy for a bit?"

"Yeh, go have your privacy in your room. I'm going to clean this up."

Ash eyed Sukhi, noticing her face was pale and her eyes were withdrawn from the usual brightness they had. He held his arm out to Sukhi, who embraced it before getting up.

"We need to talk about what happened?"

"I don't see why, I have no family and now I'm apparently knocked up."

"Because, your other family members will be after you... I have no doubt they will do whatever they can to trace you and kill you."

Sukhi sank further into a dark hole of her own misery.

"Oh God, then we are putting your family in danger."

"Honestly, it'll be fine, we aren't going to be here for very long... Before your father died, I made a promise to him that I would take care of you. He's provided me with all the access to your inheritance with this."

Ash pulled out what seemed like a USB microchip. Sukhi eyed the small device with curiosity.

"What happened to their bodies?"

"Your father and sister have been taken to a morgue in England. Unfortunately you won't be able to attend the funeral, as it might be too dangerous for you."

Sukhi was saddened that she wouldn't even have the chance to see them again.

"Doesn't it look like I murdered them? What are the police and media saying?"

"Fortunately, your father records all the footage in the house, I left a copy for Detective Darryl and asked him to get rid of the footage and ensure that you are not implicated by the media in any way."

"So what, is he going to say to keep it all secret from my family? And why did you trust the detective? How do you know he isn't working for my family?"

"Because you gave him that symbol of the Agorati, when he decided to investigate he clued up all the atrocities this group had committed against humanity. Let's just say he joined that underground group I was telling you about."

"So how is he keeping this from the rest of my family?"

"He's going to say that the footage revealed that you have been kidnapped again, and that you are officially a missing person."

"You're kidding, right?"

"I have to keep you under low-profile. Currently my father is trying to arrange new identities for us, whilst securing your inheritance to ensure no low-life family of yours tries to take it."

"I've never met your father," said Sukhi.

"He's great, you'll meet him at dinner…" Ash began to smile. "We will need to leave in few days."

"They will find me, and they will kill me. They will kill your family too if we stay here."

"I won't let that happen, to you or the baby. If there is a baby…"

"I highly doubt I'm pregnant… I think I would know," Sukhi protested.

"Really, how would you know? You have to bear in mind all the times we had… we never used a…"

"No… It can't be… NOOO!"

Ash smiled as her temper flared.

There was a small knock by the door, and two

giggles echoed from behind it.

"Ah, I never introduced you to my two siblings, Mia and Jaime." Ash began to look less like the doctor she once knew and more of a human. The two giggled louder and rushed through the door.

"Sukhi, I would like you to meet Mia, my little sister, and Jaimie, my little brother. They're twins so they get up to lots of mischief, I'm afraid."

The two children came bustling into the room, with all cheer and laughter. Sukhi couldn't stop thinking of Serena, her smile fell.

"So you going to marry Ash?" giggled Mia, swinging side to side, waiting impatiently for an answer.

"You're very pretty," said Jaimie, with bashful glee in his eyes as he hid behind Ash.

"So as you can see, Mia is the outspoken one whilst Jaimie here is a little shy."

"Will you two have children then when you do get married?"

Sukhi was taken aback by all the questions that were thrown at her. She smiled but appeared to be blushing at the thought of being married to Ash.

"I thought Mum said she was already pregnant," said Jaimie, who seemed confused.

"Don't be silly, they have to be married first," said Mia.

Sukhi blushed more.

"Ash, I can't have the…"

"Okay, you two, time to go downstairs," he said, still not listening.

But the two giggled as he tickled them and ran off downstairs. Sukhi sat down on his bed.

"Ash I can't have the baby, my family would be after it if they knew."

"Firstly, we don't know if you are pregnant, secondly they won't find out as long as we change our identities. I told you, my father is working on it."

"But I don't think I could handle it." Sukhi's eyes had lost their usual sparkle. It was clear she was in no fit state to become a mother.

Ash held her close. "I promise you, I won't let anything happen to you," he whispered as he grasped her waist, hoping to console her.

"Don't make promises you can't keep."

"Have I ever broken my promises to you?" he said, holding her in his firm grasp, ensuring there was no way she could escape.

"No... not yet."

Printed in Great Britain
by Amazon